LOVE HARD

COLORADO CLUB BILLIONAIRES
BOOK 3

LOUISE BAY

ISBN-13: 978-1-80456-049-5

BOOKS BY LOUISE BAY

Each book is a stand alone

The Hart Family Billionaires

The London Man

The Colorado Club Billionaires

Love Fast

Love Deep

Love More

The New York City Billionaires

The Boss + The Maid = Chemistry

The Play + The Pact = I Do

The Hero + Vegas = No Regrets

The Doctors Series

Dr. Off Limits

Dr. Perfect

Dr. CEO

Dr. Fake Fiancé

Dr. Single Dad

The Mister Series

Mr. Mayfair

Mr. Knightsbridge

Mr. Smithfield

Mr. Park Lane

Mr. Bloomsbury

Mr. Notting Hill

The Player Series

International Player

Private Player

The Gentleman Series

The Ruthless Gentleman

The Wrong Gentleman

The Royals Series

King of Wall Street

Park Avenue Prince

Duke of Manhattan

The British Knight

The Earl of London

The Nights Series

Indigo Nights

Promised Nights

Parisian Nights

Standalones

The Deal Maker

An American in London

14 Days of Christmas

Hollywood Scandal

Love Unexpected

Hopeful

The Empire State Series

Sign up to the Louise Bay mailing list at www.louisebay.com

ONE

Iris

Las Vegas, Las Vegas, Las Vegas, I keep saying to myself. I'm the world's worst liar, and I just know that if I'm not careful, I'm going to mention New York City when I talk to my dad. He thinks I'm going to Las Vegas to visit my best friend from school, who left Star Falls the year before graduation, a little under ten years ago. He also thinks this is an annual trip.

Fact is, I haven't seen Stephanie since she left. But she's a very convenient cover. I'm actually headed to New York City, on my own, like I do every year, to watch the opening night of the new season of the New York City Ballet.

"Iris?" Dad calls.

"In here," I say. We're coming to the end of strawberry season, and we have a minute before pears and watermelons are at their peak. But my September weekends away always come with a little more scrutiny than I'd like. I hate lying. But, even more, I hate to make my dad and brother feel guilty, which is why I don't tell them where I'm really going.

He stands in the doorway to the makeshift office I have off the barn. "I just saw Donna on the way back from the delivery to the Club."

My stomach turns over at the thought of what Dad's going to say next. No one apart from me knows I'm headed to New York, but I've thought for a while now that our neighbor, Donna has... powers. Possibly mind reading. Kidding, not kidding. It's part of the reason I avoid her at this time of year.

"Oh, how did it go at the Club? Did they like it?" We've just started supplying a local private members resort with fruit. Most stuff we sell through wholesalers, but the Colorado Club approached us just after they opened about supplying them direct. It's nice to be able to cut out the middleman. It's not big business, but it all adds up.

"Donna said Stephanie's in town."

My entire body freezes, and I have to remind myself to breathe.

Stephanie.

My best friend.

The one I'm supposed to be going to Las Vegas to visit tomorrow.

Fuck. Fuck. Fuck.

I knew hearing Donna's name wasn't a good thing.

Why in the hell is Stephanie in town? She hasn't been back here since she and her family left nearly a decade ago. So much for her being the perfect cover.

"Stephanie?" I ask, trying to buy myself some time to come up with an explanation.

"Yeah, Stephanie, who moved to Las Vegas. Why is she here if you're about to go and visit her? Does it mean you're not going? I didn't want to say anything, but we could do with an extra pair of hands around here."

There's no way I'm going to miss my trip. There aren't many things I get to do without my brother and my dad. We all live together. We all work together. But once a year, I have my trip to New York all for myself. Now that I've finally finished my correspondence course and gotten my high school diploma—ten years late—my annual trip is the only thing I have that's not about my family and Wilde's Farm. I'm not giving it up.

"Oh, Stephanie Gardener. No, I'm not going to Las Vegas to see Stephanie," I say. If Stephanie is in Star Falls, I have no idea how long she's staying. And I leave tomorrow for New York. If she's still here, my entire story falls apart.

"What are you talking about?" he asks. "You've been going to Las Vegas to see Stephanie for years now."

My brother scoots in under my dad's arm and plonks down in the visitor chair wedged in between my desk and a pile of old crates that I really need to find a home for.

"What's going on?" Bray asks.

"Doesn't Iris go to Las Vegas to see Stephanie, that girl from school, every year?" Dad asks.

"She's going tomorrow," Bray says.

Dad nods, pleased that someone's agreeing with him, and they both look at me.

"We go to Vegas together. Stephanie lives in Arizona. We meet in Vegas. But she can't make it this year. Family stuff." I'm babbling. Words are just spewing out. I have no idea if any of them make sense.

"So you're going on your own?" Bray asks.

"What are you doing in Vegas on your own?" Dad asks. "Are you gambling? You know the only person who wins is the house," he says. "You may as well just march up to the owner of the casino and give your money straight to him."

"I'm not gambling, Dad," I say, pretending to be

reading something on my computer screen, rather than desperately trying to think of who I could be in Vegas with. Stephanie is the only person I've ever known well who left Star Falls. Everyone else in this town has lived here their entire lives. Stephanie being back has completely blown my cover.

"Then why are you going?" Bray asks.

"The spa. And stuff. I told you that sometimes Stephanie's friends from Arizona come to Vegas. This year Stephanie can't go, but I'm still meeting up with them. Girls' trip." It's a possibility I may have mentioned Stephanie's friends. Part of the reason I'm a bad liar is that I can never remember what I said.

My dad looks affronted. "That doesn't seem very nice for Stephanie."

"She dropped out last minute. She insisted the rest of us go," I say with a dismissive wave of my hand.

Dad pulls his eyebrows together and looks confused.

"What did they say about the fruit at the Club?" I ask, hoping to distract everyone from the Las Vegas debacle.

"Yeah," Bray says, looking hopefully at Dad. "Did they like it? We gave them all the A-plus stuff. They won't get better."

"I don't know," Dad says. "I just left the fruit, got the signature and came home—and ran into Donna."

"Look, Dad," I say, standing up. "I have to get these boxes moved. Someone's going to have an accident while I'm away. And I still need to chase up the payment on the Oxburg account."

"Don't we have that in yet?" Bray asks. Bray never knows what's going on with the finances of the business, and that's how I'd like it to stay. He's not a spreadsheet-paperwork guy.

"Jesus, what is their problem?" Dad asks. "They know we're a small business."

"They don't care, Dad," I say. "But don't worry about it. I'm on it."

"But we need that or we can't put the down payment on the new cherry pickers. We're going to need two at least," Dad says.

"I know," I reply. Except I don't. If the cherry pickers are working, why do we need to replace them? "I'm chasing them. But you two have to let me get on with my day, or I'm never going to get all my work done before I leave for Las Vegas." Shit, I have to write all these lies down or I'm never going to remember them all.

I also have to remember to throw out all the paperwork relating to my high school studies before I go. Dad won't deliberately go poking about in my room, but it would be just my luck that he'd be trying to find a missing screwdriver or crossword puzzle and he'd find my books and papers. It's not like he'd be mad. It would just bring up too much of the past. Past that's long been forgotten.

"It's a shame you're not going to Vegas later in the year. I heard rumors Celine Dion has a new residency," Dad says. "I always wanted to take your mother to see her. You know how much she liked that song."

"I do," I reply in a soft voice. My mom and dad were the most romantic couple that have ever lived. And even now when he hears Celine sing about how she felt lifted up when she felt small, Dad gets a tear in his eye. Although, that would be the case even if my mom were still alive. He's mush to his core, my dad. I look at him and wonder if *he* ever wants to escape to Vegas or New York or somewhere away from here?

Does he want anything more? Does Bray?

"So what are you going to be doing for two nights?" Bray asks. "Sitting around in robes talking about how much the spa costs?"

I stand and point my thumb at the door. "You two need to stop chitchatting and get out of here. I'm on a one-woman mission to get a down payment for some cherry pickers, so leave me be."

They both grumble but head out. I need to chase down that payment from Oxburg, set a reminder on my phone to hide my books, and write down all the lies I just told. Hopefully they bought them. I'm not sure I have it in me to come up with an idea to reassure my dad that I'm not going to gamble away the three hundred dollars I have to my name, since I just paid for tickets to the New York City Ballet.

The only place I've ever wanted to go apart from Star Falls is New York City. For a long time, I yearned to live there, to pursue my dreams to be up there on the stage as part of a ballet company.

But now?

Now I'm on the family fruit farm, and here is where I'll stay. I've made my peace with that. But for three days and two nights out of every three hundred and sixty-five, I give myself a chance, once a year, to think about the life I used to dream about.

TWO

Jack

I'm my father's proxy. His trainee. His understudy. Tonight, he's busy, and so it's my job to accompany my mother to the New York City Ballet for the season opening.

Tomorrow, I might have to sit in on a meeting, take a call from someone he doesn't want to speak to. But tonight, it's my job to go to the ballet. Over the years, I've taken his position on a couple of charitable foundations. I also sit on the board of our family foundation.

My father isn't just my father, he's my boss. And I'm his heir.

One day I'll wake up with gray sideburns and a limp, just like he has.

It's not that I don't like the ballet. I do. And of course, trying to make the world a slightly better place through charitable endeavors isn't a bad thing. It's just my life feels like it's not my own. Because it's not. I'm being trained to head up the Alden family. Since I was born, I've been groomed to speak, act, think in a way that will ensure our family remains at the top of New York society when my father passes and I inherit.

The path has been well trodden by my father, and my grandfather, and his father before him. I know exactly how things are going to unfold. Everything is preordained.

I swirl my glass of whisky, trying to avoid eye contact with anyone in the small bar off our family's box. Because of course the Aldens have their own box. That's what happens when we donate the amount we do to the ballet. My mother is holding court on the other side of the bar. I don't have the energy to talk to anyone.

"Can I get you anything, Mr. Alden?" Greg, my mother's assistant, asks me. I hate that he calls me Mr. Alden. When he first started, I asked him to call me Jack, but when my mother heard him call me by my first name, I thought she'd had a stroke. When she regained her power of speech, she overruled me, and I've been Mr. Alden to Greg ever since.

I check my watch. The performance is often delayed on opening night, but the first bell should be about to sound.

"I'm fine," I say. The bell sounds, and I exhale at the peace I'm about to experience for the next hour or so. *Cinderella* isn't my favorite ballet but no one can question Prokofiev's music. And the New York City Ballet isn't going to do anything disastrous. It should be a pleasant evening.

I tip back my whisky, slide the glass onto the bar, and wait for my mother.

"Darling, did you see who I was talking to?" my mother asks as she approaches me.

I lift my elbow so she can take my arm, which she does. "I didn't, Mother."

She sighs in a way that tells me she's disappointed. Like

I should be following her around like a little lost sheep. I ignore it and lead us in the direction of our box.

"It was Frances Althorp," my mother says. "Her daughter, Penelope, is still single. And she's just home after a summer in Paris. You should invite her to dinner."

I close my eyes in a long blink, trying not to show any reaction. I really hope the curtain comes up as soon as we're in our seats. I know what's coming from my mother and I really want to avoid it. Frances Althorp's daughter—Penelope—is a lesbian. Not a closeted lesbian. She's out and proud and has been in a serious relationship with a performance artist from Brooklyn for about four years. Yet, still our mothers try to set us up on a semi-regular basis. I think both of them truly think we'll end up together.

"I'm not Penelope's type," I say, as we step into our box.

"Of course you are. You're an Alden. You're any woman's type."

"Not a lesbian's, Mother."

She rolls her eyes as if *I'm* being ridiculous.

"You can't stay a bachelor your entire life, Jack. You need to find an appropriate wife so you can continue our family legacy."

Now it's time to roll *my* eyes. "You know this is the twenty-first century, don't you?"

"I mean it, Jack. You know your father thinks you should be married by now."

She knows this is a low blow. She's basically telling me my father is disappointed in me. I do everything that's asked of me. Okay, I went to business school after Harvard. That had never happened in our family before. And yes, I created a successful business with my friends from business school and used some of the proceeds to buy a hotel I still own.

None of it has stopped me from fulfilling the obligations I inherited from being the only son of James Alden.

"I'll let you know when I find someone."

"One person, Jack. Not a revolving door of women. One. From a good family."

She doesn't say it, but "good family" means a family who has wealth built from legitimate sources generations ago. A Kennedy simply wouldn't do because, to my mother, they're just a bunch of bootleggers. For some reason, "tech money" isn't good enough either. You or your parents can't have made the money your family has. It has to be money from hundreds of years ago—or at least three generations. I'm still not sure why this makes a difference. But to my mother, it does.

I suppose it makes sense that to my mother, Penelope Althorp is an option. There aren't many families that fit the criteria in New York. Fewer still with single offspring who are age-appropriate.

"Jack, did you hear me?" My mother sits in the middle chair of three in our box, and I sit to her left. Greg sits to her right, nearest the stage. He realizes instantly and moves his chair between the exit and my mother, so she has a clear view. It means he'll barely be able to see.

"Yes, Mother," I say.

"Are you making any sort of effort to find yourself a wife?" she hisses under her breath.

I'm not interested in shopping for a wife. I've seen relationships can work for some people. I have a tight circle of very good friends who I met at business school. All five of them have met the women they were meant to marry. They are in love. They are better, happier, more fulfilled because of the women they're with.

I've never come close to that.

"Finding a wife isn't a priority," I reply. I let my gaze take in the theater. People glance up to see our box. Most of the audience won't know who we are. But anyone in New York high society will. I can't have this conversation with my mother here. Too many interested parties.

"You need to make it one. I'm not getting any younger. Neither is your father. We need you established."

I don't even know what that means, but it hits something in me because a familiar swirl of guilt has me keeping my mouth shut.

The lights go down and the curtain comes up.

The stage is illuminated and Meghan Furlan, one of the prima ballerinas, comes into view. She can capture an audience's attention like no one else I've ever seen perform. But I spot something in my peripheral vision. I try to ignore it. Probably just the conductor.

But I see it again, and this time, I pull my gaze from the stage.

It's a woman in the audience. She's in one of the very best seats in the house, in front of the stage about six rows back. Her hair is pulled back into a tight bun, like the woman on stage, and she's dabbing her eyes with tissues. Her profile is elegant. She has a long neck and high cheekbones. She looks like she belongs on the stage and not in the audience.

I check either side of her. On one side is Ethan Scott and his wife, who I haven't seen for a while, and I make a mental note to arrange a drink with him. To the other side of her is a woman I recognize from a New York City Ballet fundraiser.

Is she here alone?

It's not unusual for people to cry at the ballet. Even my

coldhearted mother has wept at a couple of performances. But the curtain has only just gone up.

The beautiful stranger pulls back her shoulders and lifts her chin slightly, almost defiant at her tears. She clutches her hands to her chest as Meghan Furlan performs the first pirouette of the evening. It's almost as if she thinks Meghan might fall. Of course, she doesn't, and the mystery woman breaks into a huge smile.

Inexplicably, the corners of my mouth twitch and I smile with her. I glance back at the stage, but throughout the performance, my gaze is constantly pulled back to the audience. To the beautiful woman watching the beautiful performance. I'm completely distracted by her.

Who is she?

Who *is* she?

She's so delicate, she almost doesn't seem real.

My heart is pounding and my mind is whirring, trying to think of ways I can meet the woman I've been unable to tear my gaze from. I should make a beeline for Ethan and his wife at the intermission. Or at least, that's what I can tell my mother. If I head to the main bar, I might be able to run into her. Because that's what I want, right? To talk to the woman who has me so transfixed.

I can barely think straight, and I try to organize my thoughts, try to find logical explanations for the instinct I have to race to meet her. I can't. I just know that I have to try to find her.

I'm not sure what I'll say when we come face-to-face, but I need to know who she is. There's a primal feeling in me, like nothing I've ever experienced before.

I *have* to know her.

But what if I fail? She might go to the restrooms, or I might not get down there in time. In fact, I'm *guaranteed* not to get down there in time. I'll be stopped at least five times with people wanting to make small talk or to talk about their charity or their niece or whatever.

Goddamn it.

I tap Greg on the shoulder.

"See the woman in the..." I count the rows to make sure I have it right. "In the sixth row back. In the middle with the blonde hair?"

He leans forward and narrows his eyes. "Next to Ethan Scott's wife?"

I nod. "You need to get me her name and number." I take a breath in. I'm not sure just a name will do. "And preferably the seat next to her."

He waits a beat, almost like he's waiting for me to tell him I'm joking.

I couldn't be more serious.

I lean a little farther forward and in a loud whisper, to ensure he understands the stakes, I say, "Or you're fired."

THREE

Iris

Being here tonight makes everything worth it. The cost of the airfare and hotel, not to mention the price of the ballet ticket. Even lying to my family. It's all worth it.

Every year when the curtains open, I get emotional. All my past, the sacrifices I've made, the future I might have had, comes rushing back. Tonight, it seems to have hit me harder than ever. Maybe it's my age. I'm a year older than the principal female dancer, Meghan Furlan. I gave up my dream of a dance career a long time ago, but tonight, watching Meghan, any last remnants of hope for something different have slipped away.

Meghan is the most exquisite Cinderella. How could she not be? She's an incredible dancer. But somehow it's like she was made for this part. The costumes and the choreography all elevate the performance and she borders on magical.

She deserves all the accolades.

She's magnificent.

Watching her tonight, at the peak of her career, my fingers stained with strawberry juice, everything is brought into focus. I don't know if I've been fooling myself and thinking I could still have a career in dance if I really wanted. I could train hard, make up for the time lost and still get there. But now, a woman younger than me has reached the peak of that ballet mountain. I'm seeing years and years of training paying off.

There's no catching up.

The last few strands of connection to the possibility of a different life have officially withered and died.

Maybe it's partly relief I feel. I don't have to pretend for a weekend a year that I could have been someone else.

I glance around me. Most people have left their seats during the intermission. They've headed to the restrooms or the bar. But I don't want to miss a minute of being in this auditorium. I don't like the idea of being stuck in a line and having to rush back to my seat. I want to immerse myself. I want to squeeze out every last drop of this experience.

But I need to pee.

As quickly as I can, I maneuver around people toward the restrooms. I'm not going to head to the main ones. I know that if I take the stairs at the front, usually only used by people in the boxes, there are some restrooms right there that normally have a shorter line. Nimbly, I slide through the throngs of people and get to the stairs. They're deserted. Even though I know I'll have enough time before the curtain comes up, even if there is a short line, my heartbeat ticks up in anticipation.

I get to the top of the stairs and the door to the ladies' restrooms is closed. That must be a good sign. A line isn't propping the door open. I push through the door and see just one person waiting patiently in front of me.

I know it's ridiculous, but I feel a sense of victory. I know this theater so well, I can beat most people to the restrooms. Go me.

Wow, I'm pathetic.

There's an attendant wiping down the sinks and tidying the piles of paper towels. She hums a little tune as she works. A few coins are placed on a plate on the side of the sinks. Her tips.

A lady comes out of one of the cubicles. It's a woman I saw earlier from my seat when I glanced around at the boxes. She looks like a typical New York City Ballet patron. Rich. Elegant. Head-to-toe Chanel. She transfers her quilted pink bag from one arm to the other and then washes her hands. I see her register the saucer of tips.

"They should have cloth towels," she says to the restroom worker.

"Yes, ma'am," she replies, and smiles as if she's just been paid a compliment.

Chanel lady doesn't tip.

Wow. All her money and she can't spare a little for the lady who spends her evenings in a restroom.

I use the restroom as quickly as I can, leave a five-dollar tip, and sprint back to my seat as quickly as I can.

My row is entirely empty except for two people a few seats up from me that I squeeze past on my way back to my seat, and a couple on the end on my right. Someone comes to speak to the couple on the end. They enter into a short conversation, and the couple both stand and head out. Were they given bad news? Offered a free drink or something? Why would they move? It can't be long until the curtain comes up again.

I dismiss my thoughts and turn back to the stage,

enjoying the sound of the auditorium filling up again. The ruffle of programs, the chatter of hushed voices.

It's all so comforting.

Movement on my left catches my attention. The same person who was talking to people on the other side of me is talking to the people a few seats up. I can't make out their conversation, but it seems animated. I face forward, so I don't look like I'm eavesdropping. And then *that* couple stands, just as the bell is about to sound, and they leave their seats.

How strange.

I look over my shoulder and see people filing back to their seats. People making polite excuse-me faces when they try to squeeze past each other. The auditorium is looking pretty full. I glance up to the boxes. There's the woman from the restrooms.

I smooth down my black pencil skirt that I save for important meetings and funerals. Her outfit probably costs the same as my monthly salary. Maybe my entire yearly wage.

The lights flash, indicating that the second half is about to begin, and my heart pounds. I snap my head to either side of me, and my entire row is completely empty. The five rows in front are full. I glance behind me... everywhere is full. But not my row.

Where is everyone? Does this mean that the second half is going to be interrupted as people file in late? It's so rude!

The lights dim, and I see a man stride toward me. One person! There should be at least thirty people in this row. I can't see his face as he nears, but I can't stop staring at him as he gets closer.

As he comes into focus, my stomach flips as I realize I

recognize him. That sharp jaw and full lips. The shiny thick hair that looks like it was passed down from JFK himself.

I've seen him before. I never go anywhere, so I must have seen him in Star Falls.

But he's not local.

He must be a celebrity. A movie star. Or maybe I've seen him on *Dancing with the Stars*?

For a second, I wonder if he's here to tell me I've wandered off track and to send me home.

"Good evening," he says, returning my stare. His voice is low and deep and it sends vibrations across my skin.

He sits next to me. In the seat a woman was in before the intermission.

What is happening? Before I have the chance to process what's going on, the curtains go up. I give him a final glance. He meets my gaze and gives me a small smile that flips my stomach inside out, and I turn back to the stage.

Just as Prince Charming comes to Cinderella's house, my attention is pulled from the stage as I realize that no one has filled the empty seats in my row. The guy next to me and I are the only two people in our entire row.

Prokofiev's beautiful music surges and my attention is again pulled back to the stage. It's not until the curtain comes down for a final time that I'm conscious again that there are only two people in my row.

And I'm one of them.

"A wonderful production," the man says to me as the dancers take their bows. His gaze is fixed intently on me, and I feel so hot under his stare that all I can do is nod. When Meghan comes onto the stage, I jump to my feet and applaud, as does most of the audience around me, including my next-door neighbor.

Meghan's presented with a huge bouquet of red roses

and acts like it's a total surprise and she wasn't expecting it at all. But even after all the performances she's given, it still must be a thrill to receive a standing ovation—to have everyone in the audience thank you for sharing your talent. She can't possibly get tired of the love she must feel from the audience.

"She's wonderful," I say, almost to myself.

The man next to me must hear me, because he replies, "She certainly is. She earned her position as the prima ballerina, despite her few critics."

Meghan wasn't always the darling of the New York Ballet scene. Some critics unfairly called her a pastiche of all the great dancers that came before her. She was accused of copying the elegant lines of Sylvie Guillem. And Natalia Osipova's jumps. I struggle to see why any dancer *wouldn't* try to copy the masters of their craft. Isn't it the aim of all dancers to be the best at everything they do?

I nod, and the familiar stranger holds my gaze. I turn back to the stage, trying to figure out who the man is next to me. I've definitely seen him before, but it can't be from Star Falls. It would be impossible for a guy in Star Falls, especially one as handsome as the one next to me, to be a ballet lover and for me not to know about him.

Most of the men in Star Falls are far more into pool than ballet.

He doesn't seem like he recognizes me.

After endless curtain calls, the lights in the theater finally go up.

"It was an incredible performance, wasn't it?" the man says, and I nod. "I'm Jack, by the way." He holds out his hand.

"Iris," I say, sliding my palm against his. I don't know if it's because I'm so emotional about tonight, but I feel a surge of energy as we touch, and I pull my hand back a little more quickly than is polite.

"Do you come to the ballet often?" he asks.

"Once a year," I confess. "I don't live in New York."

He nods as if I've just told him something that gives him the solution to a question he's had.

"Well, if you were just coming to one performance, that was the one to come to," he says.

"You enjoy the ballet?" I ask. Not that I don't expect men to come to the ballet. But it's unusual to see them coming alone.

"I do," he replies. "Especially here. Even the more contemporary performances."

The corners of my mouth lift. "I'd love to come more often. I don't get to see much of a range."

"You should," he says. His eyes are earnest, like he's concerned that I don't get to come to the ballet enough. It's almost like I can't look away from him. I'm trying to place him, but also, his deep blue eyes feel almost hypnotic.

"But you weren't next to me during the first half," I say, glancing down at my program. Fifteen dollars is a lot of money for a keepsake, but this once-a-year New York trip is all about indulgence.

"No," he says. "I wasn't."

It's not an explanation. "There were other people here."

"Would you like to grab a drink?" he asks, his gaze intense, like he's studying me. "I'd love to discuss the performance with you."

"Are you here alone?" I ask.

His eyes narrow a little, like he's thinking about the question. "I brought my mother. But she's heading back with someone."

My gaze dips to his mouth and his perfect Cupid's bow,

the defined line that separates his lips from the rest of his face, the fullness. It's a really pretty mouth. "Your mother?"

"Or I could walk you back to where you're going?" he suggests.

"Do we know each other?" I ask.

"No," he says, a little breathlessly. "But I'd like to get to know you a little before you disappear into the night like... Cinderella."

I can't stop my smile. I've never been likened to Cinderella before.

Maybe I got it wrong and I haven't ever seen him before. I can't imagine forgetting a man like the one in front of me.

I should make my excuses and go back to my hotel. I've taken three classes today at the Joffrey Ballet School and I'm out of shape. I spend far too long at my desk these days. I'm tired, and I should draft an email to Oxburg before I go to bed tonight. But there's something about the man in front of me that makes me want to say yes to anything he asks. It's like he might be part of my fantasy weekend, where I pretend it's still possible to live out my dreams as a principal dancer for one of the big ballet companies across the world. In my fantasy, maybe this Jack could be my supportive, devoted partner.

"A drink?" he prompts.

My heart flutters against my chest. I raise my shoulders in a little shrug. "Sure. Why not."

We make our way out. He towers over me as we walk side by side, or me before him when the corridors become too narrow. I'm in flats, but even if I was wearing my one pair of heels, I'd still be almost a foot smaller than him.

"Where's Jack?" I hear someone ask.

I turn toward the voice and see the woman who was rude to the restroom attendant during the interval.

Jack looks at me and his eyes flash and a mischievous grin unfolds on his face.

"Your mother?" I ask.

He takes my hand and pulls me in the opposite direction of the woman's shrill voice.

As we file out of the door, he drops my hand, and I wonder if he'll touch me again. And do I want him to? This man is a stranger.

We make our way out of the theater and down the steps toward the fountains. I take a deep breath in. It can't be just the pollution, but the New York air smells different—like we're on a completely different planet. It's so heavy, I can almost scoop it up in my hands.

"How often do you make it to New York?" he asks, as if he hasn't just ignored his mother.

"How often do you ignore your mother?" I ask.

He laughs. "More often than she'd like. But don't worry. She had someone else with her who told her I was leaving separately."

"But were you sitting with her for the first half of the performance? In the box?"

"Wow, you saw me?"

Now it's time for me to laugh. "I saw your mother. Not you."

"Okay, my heart just broke a little." He brings his hand to his chest. "But I won't hold a grudge. I confess, I saw *you*."

"You did?" I smile a little. I'm not sure what to make of a man who dumps his mother to come after me. Should I be flattered or horrified? "How did you end up sitting next to me? Did you switch out your ticket?"

He nods. "Something like that," he mutters. "I'm not sure I know of many places to have a drink around here that won't be overfull at this time of night. What about we head east and see what we come across? Do you want to get a cab or are you okay to walk?"

"I like to walk," I reply.

He grins at me like I just gave him the biggest compliment. "I like to walk too."

"So let's walk," I reply, and we head to the crossing.

"So where's home?" he asks.

"Where's home for you?" I counter. I don't know if I want him to know where I live. We're not in Kansas anymore. Not even Star Falls. I don't know this guy.

He lets out a small chuckle. "Home is New York. I was born here."

"Yeah, I suppose that fits," I reply. But it doesn't help me understand where I recognize him from. "And do you come to the ballet often? Or only when your mom wants you to."

We grin at each other, and the pedestrian crossing changes to green and we head across the street.

"Ahhh, the mommy jokes. Okay, bring them on." He pauses. "Actually, I enjoy the ballet. I come as often as I can."

A man who can't get enough of the ballet. Who is this guy? Prince Charming?

"I'm sorry you don't make it more than once a year," he says. "You seem to really enjoy it." He looks disappointed for me, and it hits me right in the solar plexus.

"I get to come once a year. That's more than most and I'm grateful for that."

"Right," he says, and leaves space for me to talk.

I can tell he wants to ask me again where I'm from, and now that he's shared, it feels a little more equitable. "I'm from Colorado," I say.

"Really?" he asks, like it was the last place he was expecting me to say. "I have a friend there."

"It's a big state," I say, hoping he doesn't catch the nervous edge to my voice.

"Yeah," he says. "I guess it is. Hey, why don't we cross into the park and get a drink at Tavern on the Green?"

"It's in the park?" I don't know how I feel following a stranger into a dark park in New York. Nothing about this man is anything but charming. But they say Ted Bundy was a sweetie.

He glances at me, reading my reticence immediately. "It's right on the edge of the park. You're safe, Iris. I promise you."

I sigh and give a small nod. If he's going to cut me into a thousand tiny pieces, at least he'll look good doing it.

"Do you come to New York specifically for the ballet?" he asks, as we head to the restaurant he mentioned. "Or for another reason and you try and make the ballet?"

"No, I come just for the ballet."

"Wow. That's... you're a big follower?"

I don't know why, but I want to tell him. "I used to dance, so I've always been interested in ballet."

He nods like I've just told him exactly what he was expecting, and there's something completely comforting about his response. Like it wouldn't have mattered what I had said, it would have been exactly what he wanted to hear. There's no judgement from him. No pity. It feels warm. And safe.

"You look like you belong up on that stage."

I smile. "I haven't been on a stage for a very long time," I reply. "I gave up on that dream a long time ago."

"Tell me," he says.

"What?"

"*Everything*. I want to know absolutely everything."

I laugh, and he smiles at me, like I'm completely fascinating.

We arrive at the restaurant and we order drinks. When I ask for a Diet Coke, he gets the same. I wonder if I'd wanted a glass of wine, if he would have joined me in that too.

Jack asks for cans, and when he hands me mine, he asks whether we can continue our walk while we drink.

"I like that idea," I say. I don't know if looking directly at him would be too much. But it's not just his face. He's tall and broad, but the way he moves is so graceful and confident. It wouldn't surprise me at all if he told me he had some dance training.

He opens his can of Coke and lifts it in a toast. "To unexpected evenings," he says.

I raise my can and laugh. "Unexpected evenings."

"Tell me about dancing," he says as we start to walk farther into the park. Any nervousness I felt at first has gone. Even though he's a stranger, somehow, I know I'm safe with Jack. "We can start there."

"What about you?" I ask. "Do I get to ask questions?"

"I'll answer any question you ever ask of me."

"You'll give me the truth?" I ask, narrowing my eyes.

"The whole truth and nothing but the truth. Deal?"

And somehow, I know he will.

"I wanted to dance my entire life. My parents wouldn't let me go away to ballet school. They had a family business so couldn't move the entire family. And they didn't want their daughter away at school. We were—we *are* a close family, and they wanted to keep me close."

He nods, his eyes darting from me to the path ahead.

"They said that if I finished high school, I could go

study wherever I wanted. My plan was to attend a school in New York. I took classes in... Colorado." He doesn't need to know exactly where I'm from. "I worked on my technique. I studied the masters. From Fonteyn to Misty Copeland and everyone in between. I wasn't allowed to come to New York for ballet school until I turned eighteen, but I wasn't going to let that stop my training. My ballet teacher understood my passion and let me use her studio—even when she was teaching other students. I practiced constantly, like I was three months out from auditioning for the part of my career."

"You were dedicated."

"Ballet was my entire world."

We come to a natural stop and he turns to face me. It's like he knows what I'm going to say next is going to take all my energy, and I can't walk and speak at the same time.

"Then my mother died."

He closes his eyes, like he feels my pain for a split second. He reaches out and rests his hand on my shoulder.

"There was all the grief of that—and I could have danced my way out of my pain, I think. But my brother and my father didn't have the outlet that I had. They couldn't handle their grief."

"How did she die?"

It's not a question many people ask me. Most of Star Falls knows the story of how Maureen Wilde got mowed down by a drunk driver who, despite being caught on a local camera, was never found. If people don't know the story, most of them don't ask. It's oddly a relief that Jack feels so comfortable asking me. And it makes talking about it a little less devastating.

"Drunk driver," I say.

"Fuck." He winces.

"My mom was the brains of our business. Not that my dad and brother aren't smart. They totally are. But my mom was sharp and organized and just took care of all the stuff that made the business run. I knew that without her, our entire family would go under. And we needed the business to keep us afloat or we'd all drown."

"So you stepped up," he says. "Became the brains of the business."

I shrug.

"And you gave up what you loved." He nods, like he understands.

I glance at the ground and we start walking again.

"And it still hurts," he says. "Even though if you had the choice again, you'd make the exact same decision, but you still wonder what if."

"Right," I say. "Exactly that." I couldn't have put it more perfectly myself. It's like he's stared into my soul. Like he's inside me looking out, seeing everything through my eyes. I rarely meet new people, and I've never met anyone like Jack before. Never felt anything like the way I do when he looks at me. The warmth. The understanding. The connection.

He's a man who sees me, not just the fruit farmer's daughter, but the real me. The whole me.

FOUR

Jack

I don't believe in love at first sight. I really don't.

One of my best friends, Worth, maintains that he fell in love with his wife the moment he laid eyes on her. I've always assumed he mistook lust for love.

But now I'm not so sure.

Iris instantly caught my attention. I was drawn to her in a way that was entirely inexplicable. But now? Talking to her? I never want our conversation to end. Not only is she breathtakingly beautiful. Elegant. Delicate. But now I know beneath her beauty lies a strength of character I couldn't have expected. The way she endured her mother's death so bravely, sacrificed her dreams for her family? She's got steel inside her that's hidden well.

"You still work in the family business?" I ask.

She nods her head. "Yup. You're right. Now I'm the brains." She smiles wide at me, and every time she does, it lights up something inside me, like something sleeping in me is coaxed awake.

"And once a year you come to the ballet and you let yourself remember what you sacrificed."

Her smile dims, and I wish I could put the words back and never have spoken them.

"What about you?" she asks.

"Well, I work in the family business too."

"Do you enjoy it?"

"Are we supposed to enjoy what we do?"

A flash of pity crosses her reflection. It's not a look I'm used to. Few people pity me. "I really think we are. I don't think most people do though."

"Right. So I guess I'm like most of America. I'm very privileged, in lots of ways. I have a job and I'm very lucky. That's the way I try to see it at least."

"But sometimes you *don't* see it like that?" she asks. "Working in a family business is hard. It strains relationships that should only be about love and support, and they become about money and..."

"Expectations," I say, and the word sits heavy in me. "About the next generation. Legacy."

She bursts out laughing, and I smile at her, warmed by her response. "I don't think our family thinks much about the next generation and legacy. I think we're much more about making sure everyone who should have paid has paid and ensuring we can survive another winter."

"I'm sorry," I say. "I was insensitive. My family's concerns are nothing compared to yours."

She shakes her head and places her hand on my arm. I feel it heat my entire body, like her touch is breathing new life into me. "You weren't at all. *I* was being insensitive. Just because we're not worried about the same things doesn't mean your worries aren't valid."

"It's different," I say. "You're right. I suppose we still

operate within certain constraints. Except yours are dictated by bills and payments and mine are dictated by... expectations and..."

"Expectations of who?"

"My mother and father."

"And you don't want to disappoint them?"

"I really don't. Or my ancestors. My grandfather and his father before him and then his before him. I come from a line of men who worked hard to give me the opportunities I've been afforded. Now I have an obligation to pay it forward and make sure future generations of my family have those same opportunities."

She raises her eyebrows. She must think I sound like a spoiled brat. "That's quite the burden."

She's not being sarcastic. Her tone is comforting and soft. There are plenty of people who would be eager to tell me how spoiled I sound. It's a first-world problem and I know it is. I feel ungrateful for being so miserable about my situation because I know most of America would love to be in my position.

"But you feel guilty for letting it feel like a burden."

I huff out a half laugh. I wasn't expecting her to say that. "That's exactly how I feel. I don't think I've ever told anyone that."

"I understand why you wouldn't want to share it. You don't want to appear ungrateful. But my dad has a saying that if you don't allow yourself to feel sad, just because there are people who are worse off than you, then you can never be happy if there are people in the world happier than you."

I chuckle. "Wow. That's..."

"It makes perfect sense, right? If you feel a lack of freedom because you haven't chosen your path, then that's entirely understandable." She slides her hand into mine, and it's as if she's connected me to an electrical charge. I feel her warmth across my entire body. She hasn't touched me since I pulled her away from my mother, and I can't believe I'm lucky enough to be the guy holding her hand.

Telling her things is oddly comforting. It's as if we're reconnecting after years apart. It's like I've known this woman a thousand years and I'll know her a thousand more.

We wander in silence for a few minutes. Her thumb strokes my wrist, my fingers wrapped around hers. I don't think I've ever had a more perfect evening.

"How long are you staying in town for?" I ask eventually. I want tonight to last forever, and then I want to see her again tomorrow and do it all over again.

"I leave the day after tomorrow," she says.

It's like someone's punched me in the stomach, and I fight for breath.

"Really?" I ask, hoping I misheard her. "The day after tomorrow?"

"Three thirty out of Newark."

"Say you'll have breakfast with me tomorrow morning," I say. "I'll pick you up from your hotel. Where are you staying?"

She focuses on the path right in front of us. "I can meet you back here. Maybe that restaurant where we just got our beverages."

"Sure. But I can pick you up," I say. "Are you in Manhattan?"

The air shifts. I've said something wrong, and I'm not quite sure what.

"Yeah, just in Times Square, but I can meet you at that place back there," she says.

I stop and turn so I'm facing her. I want to see in her eyes what I've done.

She searches my face. "I'm not some girl with a family legacy, Jack. I'm staying at a pretty gross hotel in Times Square. You don't need to see it."

I close my eyes as realization dawns. She doesn't want me to see where she's staying. Does she think that I'm such a snob that I wouldn't want to spend time with her if I knew she was staying in a shitty hotel?

Her palm on my face makes me open my eyes. "I think maybe I want to stay in this fantasy a little longer," she says, her chocolate-brown eyes gazing into mine. "My accommodation doesn't meet the criteria for any kind of fantasy that I want to indulge."

I smile, because *she's* smiling and I can't not. But inside me, sadness swirls.

She's thinking ahead and has condemned tonight to being the beginning and the end. To being a fantasy that will be over before it's even begun. When I look at her, I can't think of anything but this moment, right now, between us. It doesn't feel like a fantasy. She feels more real to me than any woman ever has.

But I'll do whatever she asks me.

"Okay," I say. "Tavern on the Green. But the night's not over. Not yet. Tell me the name of your first crush."

"Easy. Nureyev, of course."

I laugh. Of course she'd pick the most famous male dancer of all time, and we start walking. "Of course. You can't fault those cheekbones."

"Oh, I don't think you did too badly with your bone structure. You don't need to be jealous." Her eyes twinkle as she speaks.

"Plus he's dead. And I'm here with you."

Even in the lamplight, I can see her reddened cheeks. "That's the weirdest and best compliment I've ever had."

"I'm glad," I say. "I'm auditioning for a recurring part in your annual fantasy."

She shakes her head as if I'm simply incorrigible.

"Tell me about your mother," she asks.

"Way to kill the vibe," I say on a laugh.

"Come on, Jack. You love her. You bring her to the ballet, after all. Tell me you didn't leave her alone to come and chase after me."

"No, she had her trusty assistant with her and her driver waiting at the curb."

"Oh, you're... I see. She has a driver. Of course she does. Because... legacy. I'm getting the picture now."

"I told you I'm spoiled," I confess.

"I don't think you're spoiled," she says. "I think you might be the perfect gentleman. A Prince Charming type."

She makes me want to be Prince Charming. For her. "I'll take that."

"Who was *your* first crush?" she asks.

"A girl called Sally Frampton. I was twelve, and she lived in the townhouse opposite ours. She was fourteen and wore lipstick and a lot of pink. I could see into her bedroom if I angled myself right from the landing window." I wince. "That makes me sound like a pervert. I wasn't hoping she was naked. I probably would have died of shame if she had been. She had a dressing table against her window and I used to like watching her putting on lipstick."

"Sounds very low-key stalker. Like stage one. Did you ever up your game?"

I chuckle. "Never graduated past stage one, I'm afraid."

"First love?" she asks.

I hold her gaze a little longer than I should. I'm looking for something from her. Some kind of indication that she's feeling what I'm feeling right now. She's asked me a question, and I think she might be the answer. I think Iris might be my first love.

It seems ridiculous to be even thinking such a thing, but I feel so comfortable with her. We have no friends in common. I laid eyes on her for the first time just a few hours ago, but I have this deep-rooted feeling that we've been orbiting each other for lifetimes, waiting for the perfect moment to collide. And tonight's that night.

"I'm not sure," I say, chickening out of telling her my real answer.

"You're not saying something," she says, immediately latching on to me holding back.

I sigh. "You're right. Dating and I have a complicated history."

"You and dating? Are you a couple?"

I chuckle. "It feels like I date to keep my mother happy." I scrub my free hand over my face. Did I really just confess that to the woman beside me, who I might be in love with? It might be a good idea to try to impress her rather than tell her all the bad shit about myself. For some reason, I have to tell her.

"Is this the bit when you tell me you're gay and you're looking for a beard when you date?"

"I think that would be easier. I'm not gay. But my mother wants me to find someone who's... suitable in her eyes." Iris doesn't react. There's no raised eyebrows or incredulous laugh. I'm grateful. "She's from another era. It's not just her. In the circles where I was raised, marrying a suitable person is expected. Required."

She stares at the ground as we continue our walk.

"I know it sounds old fashioned, but my mother has certain expectations of the woman I marry. So most of the women I date fit within some strict boundaries."

"So they're from certain families?" she asks. Her tone isn't judgmental. Just interested.

I pull in a breath. "Yes. They have certain surnames."

"Lineage."

I don't say anything. She's not wrong.

"You want someone who's the opposite of what your mother would like?"

I think about her question for a few seconds. I don't want to answer right away. Not because I want to give her the answer she wants. I'm going to be truthful with her, but I'm not sure what my truth is. "I want someone *I* choose," I say.

"Does that mean you automatically rule anyone out who fits what your mom wants?"

I let out a groan. It's such a challenging question. But it gets right to the core of my issue with dating. "If I'm honest, I'm not sure. Everyone I take to dinner either fits or doesn't fit. You know? If they fit, I sort of resent them. It's impossible to find a real connection because all I can think is that they fit my mother's criteria. And if they don't fit, that's all I think about too. This must sound wild to you."

She starts to laugh, and it's the sweetest sound I ever heard. "Kinda wild."

Out of habit, I've been leading us through the park to the Bethesda Fountain. We get to the top of the steps.

"Wow," she says as she looks out onto the fountain, lit up in warm yellow. "This is... Shall we sit?"

I glance around for a bench, but she takes a few steps down and sits right on the stone. I take a seat next to her and look out onto the fountain. I don't think I've ever sat on the ground in New York. Not even as a kid.

"What about you?" I ask. "What's your dating history?"

"Oh, I don't have much of a history. A high school sweetheart who turned out to be not so sweet. He had anger issues. Although, he seems to have reformed. He's married now. Two kids."

"He was violent?" I ask, horrified at the thought.

"Never with me. But he used to like going out, getting drunk and getting in trouble. Anyway, that fizzled out after my mom died. Since then, there's not been anyone serious. A guy who owns the local auto repair shop asks me out a couple of times a year. He's older and..." She shrugs. "He's a nice guy and all, but I don't want to get into anything romantic with him. We had one date years back, but since then, I always say no. But he keeps on asking."

I think if I was that guy, I'd keep on asking too.

"What do you do for fun?" she asks. The question takes me off guard.

"Fun?" I ask.

Her eyes flash wide and her smile is so broad, it makes me want to get closer to her—tell her everything. "Jack, don't tell me you never have fun."

"I'm a lucky guy. I have five close friends. They're like brothers to me. When I hang out with them, I always have fun."

"That's so nice. I can tell you for free, having a real brother isn't always so fun."

"Tell me about him," I ask.

"About Bray?" She dissolves into giggles. "You don't want to hear about my brother. He's bad-tempered before two cups of coffee. Messy as hell. Annoying on an hourly basis." She sighs. "He's a good guy. A kind heart. He really cares about the people who work on the farm. And actually, he cooks a great chili."

I laugh at the description. It feels warm and familial. Like something I'd see in a movie.

"You don't have any siblings?"

She looks at me like she's taking me in for the first time, or as if she's making some kind of mathematical equation in her head. She sweeps her fingertips over my forehead. "Heavy is the head that wears the crown."

"Did you just quote *Henry IV* at me?" I ask her.

"Actually no. The quote from *Henry IV* is, 'Uneasy lies the head that wears a crown.' So, I'm paraphrasing."

"It's like I'm sitting right next to CliffsNotes."

She laughs and nudges me. "I always liked a tragedy. If you think about it, all the great ballets are so sad. *Gizelle. Romeo and Juliet. Swan Lake.*"

"You like the dark stuff?" I ask her.

She takes a beat, like she's thinking. "I like that the stories create all this feeling in the dancer and in the audience and it connects them. And then at the end, the lights go up, and the dancers all take their bows. It's all fine. None of it's real."

"Even though the endings might not be happy, it's all okay?" I suggest.

Our gazes lock.

"Exactly."

We've known each other an amount of time that can still be counted in minutes, but our conversation isn't cursory. We're right at the heart of who we are. Who we want to be.

Even with my closest friends, I'm not sure I've felt this connected.

She stares out onto the fountain. "You know I've never been into Central Park." The conversation shifts.

"Really?" I ask. "Despite your annual trips to New York?"

"Yeah. Maybe I don't want to believe that I could have been happy here, you know? I don't want to start feeling too familiar with the place."

Her words burrow into me, leaving contrails of sadness in my chest. She sacrificed so much for her family.

"Colorado is beautiful," she says. "I know I'd miss the mountains and the valleys if I was to ever leave. I don't think I ever wanted to know if Central Park would fill up that part of me that needed the green. The nature."

"So it's good you're seeing it in the dark."

She laughs. "Right." She stands, taking my hand. "Let's go closer to the fountain." She glances at the sky. "I want to see something."

I follow her as she races down the steps and stares into the water surrounding the fountain. She looks between the sky and the pool.

"Even with all the lights, you can still see the reflection of the moon." She grins, turning to me, urging me to see what she sees. Her sense of excitement is contagious and I smile, so widely and out of the ordinary that my cheeks hurt.

"The moonlight's reflection," she says on a sigh. "There's something magical about it, don't you think?"

I've never thought about it. Not until right now. "I don't think much about moonlight."

She tilts her head, like I'm giving her new information about myself, but is it really so remarkable? Who goes around thinking about moonlight?

Iris. That's who.

"I think you're right," I say. My eyes dip to the pool surrounding the fountain and then back at her. She's lit up by the streetlamps around the celebrated Bethesda Fountain, but still finds the most magical thing about our surroundings, the moonlight reflected in the water.

I can't help but think *she's* the most magical thing in New York. And she's in front of me. I have an overwhelming need to be closer to her.

"I want to kiss you," I say, stepping closer.

She reaches out and presses her palm against my cheek.

Our eyes lock and my chest expands. Warmth surges through my body, and I close my eyes and press my lips to hers. I can taste summer meadows and sunshine on her lips. We shift so we're closer, and I deepen our kiss, my tongue pushing through her lips, meeting hers, and I can't hold back a groan. It's like I've waited a lifetime for this kiss. She's warm and soft and sweet and so goddamn real. And I'm not thinking about anything but her. She blocks out any thoughts about real life and makes it all about the here and now.

Her hands slide down to my chest, and I wish I could rip off my shirt and give her full access to my body, like she's had to my soul all evening. I want to show her everything. I want her to know me like it feels like she might already.

She pulls back first. I'm not ready for our kiss to end, but I'm not sure if I'll ever be ready. I want to dive back in and lose myself in her.

Her lips are red and swollen, her breaths coming fast and shallow.

"Jack," she whispers.

I gaze at her, wondering how it's possible to be feeling as strongly about a woman I only met this evening.

She tilts her chin up slightly, and it's all the invitation I need. I cup her face in my hands and kiss her again. She sinks against me, as if she's surrendering to me, and my cock presses urgently against the zip of my trousers.

Her delicate fingers hook into my shirt, her fingertips skirting my chest. It's too much and not enough at the same time.

Again, she pulls away first.

My chest rises and falls. It's just a kiss. But it feels like everything. Or the start of everything.

"I really like you," I say, before I can stop myself.

She grins at me. "I really like you." She shakes her head. "It feels like I've known you... more than just a few hours."

"It really does. Like there's history between us."

She nods in agreement. "I don't think I ever believed in past lives before," she says. "But it's like I know you. And you know me."

She's echoing my exact thoughts. I sit on the side of the fountain and pull her onto my lap. If I could unzip myself and pull her inside me, I don't think she'd be close enough.

I don't think I could know her long enough to ever feel satiated.

I never want to let her go.

Eventually, after kissing for days, we head out of the park. When we get to the road, she won't let me see her back to her hotel. I don't invite her back to my place. I don't want this to be about anything but what it is between us. And it's so much more than sex. Yes, I'm attracted to her. It might be a month before my hard-on subsides, but I don't want tonight to be muddied by going to my apartment. What we've shared tonight is connection and that transcends a night naked in my bed.

Although if she suggested it, I'm not sure I'd be able to say no.

"I'll see you tomorrow," I say, when she rolls down the window of her taxi. She wouldn't let me order her an Uber, so I handed the driver fifty dollars and told him to get her back safely. "I'll be waiting on the curb."

"See you tomorrow." She smiles and presses her fingers to her lips and blows me a kiss.

It hits me right in the heart.

FIVE

Iris

I wake to my phone ringing. I sit up and grab it from my nightstand just as the screen goes dark. I've missed it.

Then I remember what happened last night.

The ballet.

Central Park.

Jack.

And how Jack and I didn't swap numbers.

Jack.

Jack.

Jack.

I can't help but smile, just from thinking about him. About how I'm going to see him again this morning. About the way he sat next to me at the ballet. He never really explained that. I make a mental note to ask him about it.

My phone starts to ring as I'm holding it.

It's my dad. "You okay?"

"Yeah, but Bray broke his goddamn leg."

I wince at the thought. "Is *he* okay?"

"He's fine. Or he will be. He got his leg stuck coming off the big tractor and fell back."

I wince at the image.

"I hate to do this to you, but any chance you could get back today? I have to focus on getting the last of the strawberries picked and packed. And with a pair of hands down, I just don't think we're going to make it. I've been up all night at the hospital and—"

A ring around my chest tightens and tightens, as if something's trying to hold everything in place. Suddenly it releases, and my heart drops through the floor.

"It's okay, Dad. I'll see if I can move my flight." My entire body feels heavy at the realization that I'm not going to be able to spend more of the day with Jack. Of course I feel bad for my brother and dad, but I feel bad for me too. "Let me check with the airline and I'll let you know when I'll be home."

"You're a wonder, Iris."

I smile. We don't talk about me giving up dance and a life in New York. But he knows.

We hang up and I start scrolling flights back to Colorado. Last minute, they're all so expensive. The only one I can find that I can afford leaves at ten out of LaGuardia.

I squeeze my eyes shut in frustration. It means I won't be able to make Tavern on the Green with Jack. I won't see him again.

The fantasy is over.

Star Falls calls.

I push down the panic, the disappointment, the memories of last night and book the flight. It's six now. It will take me an hour to get there. Maybe if I'm quick, I can drop by Tavern on the Green and leave a note to give to Jack.

I pull on some clothes and throw everything I brought into a suitcase. My program from last night sits on top of the bundle of clothes and toiletries, and I flip closed the lid to my suitcase.

I've checked out and I'm in a cab within ten minutes. The cab driver last night insisted on giving me the change from the money Jack gave him. I gave him a generous tip before I accepted the rest. There are plenty of homeless people around Times Square, and I figured I'd distribute the ten bucks before I left this morning. Instead, it's paying half of my cab fare to Tavern on the Green.

When I arrive, there's no one about. The restaurant is locked up. I bang on the door but no one answers.

I didn't think this through.

I glance around. Maybe I can post a note under the door and hope someone takes pity on me and gives it to Jack when he arrives. But he said he'd be waiting on the curb. If I don't show, will he even go into the restaurant?

He might. And hope is all I have right now.

I grabbed the hotel notepad and pencil from beside my bed before I left, and now I pull it out of my jeans pocket. I check the time. I don't have long, so, leaning against the wall of the restaurant, I scribble out a note, telling him how my brother's injured and I've had to leave New York early. And then just as I'm about to scrawl my cell number, I pause.

What am I doing?

Am I really expecting him to call? And won't I be devastated if he doesn't? I won't ever know if he didn't get the note or if he did and just didn't call. Didn't call because last night didn't mean as much to him as it did to me.

I fell under Jack's spell so quickly.

Before this trip to New York, I would have rolled my eyes at anyone who told me they had a whirlwind evening with a handsome, ballet-loving New Yorker with a family legacy to maintain.

A family legacy, which is another reason why I shouldn't write down my number. Last night was wonderful. Jack was wonderful. It lifted me up and filled my soul in a way I've never experienced with anyone before. But it was a fantasy. A story with no chance of a happy ending.

Jack and I don't exist in real life. We can't.

It's impossible.

Not only do we live at opposite ends of the country, but he has to find a woman from the right family. A woman with the right surname, the right connections, manners, and background.

I'm never going to be anything but a fantasy for Jack. And he for me.

I stare at the note. Maybe I should have gone right to LaGuardia. Why am I here writing love notes like some crazed teenager? I'm an adult, and my very real world is waiting for me back in Star Falls.

I go to crumple up the note, but somehow I can't. Jack may never find the note, but I have to at least try to tell him that I didn't stand him up. At least, not because I wanted to.

My heart sits heavy in my chest. I turn and slump against the wall of the restaurant.

Maybe it would have been better if I'd said no when Jack asked me to join him for a walk. It would have made leaving New York easier.

As I'm about to leave, a short guy in a baseball cap smoking a cigarette comes toward me. He pulls out a huge bunch of keys.

"Do you work here?" I ask.

"Sure do," he snaps.

"I was supposed to meet someone here for breakfast.

But I can't make it. I was wondering if I could leave this note with you?"

He looks at me, one corner of his mouth lifted like he's looking at moldy raspberries.

"Send 'em a text."

"I don't have their number." I shake my head. "It's a long story. But if someone called Jack comes in, could you give him this note?"

He rolls his eyes and snatches the note from my hand. "Sure." He unlocks the door and goes inside.

My entire body sags as I watch him go inside. It's like he's taking my fantasy with him, crumpled up in his hand.

There's no way Jack is ever getting that note.

SIX

Jack

Why the hell didn't I get Iris's number last night?

I'd been so thrilled she'd agreed to meet me this morning, so keen not to push her into letting me pick her up that I didn't think to ask for her number. I've barely slept. I could have stayed up all night with her, just talking. Just holding her.

I check my watch. She's only ten minutes late, but what if something's happened to her? She's not used to New York. And I sent her in a cab to Times Square! What was I thinking? She might be in a dumpster right now. Now I wish I'd insisted she spend the night at my place. I should have insisted we go back to her hotel, pack up her stuff and bring it all to my apartment. That way I would have known she was safe. I would have been sure.

I fist my hands and scan Central Park West for taxis, trying to gauge whether any of them are slowing down.

Where is she?

The minutes tick by. Soon it's an hour after the time we'd agreed to meet.

The disappointment that she's not coming weighs me down. I should never have let her go last night. I should have held on to her.

How could I have been so stupid?

My heartbeat starts to race, like an impatient fist banging on my chest. Should I go to Times Square? I could call our security team and get them to check the area. I could get them to find out where she lives. Iris...

She never gave me her last name.

Fuck. How could I feel so close to a stranger. So completely seen and understood by someone and not even know their last name?

I push my hands through my hair. I can't stand feeling so helpless and out of control.

I hail a cab and ask for them to take me to Times Square. She didn't tell me the name of the hotel. I don't even know if she was in Times Square or just nearby. But I can't just stand around wondering if she might be there.

As we pull off, I take out my phone and do an internet search for Iris Colorado. It's not the most common name. Maybe it will bring up something. Dread trickles through my body as the results load on the page. There's an iris flower called the Colorado Ambrosia. Fitting but no help at all.

It's hopeless.

I stare out of the window, trying to think of a solution—and then, on the street up ahead, I see her. My heart leaps into my throat as I take in her blonde hair up in a neat bun like last night.

"Stop!" I yell to the driver, my blood pulsing in my veins. I can't believe I've found her. "Pull over."

We come to a stop just ahead of Iris and I leap out of the cab.

My heart drops as we come face-to-face and I fist my hands.

It's not Iris.

The woman doesn't even look like her. She's tall and her hair is dark not blonde. I don't know how I mistook her for Iris. I'm hallucinating.

The cab door is still open and I slide back onto the back seat. "Sorry. Times Square again, please."

The driver doesn't say a word. He just starts driving like he can take whatever crazy New Yorkers throw at him.

As we continue our journey south, I try and think about the details Iris shared with me. Is there any way I could track her down? She talked about her father and brother and their family business. What was it? An auto repair shop? No, that was her first love or the guy who asks her out a few times a year. But maybe that would help. What did she say his name was? I sigh as I realize she didn't share his name.

When we get to Times Square, I almost don't get out of the cab. It's so vast, there's no way I'm going to find Iris here. Even now, this early on a Sunday, it's busy. There are people everywhere and the lights from the surrounding billboards are almost blinding even in the sun.

I feel like I know the woman I met last night to her bones. But at the same time, I don't know anything about her.

I don't even know if she's alive or dead.

My phone buzzes in my hand and my stomach surges in anticipation. When I glance at the screen, it's Worth who's calling. Why was I expecting it to be Iris? I didn't give her my number either.

I'm an idiot.

I press accept. "Hey."

"Avril said she saw you thirty minutes ago on Central Park West. Was it you?"

And here I was thinking it was possible to disappear without a trace in New York City. "Yeah, it was me. I was waiting for someone. They didn't show."

"A date?" he asks.

I sigh. Was it a date? The most fascinating woman I've ever met? The love of my life?

"We just got to Tavern on the Green for brunch," Worth continues when I don't respond. "Why don't you join us? It's just Sophia, Avril, Poppy, and me."

"I left," I say. I don't tell him I'm in Times Square. How would I possibly explain that?

"So get back here. I want to know who'd stand Jack Alden up for a date."

I sigh, my chest hollow, my mind racing. I'm no more likely to find Iris wandering about in Times Square as I am walking up and down Main Street in Aspen. Brunch with one of my best friends might help take my mind off of being stood up. Or... who knows what happened. "I'll be there."

The journey back to Central Park passes in a blur. I mentally analyze our conversations from last night and try to think of something, anything that might help me if I wanted to find Iris again. But I don't come up with anything.

When I enter Tavern on the Green, I see Worth immediately, and I can tell by his expression that I'm not covering up my disappointment very well.

"We're going to need a round of Bloody Marys for the table," Worth says to the waitress, who's standing at the table before he's even said hello.

He knows exactly how I'm feeling with a single glance.

I put on a smile and greet Worth's wife, Sophia, and Worth's two sisters. I'm grateful the three of the women seem deeply ensconced in some debate and go back to it as soon as we're all seated.

"What's going on?" Worth says.

"I'm not sure," I reply honestly. How I'm feeling doesn't make any sense to me. I'm not sure how I'm supposed to explain it to someone else.

"Okay," he says. "That's out of character, for a start. You'd normally reply that everything's great."

"Because most of the time, everything's just fine. Most of the time I don't have any complaints."

"Not even about your mother?" he asks.

"That's just everyday background noise. Nothing to report in about."

"But today's different," Worth says.

Today is different. At least I thought it was going to be.

"I met a woman," I say. "Last night."

Worth is one of the few people who is as comfortable with silence as I am. I scan the menu as I think about last night. About first spotting her in the audience—her long, elegant neck. I could see the softness in her—her kindness—even before we'd exchanged a word.

"At the ballet," I go on. "I saw her and..." I shake my head because the thoughts that are running through my mind seem too far-fetched to say out loud. "I felt something," I say. "I know that sounds stupid, but—"

"It doesn't sound stupid. If you felt something, you felt something."

I nod. "I definitely did. And then I got to speak to her." I leave out the bit where I threatened to fire Greg if he didn't get me seated right next to her. Somehow he got the entire row cleared out. He deserves a raise.

"She was... it was as if I'd known her before. As if we'd known each other our entire lives. It was..."

"And she felt this too?"

I nod. "At least I think she did." Was I kidding myself? Was I projecting my feelings on her? I don't think so. My feelings felt entirely reciprocated last night. But maybe I was imagining that.

"And the sex?"

"I didn't sleep with her," I say quickly. "Not because I didn't want to, more that I didn't want her to think that's what it was between us. I was sexually attracted to her, but I was also drawn to her down to my soul." I realize I'm talking out loud rather than just having thoughts, and I clear my throat and shift in my seat. I sound certifiable.

"You don't need to feel uncomfortable, Jack. You don't need to pretend otherwise or hold back. I'm your friend. And you know how I fell in love with Sophia the moment I met her."

I sigh and then let out a half laugh. "Yeah, I always thought you were full of shit when you told that story. I've seen plenty of women and wanted to sleep with them the moment I met them, but it wasn't until I met Iris that I thought it was possible to feel real, raw emotion for someone you've only just met." I pause. "I hadn't even spoken to her, but I knew I had to. And when we talked, I just wanted more. And she seemed to know me."

"So what happened this morning?"

I tell him how I didn't get her number last night. "I think we felt so connected that a phone number seemed unnecessary. God, I sound like an idiot."

"And she just disappeared into the night, without even leaving a glass slipper," Worth says.

I narrow my eyes until what he's saying comes into focus.

Cinderella.

That's who Iris was.

"Maybe she got the time wrong. Or couldn't find your meeting place," Worth suggests.

The waitress comes back to the table with our drinks and, after setting five Bloody Marys onto the table, she pulls out her pad, ready to take our order.

"Sophia, do you want to go first?" he asks.

She shakes her head. "I've not even looked. You and Jack go and come back to us."

"Jack?" the waitress says, looking between me and Worth.

"I'm Jack," I say. "I'll take the steak and eggs."

"This is going to sound really weird, but the chef has a note for a Jack. Some woman left it with him this morning. He told me to see if any Jacks came in."

"A note?" I push my chair back as if I'm going to stand, and then I take a breath. It has to be from Iris.

"I'll get it for you," the waitress says. "Unless it's been given out already. Let me find out when I've put your orders in."

Fuck. Can't she go now?

Worth orders quickly, like he can feel my impatience, and then it's down to Sophia and Worth's sisters. Finally, the waitress takes our menus, and as I hand her mine, I say, "I'll just wait here." I'm not sure if I'm reassuring her that I'm not going anywhere or reminding her to make the note a priority. Both, I think.

I watch as she goes back to the cash register area, tucks the menus into their home, and then starts to tap away on the register. Presumably she's putting in our order, but it feels like she's transcribing *War and Peace*. How long can it take?

When she's finished, she disappears through the doors that lead to the kitchens.

Maybe I should have gone with her.

"How's your love life, Jack?" Sophia asks me from across the table.

I glance at her, lightning fast, then pin my gaze to the kitchen door. I want that note as soon as possible. "It's good. Totally fine," I answer absentmindedly. I want to be sure that when our waitress returns, she's holding the note.

Iris's note.

It has to be.

She'd never want to stand me up. Something must have happened, which meant she couldn't make it. That has to be the reason, and without having my number or even my last name, how would she be able to explain?

"Good talk," I hear her say, and then Worth says something to her.

I'm not a guy who likes to be rude. Not to anyone. My mother is rude enough for all the rest of the Alden family put together. But I don't want to focus on anything but the note I just know I'm going to get.

The waitress seems to take three hours, but finally she comes back through the kitchen doors, clutching a piece of paper. One of the other waitstaff stops her as she heads over to me. They chat, and it takes all my self-control not to stand up, march over to her, and take the note from her hand.

Eventually she arrives back at our table.

"Were you expecting something?" she asks.

I hold out my hand. "Maybe."

She gives me the piece of paper that's folded in half, with my name on the front, with an exaggerated J. Just the curve of a single letter makes me smile.

It has to be from her, doesn't it?

I want everyone in the restaurant to disappear so I can read the note in private. If it's not from Iris, I'll be disappointed. If it is...

I unfold the paper.

Dear Jack

I've been called back to Colorado early because my brother is injured. I'm sorry. I don't know if you'll get this note, but I hope you know I had the best evening of my life with you.

Yours, Iris

My heart seizes like it's trapped in a net.

She's gone. But I wasn't projecting. She felt it too.

My eyes snag on the word...

Yours

Yours

Yours

I can't see anything else.

"Is it from her?" Worth asks.

I can't tear my gaze from the page, but I nod. "She got called away."

"Did she leave a number?" he asks.

The question hits me like I'm the kettle drum and Worth's the mallet. Even though I know she didn't put her number on the note, I still scan the paper like I could have missed it. I shake my head.

"Really?" Worth asks.

I hand him the note. I don't have the energy to tell him.

"It's a really nice note. I wonder why she didn't leave a number. Seems weird."

And then I realize. Once a year, she lets herself have a fantasy about what her life might have been if her mother hadn't died. It would have been too painful to prolong it. She wants to shut down and get on with real life back in Colorado.

"It's not weird," I say. "I understand why she didn't leave her number." I don't like it, but I understand her. There's a pain inside me I haven't experienced before. It's like I'm empty and I'm falling into nothingness. It's a pain that breaks into hopelessness. Like I know that I won't ever be happy now that Iris's gone.

The waitress arrives with our food.

"Was the note for you?" she asks.

"Yes, thank you very much." It wasn't exactly the note I wanted, but she'll get a very generous tip from me.

"Oh, I'm just pleased the note found its way to its rightful owner," she says, putting my steak and eggs in front of me.

The last thing I want to do right now is eat. I want to disappear. If I can't be with Iris, I want to be alone.

"I'm going to head out," I say. "I don't want to kill the vibe."

"Stay," Sophia says. "We're your friends, Jack. If you're feeling sad, we want to be able to be there for you."

As much as I'm grateful, no one can help me feel better. I just want to get out of here and disappear.

"I need to think," I say. "Be on my own for a bit."

Sophia looks concerned, but Worth interrupts before she can say anything. "Maybe you should get out of New York. Have you thought about going to the Club? A change of scene might be good for you."

I pull my mouth into a fake grin. "Good suggestion," I lie. "I'll think about it." I want Worth to know I'm grateful for his concern, but being in Colorado would make things worse, not better. It would remind me that I've met the woman it feels like I'm meant to be with, who's disappeared.

For the first time in my life, my heart cracks clean open —smashed into smithereens and I'm not sure what it's going to take, if it's even possible, for it to heal.

SEVEN

Iris

In most ways, it's like I've never been away from Wilde's Farm.

I'm still chasing Oxburg for payment.

My dad is still complaining.

And everyone's commenting on how the September sun is hotter than usual.

The only difference is my brother is slumped on the chair in my office, his leg in a boot.

Oh, and my heart is broken.

I know I was only away for two nights but it feels like it might have been a month. Something inside me has rearranged itself. I'm different. For the first time after a trip to New York, I've brought the Big Apple back home with me.

Usually, I say goodbye at the airport and I'm able to put the trip, the ballet, the different sights, sounds, and smells to the back of my mind and not think about them again until the next year. I store away my fantasy—my taste—of a different life. It allows me to get back to the farm like I never left.

This time it's different. Now, every time I blink, I see Jack. I feel his hand on my face, his lips on mine. Every now and then I turn my head and I catch his scent. I know it's impossible. I've showered twice since I saw him and washed everything I was wearing, but sometimes it almost seems like he's here. Lingering.

Thoughts of him.

His scent.

He's all around me.

Being back in Colorado is harder this time. Today in the office has been difficult. Despite being busier than usual because of my brother's leg, the hours have dragged. I can't wait for the end of the day, but at the same time, I don't want to go home. Still living with Dad and Bray has never bothered me. A couple of times, I've had the opportunity to move out, but the money it would cost would probably mean I couldn't afford to go to New York and so it's never seemed worth it.

But today, all I want is a place of my own.

"I'm not going to be able to cook," Bray says. "Or play hockey."

"I'll inform the NHL," I snap.

"Wow, thanks for the sympathy. I know you cut your trip short, but it's not like I took a mallet to my own leg."

I sigh. I know I'm being snappy. I need to box up thoughts of New York and Jack and toss them into La Poudre Pass and hope they end up in the Gulf of Mexico. But it's harder than it should be. I gave up on my dreams of dancing a long time ago. I grieved them along with my mother.

For a long time I wanted more than I had.

I wanted my mother back.

I wanted my career back.

Eventually I made peace with what I was able to have. I learned to live with what I had rather than what I wanted.

But now, meeting Jack? It's brought all those old feelings to the surface. I could never have Jack, however much I might want him. I could never have a life with him. I know I have no right to want more. We have a roof over our heads, food in our stomachs, and a job to go to. We're a lot luckier than a lot of people.

New York just made me yearn for more.

No doubt I will get over it. Over *him*. It just might take me a while. And I might be a cranky grump until then.

"Right," I say. "I'm sorry. I just really want Oxburg to pay up. I'm going to try them one last time." I dial the number of their finance department, just like I've done at least a dozen times today. Most of the time no one answers. When they do, I leave a message for Karen to call me back, but she never does.

Miraculously, someone answers, and I ask to speak to the elusive Karen.

"This is Karen speaking," a voice says into the phone.

It takes a second for my brain to catch up to the fact that I'm actually speaking to the person I've been trying to speak to for weeks now.

"Karen, this is Iris Wilde from Wilde's Farm. I'm following up on two invoices that have been outstanding over ninety days. Can I give you their numbers?"

"Sure thing."

After I give her the numbers, she asks me to hold. She's gone so long, I half wonder if she's just hung up and I haven't realized it.

I glance at my brother wondering what I can do to get him out of my office.

"So are you going to cook?" Bray asks when he catches me giving him death stares. "I could use a steak. I need the protein to help me heal."

"You need to figure it out with Dad. I'm going out." I have no plans to go out, but I don't want to be at home, cooking. My resentment will build and there's a real chance I might explode.

"Dad can't cook steak."

"Then have a peanut butter and jelly sandwich. I'm not your mom or your girlfriend. And I have enough to do already without adding Wilde's Catering to my résumé." I know I'm being a bitch before Bray has to tell me. "I'm sorry. I'm stressed out by these invoices. And I just need a minute."

"Iris?" Karen asks from the other end of the phone.

"Yes?" I ask hopefully.

"I just found one of the invoices in our system. It's been stuck waiting approval. I just need to check we received the order and my boss is happy. I can't find the other one, though. Can you send it again? I can give you my direct email."

"Sure," I say. I guess it's progress, but there's no certainty we're going to get payment on either invoice. Dad is really counting on getting payment on these so he can get the cherry pickers. "I'm going to follow up in a couple of days."

"No problem," Karen says. "Thank you for your patience."

Patience.

That's what I need. If I can just ride this deep sense of disappointment, things will get better. Or back to normal at least. I'll stop thinking about Jack. About New York. About a different life.

Bray tries to get to his feet but is fumbling for his crutches. I go over and help him, pulling him to his feet.

"I'll drop you off before I head to Grizzly's, so you don't have to wait for Dad," I say.

"Thanks, Iris," he says. "I'm sorry you had to cut your trip short for me."

I sigh and pull my mouth into a small smile. "Thanks."

Our home is adjacent to the farm, so it doesn't take long before I've helped Bray into the house and gotten him some snacks to keep him from withering away until Dad gets home.

"Who you meeting at Grizzly's?" he asks. "Your school friend? She still in town?" He raises his eyebrows, almost like he's daring me to say yes. "Oh no, you didn't go to Vegas with her in the end, did you?"

"If you've got something to say, just say it. Otherwise, eat another chip and I'll be on my way."

"You messing around with some married man or something?"

"What?" I yell. "Why on earth would you think I'm messing around with a married man? I would never."

"You're hiding something. You could never tell a lie. I'll bet you've *never* been to Vegas. I just don't know where you disappear off to every year."

"Well, you have a think about that. I'm going to get myself some chicken wings."

"Awww, bring us back some," he calls as I head out.

"I might," I say over my shoulder, and I push through the front door.

I'm not sure I'm even going to Grizzly's. I could grab a pizza at Pizza Meet Ya. I've never been to either place on my own. When I go to New York, I quite enjoy eating at a restaurant by myself, but here, in Star Falls, I'm pretty sure people would think I'd lost my mind if I asked for a table for one.

All the same, I pull into Grizzly's parking lot. I can't be on my own with my thoughts tonight. I need to be around people. Just not the people I gave up everything for. Tonight, I need space from Bray and Dad. I need to forget about everything.

I need to forget about Jack.

EIGHT

Jack

I've been summoned.

Greg reached out this morning and informed me that my mother would like me to join her for lunch.

Why my mother couldn't send me a text, like a normal person, I don't know. She claims she doesn't know how to text. Sometimes I think she's deliberately trying to hurtle back to the nineteenth century.

"Good afternoon, sir," Cooper, our house manager, says when he opens the door.

"Hi, Cooper. How are you?"

"Can't complain, sir. Your mother is in the morning room."

I really wish he wouldn't call me sir. I've given up asking him to call me Jack. Ever since I turned eighteen, it's been *sir*.

I take the stairs to the second floor, where the morning room and the dining room are. My mother even has Cooper set up the dining room when she's alone. I have no idea why she doesn't just eat at the kitchen counter.

As I approach the double doors to the morning room, I realize my mother isn't alone. And she's not talking to staff. There's a different tone she uses with them.

I open the door to find my mother, Frieda Campbell, and her daughter, Gabriella, sitting and chatting.

It feels like I've walked into an ambush.

"Oh, Jack, so lovely that you could join us," my mother says.

I plaster on a smile and go to kiss my mother on the cheek. "Mother. How are you?" Of course, I would never want anyone to feel uncomfortable, so I don't mention that I was expecting this lunch to be just the two of us, and that Frieda and Gabriella were the last people I was expecting to see.

"I think I mentioned to you that Gabriella was back from Harvard finally."

I then work my way around the room, kissing Frieda and Gabriella on the cheeks. "How lovely to see you both."

I've known the Campbells for years. My entire life in fact. They're one of the handful of New York families that move in the same circles. I was at the same prep school with Gabriella's brother, Francis, although he was a year below me. One of my friends from school dated Gabriella after she graduated college. She went to Princeton for her undergraduate degree.

Gabriella Campbell would be a perfect match for me as far as my mother's concerned. She's impeccably well-mannered, has an acceptable surname and would ensure the Alden family name is continued in just the way my mother expects.

Except I don't see Gabriella in that way. At all. I never

have. It's not that there's anything wrong with her. She's pretty. Clever. I just... I don't find her attractive.

"Your mother was just telling us about the ballet," Frieda says, and my heart jolts in my chest.

"It was beautiful," I say. "A great production."

"Not that you saw the second half," my mother replies testily.

"What I saw of it was wonderful," I say with a smile.

"I love the ballet," Gabriella says neutrally like she doesn't love it at all, but thinks she has to say she does. I'm not sure it's fair to compare, but Gabriella doesn't love the ballet like Iris likes the ballet. I bet she doesn't *feel* it the way Iris does.

It's been weeks now, but Iris's still on my mind all day, every day. I keep catching glimpses of her in restaurants and walking in the park. But of course, it never turns out to be her. She's long gone. But for the second or two that I think I've found her again, I feel happy.

It's the in-between times that are a problem.

It's like I have a black cloud hovering over my head, constantly threatening rain. Even my insides feel dark and cloudy. I used to take life in my stride. But now? Now there's a veneer of gloom spread across each day and I can't seem to shake it off.

I tried to find out Iris's surname and contact details from the New York City Ballet. I figured, they must have records from when she paid. I pulled every string the Aldens have with the organization, but came up with nothing. They told me repeatedly that unless it was members who booked, they didn't keep details of attendees.

"Jack will take you, won't you, Jack. We have our box, of course. I'm sure you can find a suitable date." My mother stares at me pointedly.

"I'll check my calendar," I say.

Gabriella smiles widely at me. Is she really interested in me? And if she is, why wouldn't she just message me and suggest a drink? Why would she go along with this weird lunch where it's clear we're being set up but nobody can mention it? It's not like we don't know each other. She's probably just trying to please her mother, just like I try to please mine.

Cooper comes in and announces lunch is ready. We all head into the dining room. Even if my mind wasn't full of Iris, I wouldn't be interested in Gabriella. This is just a huge waste of time.

The first dish is served, and Frieda and Gabriella comment on the beautiful presentation and the delicate china. I can tell my mother is imagining our intermingled lives. In New York's strict social hierarchy, the Alden family is probably a tier above the Campbells. Not from a financial perspective. Generations ago, the Campbells made a lot of money through imports and exports from Europe and Asia. But just from the historic relationships that the Aldens have throughout the world. My great-uncle married a Norwegian princess. It always helps to have a little royal blood in your family tree. And the Aldens support the arts in New York in a way that no other family does. Our patronage of the New York City Ballet goes back since its inception.

But my mother will think this a good match. Gabriella is young enough to have as many children as it takes to get a boy—vital for the Alden name to continue. And my mother gets on well with Frieda. She understands and respects the hierarchy.

"How was Harvard?" I ask Gabriella, who's seated next to me. My mother is deliberately engaging Frieda in conversation to allow Gabriella and me to talk. It's painful.

"I enjoyed it," she says. "The campus is beautiful and Boston isn't far from New York."

I let out a genuine laugh to this. I'm usually the one who measures any place that isn't New York by the distance it is to Manhattan.

"I actually really did love the weekends spent on the Cape. I would even consider having a regular home there. It really is lovely."

"We have a place on the Vineyard," I say. I'm sure she knows about our family vacation home there and that's why she mentioned it.

We chitchat about Boston and the Vineyard. It's polite. Friendly even. But nothing more.

"So what's your plan, now that you've finished your master's?"

She pulls in a breath, while shooting a glance at her mother. She lowers her voice. "Well, I'd like to go to Europe. I've never spent any extended time there. I'd like to go to museums, hang out in Parisian cafes. Just for a little bit. You know?" She smiles at me, and I can tell it's genuine.

"It's a secret?" I ask her, lowering my voice to match hers.

She shrugs. "Mother thinks I'm getting old. She's worried I'm going to get left on the shelf." She rolls her eyes. "What is the shelf, anyway? That's what I want to know. I'm twenty-six. I don't want to be having children for a decade. I've got a life to live."

I stifle a chuckle. If my mother knew Gabriella didn't want kids for ten years, I don't think she'd let them finish their first course before she had them both escorted out.

"You should go to Europe," I say. "You never know who you might meet."

"Well, exactly. I'm so bored of New York guys," she says. She blushes. "I don't mean to be rude."

I shake my head. "No offense taken." It's a relief to know that Gabriella is as uninterested in me as I am in her. "If you want to go to Europe, that's what you should do. Don't give up on that just because of... parental expectations."

She smiles. "Easier said than done. You know that."

"I do," I reply. "Seeing as you've told me a secret, I'll share one with you. I had no idea you and your mother would be here today. My mother summoned me to a one-on-one lunch this morning."

Her face freezes, her mouth in a hard line. "I was told you were the one who suggested the lunch. As if we can be tricked into liking each other."

I laugh. "Turns out I *do* like you."

"But I mean romantically." It's clear we're both on the same page as it concerns our compatibility as life partners.

"What are you two so deep in conversation about over there?" my mother asks. She turns to Frieda. "I knew they would find lots in common."

"We're just chitchatting about the house on the Vineyard."

Mother nods and resumes her conversation with Frieda.

"So what about you, Jack?" Gabriella says. "I want to go to Europe. What do you want to do?"

Her question gets my attention. Gabriella wants to escape to Paris. It's never even occurred to me that I could leave New York. Not for any extended period of time.

I admire her for thinking outside the expectations of her. I hope she makes it to Paris.

When Frieda and Gabriella have left, my phone buzzes.

It's from Byron in our group chat with Bennett, Worth, Fisher, and Leo.

"Pack your bags, Jack. We're heading to Colorado. Tomorrow. We're taking Bennett's new plane. Wheels up at 9 a.m. No excuses."

When Worth suggested I go to the Club right after meeting Iris, it was the last place I wanted to be, but now? For the first time the two weeks since I met Iris, my chest loosens at the thought of not being in New York, and I realize a break from New York with my best friends is just what I need.

It might not be Paris, but anywhere but here will do.

NINE

Iris

I can now add delivery driver to my résumé. Since Bray's accident, he can't drive. On the farm, enough of the pickers can operate the machinery that it doesn't matter. But Bray takes the deliveries to the Colorado Club. And I've inherited that particular job.

The Club likes to be able to tell their members that their fruit was picked this morning, so now I have to get into work earlier so I can be up the mountain by six thirty.

If it didn't mean more work for me, I might be tempted to take a mallet to my brother's other leg.

Lucky for me, the truck is loaded with the fruit, so I just need to find the key and go.

When I arrive, the truck is having the last few bits of fruit added, and then in a matter of minutes, I'm off, up the mountain.

I pass by Beth and Mike's cabins, although they don't own them anymore—Byron Miller does. Despite him owning most of the mountain, he's building a house down in

Star Falls. Of all the people who've left our town, he's the one I never expected to see again. Apparently no one ever leaves this town.

There's a huge yellow crane set up right on the edge of his land. I really hope it's not going to block the road on the way back down. I've got things to do. I'm going to follow up with Karen today. It might kill me, but I need to get those damn invoices paid so we can place the order for the new machinery. Anything to stop my dad's constant complaints. I also need to fill in my course enrollment forms for the course I've found on the Deer Valley Community College website.

I take the road before the main entrance to the Club. It's the one for goods and deliveries. I pull up in front of the kitchen entrance. There's not usually anyone out here, but this morning, there're a couple of staff outside who look like they're having an argument. They don't even notice I'm here.

"He's bringing his entire crew from New York," one says to the other. "We can't use that shitty steak."

Yikes. I'm pleased I don't work here. And I'm *really* pleased I'm not delivering shitty fruit. The fruit we bring up to the Colorado Club is the best. All the fruit from Wilde's Farm is great, but the Colorado Club gets the top-tier stuff.

I open the truck and pull out one of the crates. There are five to bring in. Hopefully I'll find someone in the kitchen who's in a better mood than the two guys whose argument is still going on.

I enter the door that leads to the kitchen. There's a corridor, and on the left the room that leads to the huge walk-in refrigerator, and on the right, the entrance to the kitchen that's been propped open with a large box that says it contains olive oil. I hover outside. "Hello!" I call. "Fruit delivery."

No one answers. There's usually more people around and it's easy to find one of the kitchen staff who will sign for the delivery. Today the atmosphere seems a little different.

I slide the crate into the store room and poke my head into the kitchen. People are huddled over on the other side, all listening to a guy wearing a white bandana talk. They're all nodding and looking very serious. The swing doors that lead out of the other side of the kitchen—presumably to the restaurant—opens and a familiar face dressed in black trousers and a white shirt enters.

We lock eyes.

"Stephanie?" I ask. Stephanie, who moved to Vegas. Who, until this year, my family thought I visited every year. What's she doing at the Colorado Club?

"Iris!" she says, beaming, and she comes over and we hug.

"What are you doing here?" I ask. "I heard you were in town."

"I keep hearing your name too. I'm so glad we ran into each other. What are *you* doing here?"

"Delivering fruit."

"Oh, I can help you with that," she says. "The chefs are having their daily meltdown early today." She rolls her eyes. "And all at the same time. You won't get any help out of them."

"You work here?" I ask as we head out to the truck.

"Yeah, I got a job as restaurant manager. It's weird to be back. But not quite back, if you know what I mean."

"So you're here to stay?"

She grins. "Unless I get fired!"

"Wow, I had no idea."

We get to my truck and I pull off a crate and hand it to her, taking another for myself.

"I was hoping I'd run into you, actually," she says, leading us back to the kitchen. "From what I've heard, people think we're still close. I've spoken to a few who think you came out to visit me in Vegas."

My cheeks burn hot, and I don't know what to say. I'm such a horrible liar. If I deny it, my blush would be enough to give me away.

"Oh, yeah," I say.

Stephanie puts her crate next to my first one in the store room. I slot mine on top.

She stands, looking at me, waiting for me to say more.

I take in a breath and try not to wince. "I've told people I go and visit you in Vegas once a year."

She lets out a small laugh. "Okay," she says. "So I've acted as a cover without even knowing it."

"I didn't expect you'd be back in town, given your entire family left."

"Apparently not. Well, I've managed to give vague responses, so I haven't blown your cover. But now I'm intrigued."

I head out first this time. There are two crates left in the truck.

"I just need a weekend to myself," I say. That's the truth. Sort of. "I always thought I'd leave Star Falls after high school, then my mom died and I ended up staying. I just take a weekend every year to... I don't know. Spread my wings or something."

She leans against the truck, ready to chat rather than reach for the last of the crates. "I heard about your mom. I'm sorry. She was always really kind to me."

I smile, genuinely thankful for her words. It's been a

while since I've had condolences for my mother's death. "Thanks."

"You were going to go to ballet school, weren't you?"

"You have a good memory," I say.

"You were obsessed. When you weren't training, you were watching ballet."

"Not much time for any of that now."

"You don't dance at all?"

"Nope," I say, and pick up one of the last two crates and head back inside.

Once a year in New York doesn't count.

"Do you miss it?" she asks from behind me.

We stow the last of the crates and I pull out the delivery note from my back pocket. "I don't have a pen."

She reaches into her pocket and pulls out a pen and takes the delivery note from me, before signing it and giving it back to me. I give her a copy.

"I allow myself to miss it once a year," I say, standing as straight as I can. "I go to New York. Watch the New York City Ballet. Take a class or two at Joffrey Ballet School and then I put it away for another year and come home to the farm."

Her eyebrows pull together and pity fills her face.

I don't want her to feel sorry for me. "The look on your face right now is why I don't tell anyone where I'm going and what I'm doing."

"You don't want anyone to feel bad that you stayed?"

"My dad and brother, mainly. They couldn't have coped on their own. They needed me to stay, and that's okay. I made the right decision. I don't regret it. I don't want them to carry any guilt about it. I did what was best for my family and I stand by it."

"You can't tell them that?"

"I think Dad would have tried to pack me off to New York, and if I'd let him, the farm would have gone under."

"Maybe," Stephanie says. "But time has moved on."

"Right. And any hope I had of making dance my career has passed. So what's the point in dredging it up?"

"I don't know. Maybe your dad and brother deserve you to be open with them. Maybe they want to comfort you because it must be hard to give up something you cared so passionately about. It must still hurt if you go back to New York to relive that every year. Maybe they won't want to turn back the clock, but perhaps they'd just want to hug you. Like I want to do right now."

Tears gather in my throat. I came here to make a fruit delivery, not spill my guts to a woman I haven't seen since high school.

She pulls me into a hug, and I hug her back.

"I missed you when we left," she whispers as she hugs me.

"Me too," I say. I don't add that it didn't last long because the grief of losing my best friend was soon overshadowed by the grief of losing my mother. It's hard to care about anything when one minute your mom still comes and kisses you good night before bed, and then you're standing over her grave.

But it feels good to have Stephanie back.

She pulls back and holds my shoulders with both hands. "I'm absolutely frantic at the moment because we've got some VIP arrivals, but we should meet up. Go to Grizzly's or something."

"Don't you always have VIP arrivals?"

She laughs. "Yeah, but everyone's freaking out about this particular party. But once they've left, let's hang out.

Catch up. Honestly, chatting like this, it feels like I saw you a couple of months ago, not over a decade."

It's true. It's easy between us. Maybe because she knew me when I was a teenager before I bore the scars of becoming an adult and all that has entailed for me. "Maybe I've been manifesting our connection by pretending I'd visit you."

She grins at me. "That manifesting shit works, man."

"Well, I hope it goes well with your VIPs. I'll probably run into you in the meantime. I'm doing the deliveries up here at the moment three times a week because Bray broke his leg."

She rolls her eyes. "Of course he did."

Her reaction isn't surprising. Bray was a true daredevil as a kid. He was always coming home from the end of the day covered in bumps and scratches. And more than once he dislocated his shoulder on the hockey rink. A broken toe was a weekly occurrence.

"He's not as bad as he used to be. This time he just toppled off a tractor."

She blushes and lowers her voice. "I don't think I ever told you that we kissed back in the day."

"You and Bray? I didn't know that."

"I swore him to secrecy. I knew my best friend's brother was strictly off-limits."

I laugh. I would have probably hated the idea of Stephanie and Bray together. Mainly because I would have felt left out. Now the idea feels oddly comforting.

"Let's swap numbers and we can get a night a Grizzly's in the calendar."

Once we've exchanged our details, we have another hug, and I get back into the truck. I only expected to drop off some fruit this morning. The last thing I was expecting was to get my best friend back. For the first time since New York, I feel a little lighter.

TEN

Jack

I don't like to complain, but if we're traveling on a private plane, I don't understand why we have to leave so early. I haven't slept well since I met Iris. I wonder if I ever will again.

"Leaving so early means we get the entire Friday to enjoy at the Club," Fisher says as we come into view of the airport. "This was great planning, Bennett."

I love my friends for arranging this trip. I know how busy they are, how their schedules are booked up weeks, months, and years in advance. It will have taken a lot for all five of them to drop everything to be here.

They might not have said it directly, but they're doing this for me. I need to stop being so ungrateful. I needed to leave New York. I still keep seeing Iris everywhere I go and I swear it's slowly sending me insane. Hopefully in Colorado, the hallucinations will stop and I can forget about her.

I might be able to sleep.

Stop faking my smile.

"An early morning hike seems like a good idea," Worth says.

"Said nobody ever," I reply.

"As you know, the helicopter to the Club takes about ten minutes. So we'll get there about nine local time," Byron says. "We can do anything we want. Hike. Eat. Go into town."

"Grizzly's!" Fisher says.

"Doesn't open until lunchtime," Byron says. "You'll have to wait for your wings."

"We could go to the diner," Fisher says. "Get some breakfast. The waffles there are great."

"I could take offense, you know," Byron says. "The Club does waffles. And they have better fruit than the diner."

We all try to stifle our laughs. I don't know why Byron is getting worked up. Obviously, the food at the Club is insanely good. The diner is just a change of scene for Fisher. Because he now lives between Star Falls and New York, he gets to appreciate it more.

"Do you feel like a local?" I ask Fisher.

"Not even close," he says. "Not because everyone isn't welcoming, but just because New York is always going to feel like home. But I have to say, I didn't expect to love Star Falls the way I do. Even if we could be full-time in New York, I wouldn't want to. It's good to head west, breathe some mountain air and unwind."

Mountain air is a little overrated, as far as I'm concerned. Martha's Vineyard is not a four-hour plane ride and the air is just as fresh.

"We can go right to the diner," Bennett says, always the most likely of us to take control of the itinerary. "Have some breakfast. We can go get some hiking gear for Jack, because we all know his housekeeper didn't pack anything. That place with the moose outside it. Then we can come back to the Club and hike. Then have lunch and chill out this afternoon."

"*Chill out* is Bennett-code for catch up on emails," Leo says.

"You're hardly one to talk," Worth replies.

"None of us have any room to talk," I say. "But yes, let's follow Bennett's plan." I like the idea of being busy. If I'm out of contact this morning, the office will want to speak to me this afternoon. It might mean I have a real shot of not obsessing over Iris for a few hours.

After the plane lands, we take a helicopter to the Colorado Club. When we land, two SUVs are waiting to take us for breakfast.

"I'll drive one," says Byron. "You can ride shotgun." He lifts his chin to me as he speaks. "It's better if you don't drive."

"I can drive," I say.

"I didn't say you couldn't. I just said it's better if you don't. I mean, how often do you actually ever drive yourself?"

"In Martha's Vineyard."

He chuckles but doesn't respond, and Worth gets in the back with Byron and me in the front. Leo, Bennett, and Fisher are in the second car.

A member of staff hands Byron the key. "The road is closed at Beth and Mike's place because of the crane. You'll need to take the long route."

"What a pain," spits Byron. "It's our crane, but it's a

pain in the ass to go the back route past Wilde's Farm. Are you sure you want to go to the diner?"

"I don't care," I say.

"Let's just stick to the plan," Worth says from the back. "A few back roads might be nice. It can get us into the Star Falls mindset."

Byron pulls off the main road a couple of miles outside the grounds of the Club.

"How long until you move in to the new place?" I ask Byron.

"Six months. Probably means a year given the fit out, factoring in delays."

"Well, it's not like you're slumming it at the Club, is it?"

"No. But I'm looking forward to not being on the grounds. It will be nice to switch off," he says.

Switch off. That's what I need to do. Switch off from Iris. I just wish I could find a button that could erase her from my mind. I've done everything I can to find her. I even spoke to a private detective who said without more to go on, he couldn't help me.

She doesn't want to be found. I have to accept that.

I've always been so good at not fighting against things I can't change. I've never wanted to waste my energy. Why am I finding it so difficult this time?

As we get to the bottom of the mountain, the ground flattens out and simple wooden fencing appears on Byron's side of the vehicle.

"This is a fruit farm," he says. "The Wildes are a good family. You know they still don't grow apples because that was my family farm's fruit."

"An unspoken agreement?" I ask.

"Yeah. And now we're getting the orchard back up and running, it won't be for nothing."

"You're getting your family's orchard up and running?" I ask.

"Not me. Not really. I donated the land to the town, so it's like a cooperative of the people who want to be involved."

"That's a lovely idea," Worth says from the back seat.

Byron slows down as we pass the entrance to the farm. "Yeah. So the two fruit farms will still exist in harmony."

Farther up the drive into the farm, there are a couple of vehicles parked and a woman with long blonde hair is putting something in the back of a truck.

I swear, it looks exactly like Iris.

Not that I've even ever seen her with her hair down. I turn away from the window and close my eyes. Images of Iris have followed me to Star Falls. I'd hoped a change of scene would keep them away.

"Do they supply the Club?" Worth asks from the back.

"Yeah. We use as many local suppliers as possible. Anyway, the fruit from Wilde's is incredible. If we were having breakfast at the Club, that's where it would be from."

I bite back a grin at Byron trying to sell the Club to us, like we don't know it's the best, and I keep my gaze straight ahead. I don't want to catch a glimpse of any more Irises.

Byron made the road sound like some monster truck route without the monster truck, but we're pulling up outside the diner in no time.

Fisher pulls up right next to us. "Waffles!" he says as he gets out of the car, gazing at the diner like he's possessed.

Byron tugs at my jacket. "Let's go see Marv and his owner, Marge, get you some hiking gear, and then join the rest of them."

I shrug. I don't have much of an appetite anyway.

"Marge will have you set up in ten minutes. The rest of them can wait to order."

Byron was right, Marge looked me up and down and the only thing she made me try on was shoes—which fit perfectly. So I pay, and ten minutes after we left them, Byron and I join the rest of the group in the diner.

As we enter, the redheaded waitress who always gives Byron shit has her back to us, talking to someone in front of her. She turns and steps toward us, revealing who she was talking to.

A petite woman with long blonde hair comes into focus.

More images of Iris.

I just can't shake them. I can only see her in profile as she's talking to someone through the kitchen pass, but it looks just like her.

It *really* looks like her.

Iris?

It can't be.

I must be mistaken. When she turns, I'll realize it's not my Iris. Then I might have to make an appointment to see a neurologist. Or a shrink or something.

I'm rooted to the spot, waiting for her to turn, waiting for my madness to be confirmed. I can't move. I can't even turn my head so I can focus on something else. It can't actually be Iris. These goddamn hallucinations.

I'm vaguely aware of someone—Worth, I think—calling my name, but I can't answer. I can't focus on anything but the woman in front of me and the curve of her neck. The jut of her chin and her elegant profile. It *really* looks like her.

The room tilts a little, and I can't seem to get my breath. I can't tell what's real and what's not anymore.

The woman laughs and I want to reach out to her, move her to face me so I can see for certain that it's not Iris.

What seems like hours later, she finally turns.

And screams.

Fruit hits me in the face and the chest and everyone around Iris and me charges into action.

It's only me who doesn't move.

Me and Iris.

ELEVEN

Iris

Two universes collide inside me and I can't breathe as the energy from both crash together. Waves of confusion and excitement and horror collide. I'm hot. And cold. And I feel nothing and everything at the same time.

Jack's here. Jack's here. Jack's here.

In Star Falls.

Right in front of me.

When I met him two weeks ago in New York, I thought he looked familiar. Jack isn't a celebrity. Just a friend of Byron's. People say it's a small world. But it really isn't. Not at all. How is he here?

Is it coincidence? Or fate?

"Sorry," I say, bending to pick up the raspberries I've just thrown.

"It's fine," Donna says. "These guys are scary, I get it."

The raspberries have been rescued from the floor, but as I straighten and stare back at Jack, I'm aware that he has splodges of raspberry juice all over his white shirt.

One of his friends pats him on the shoulder. "We'll just take a seat, Donna."

"Sure," she says.

My gaze lifts and we lock eyes.

"Iris, you okay?" Donna asks.

Jack and I keep staring at each other.

"I'm not sure."

I may well be about to vomit. Or faint. Or both.

Jack was the very last person I expected to see today. And although he looks so incredible—his JFK-brown hair shiny and thick, his eyes as piercing as ever—honestly, he's not who I wanted to see.

Leaving New York was worse this time than it's ever been before. Partly because I was called back early and I wasn't mentally prepared to pack up all my lost dreams by the time I left. But mainly because of Jack. He renewed that sense of knowing there was something out there for me that I couldn't have. The sense of loss that I've carried with me since my mother died.

"Do you two know each other?" Byron says from somewhere.

"Cinderella," Jack replies.

"*Iris* is Cinderella?" someone says.

Finally, I'm pulled out of this trance that seeing Jack has put me in. "Jack," I say. "What are you doing here?"

"Byron's my friend," he says. He hasn't taken his eyes from mine since he saw me. It's like he can't quite believe what he's seeing.

I know how he feels. We weren't ever meant to see each other again. I was supposed to come back to Star Falls and we were both supposed to get on with our lives.

"We're here to mend his broken heart," Byron says. "But, we're redundant."

My heart lifts in my chest at the idea that by meeting like this, we're somehow fixed. But the heaviness inside me is insistent. It presses down, bringing my heart back down to the floor. Byron's talking like Jack and I running into each other solves everything. Like now we can ride off into the sunset and have our happy ever after. But of course, that's not true.

Seeing him again just makes it harder. Makes it more frustrating that I'm stuck here in Star Falls. I need to remain in reality. Fantasies are for New York. Not Star Falls.

"I need to get back," I say, glancing down at the empty box that held raspberries that I brought in for the diner. They were too ripe to do anything with other than eat.

"Iris," Jack says, like he can't believe I might just walk out. "I got your note."

"You did?" I ask, surprised. I never expected him to actually get it.

There're murmurings behind us. His friends discussing me. And Jack. "It was nice to see you," I say, and offer him a small smile. What else can I do?

I shake my head and reach for the door. I need some air. I feel like my entire life just exploded and I need some time to put things back in their proper place.

I take the steps toward the truck, which is parked right outside, and just as I hit the sidewalk, Jack calls my name. I stop, but I don't turn around.

He's next to me in a second. "You're just going to walk away? You don't want to talk? To tell me why you had to leave? To—"

"To what, Jack? I was planning to meet you the next morning. My brother broke his leg. Dad asked me to come back to help. How could I say no?"

"I'm not saying you could say no. But somehow, for

some miraculous reason, we've run into each other again. And..."

"And what?"

He pulls back and contorts his face into a scowl. "I thought we had... a connection."

"I thought so too," I mumble.

"I thought you would be pleased to see me. I know I'm—"

I can't hold it back any longer. I drop the small box I'm holding and press the heels of my hands against my eyes, blocking any tears from falling. The last thing I want to do is cry.

"Iris." His voice is soft and concerned. He closes the distance between us and his hand is on my back. He's trying to make me feel better, but all he's doing is making everything worse.

"I could have left my number on the note. There were ways we could have stayed in touch." He searches my face, waiting for what I'm going to say next. "But I didn't. Deliberately."

His face darkens, like I've slapped him.

"Because what then?" I plead. "We come from two very different worlds on different ends of the country. There's no point in dragging this out." It feels like a knife slicing into my gut and I'm the one gripping the handle. "I had a wonderful evening with you. But it was a fantasy. There was nothing about it that was real."

As I say the words, I'm not sure they're true. It was all real to me. The way I felt like he knew me when we'd barely spoken. The way that he made me feel. It all felt as real as anything could.

"It's easier not to pretend that you and I can exist beyond that fantasy." The knife sinks deep and twists. I glance down at the ground, trying to gather my strength. "Enjoy your breakfast, Jack."

Before he can say anything that might change my mind, I slide into the truck and head out. I can't look in my rearview mirror. I don't want to see his face again. Seeing him again has made this all so much harder. Jack belongs in New York with my fantasies of what life could have been. It's easy to carry on with life when you don't know what the alternatives are. It's easy being single, when the perfect guy isn't standing on the roadside wanting to be with you.

I have to protect myself. I've had enough disappointment and heartache in this lifetime. I just want to keep my head down and survive. I'm done with ups and downs. With disappointments and surprises. I'm done with hoping for more. I just want a straight road. A road back to Wilde's Farm to get on with my life.

The only problem with a straight road is that it's easy to glance back and see what you left behind.

TWELVE

Jack

I'm usually the guy with all the answers. But today, I don't even know what the questions are.

Fisher wants to go to Grizzly's, so that's where we're headed. I'd say it's partly the wings and partly because he wants to see Juniper. I can't blame him. Doing long distance must be tricky. I know they're normally in Star Falls when Juniper's eight-year-old daughter, Riley, is in school, but Fisher does have to come back to New York regularly. It's been a few days since he saw Juniper. And he's newly in love. It's understandable.

Somehow, even though I got shot down in flames by Iris today at the diner, I'm sympathetic to Fisher's request that we go into town. I'm rooting for Fisher and Juniper's relationship. Since meeting Iris, I'm somehow less cynical about Fisher settling down. I'm less skeptical about Worth falling for Sophia the first time he laid eyes on her. I may only have had one evening with Iris, but she changed me.

After seeing Iris at the diner, I thought all my Christmases had come at once. I couldn't believe my luck that instead of all these imagined Irises, I was standing in front of the real one.

What are the odds?

At least she explained why she didn't leave her number. It still hurts, but I get it. I understand why she wants to keep her once-a-year-New York world separate from the rest of her life. It's helped her survive.

But I still want her.

Maybe she doesn't want me, but right now, I'm in Star Falls, and I'm not going to leave without trying to convince her that I'm the right guy for her.

What's the worst that can happen? She already broke my heart.

Maybe that's why I can't just stay in my room tonight and lick my wounds. I know there's a possibility that Iris might be in Grizzly's. And I'll do just about anything to see her again.

The cars park outside Grizzly's and we step out. "Smell that fresh mountain air?" Fisher says, pulling in a breath.

"Smells a lot like stale beer and sweat to me," Byron says. "The Colorado Club has a better scent, but even I can admit that the wings at Grizzly's can't be matched."

We head inside and I scan the bar, trying to spot the golden hair I saw this morning at the diner. She looked different with her hair down. It's longer than I imagined it would be. The ends go to her elbows. It's kinda cute she doesn't tie it back for work but does to go to the ballet. I must ask her about it. If she'll talk to me. If she'll even be here.

But somehow, I know she'll be here at some point this evening, even if she's not here now.

Yeah, she walked away without giving me her number. But I'm not so sure she'll be able to *keep* away, knowing I'm here. Whatever it is we have between us is way too powerful. I don't believe she's willing to turn her back on me, even if she thinks it's the right thing to do.

If she doesn't show, then I'll have my answer. I'll be back to New York on the first flight out of here.

We grab a booth and slide into our seats.

"Is this the right place to be?" Byron asks. "Maybe we should have stayed at the Club."

"And deny us of the wings?" asks Fisher. "I'm sorry, I consider myself a good friend, but not even Jack's broken heart can override Grizzly's wings."

"It's good to have boundaries," I say. The fact is, I'm happy to be down in town. I need to know there's hope for me and Iris. If she comes into Grizzly's tonight, I'll know that she wants me like I want her. I don't know why, but I have faith that she'll know that I'll be here tonight. If she wants to avoid me, she'll stay home.

"Tequila?" Bennett suggests. "I'll get a bottle."

Honestly, I'd prefer a really nice glass of red wine, a burgundy. Chateau Margaux perhaps. But even though my friends accept me for the snob I can be, I'm not going to feed them with fodder for their jokes.

"Tequila sounds good," I say.

"They have a nice one," Byron says.

"They keep it just for you?" Worth asks.

"It's much worse than that. The Club gets it in. The Club sells it to Grizzly's and then Grizzly's charges me double to buy it back."

I can't help but chuckle. "That's called entrepreneurship."

We get a bottle of tequila, a tray of beers, and some shot

glasses, and take the two trays over to a table. I'm not quite sure why we've not used the table service, but I'm not going to argue.

"Pool, anyone?" Fisher asks.

I shake my head. I'm terrible at pool and I don't enjoy it. Plus, I've given myself a seat with a view to the entrance. I'm not moving unless it's to greet Iris.

Leo joins Fisher for a game of pool, leaving the four of us at the table.

"Are you sure you didn't recognize Iris?" Byron asks me. "You must have been in Grizzly's at the same time."

"I'm sure. If I'd seen her before, I would have known."

"You think she looks a little different in New York?" he asks.

"Maybe. Probably. But this morning in the diner she looked exactly the same. But better. I know you think this is just about physical attraction. I'm not saying that's not part of it. But it's more than that. We... connected. Before we even spoke." I stop talking because if I carry on, I'm going to say something that sounds pathetic. Something like how it was as if our souls connected before we'd even met, and I can't let myself say that out loud. It doesn't make logical sense. I get that.

"She's pretty," Bennett says.

"Yeah. She's beautiful," I reply. "And incredibly kind. And thoughtful."

"Do you have a plan?" Byron asks.

"To win her over?" I ask.

Byron pulls in a breath. "Yeah, but also, what then? Okay, so maybe the two of you have this connection. Maybe she's on board. You both want to be together. Then what?"

I haven't really thought past seeing her again tonight. "Then what? What should my plan be?"

"I think you need a plan," Byron says.

"But you didn't have a plan. Fisher didn't have a plan. You've managed to make it work."

"So, this is it? This is the woman you want to spend the rest of your life with?" Worth asks.

It feels like a trick question. Of course it sounds ridiculous to say yes. I haven't spent more than a couple of hours with the woman. We haven't slept together. In so many ways we barely know each other. But I can't help how I feel.

"I've never felt so strongly about a woman," I say, skirting the question.

"Okay," Bennett says. "So let's play this out to the conclusion. You spend some more time with Iris. You figure out she's the one. Do you move to Star Falls?"

Is he actually serious? I pull my eyebrows together. "I'm not sure I'm cut out for farm life," I say.

"So you're expecting her to move?" he says.

I shift a little in my seat. "She loves New York. She wanted to move to the city when she graduated high school."

Byron's eyes widen, like I'm missing something. "But she didn't," he says.

"Because her mother died and her brother and father needed her at the farm. I can get someone to help them out."

Bennett fixes me with a look. "It's not a farmhand they're after."

"I know," I say. "She does all the administration and the finance. The business side of the farm. From what I can tell, her dad and brother do the horticulture side."

"Right. So it's more than an admin job. She runs the farm. And even if you could replace the job she does, maybe she's their emotional support as well. And vice versa."

Okay, so maybe it's not as easy as we'll just move to New York. But there's a solution. There's got to be. And it doesn't involve me moving to Star Falls.

"Say you do convince her to move to New York," Bennett says. "And dad and brother are happy. Are you going to marry her? How's that going to go down with Joan?"

I roll my eyes. "I don't need to ask my mother's permission about who I marry." As I say the words, they come out hollow. Technically, I don't need my mother's permission. I don't need anyone's permission. But honestly, if I was to marry Iris, my mother would have something to say about it.

"She wouldn't be happy," I concede. "But that wouldn't stop me from doing what I wanted."

"It might make life very difficult for the both of you," Bennett says.

"Difficult, but not impossible." Honestly, she could make life close to impossible for Iris. As could New York society. People in my life aren't warm, fuzzy folks. They're hard and suspicious and the exact opposite of Iris. No one in my life would accept Iris.

My thoughts are interrupted as the door to Grizzly's opens and in walks a girl I swear I've seen up at the Colorado Club, together with the only woman I *want* to see —Iris.

My heart pushes against my chest and my breath leaves my body.

She looks incredible. She's wearing a white shirt and jeans. Her hair falls down her back. Without it pulled back from her face, she looks a little younger than she did in New York. More carefree. It suits her.

She's smiling as she comes through the door, like the woman she's with just told her a joke.

Leo mumbles under his breath. "I think this means we can all go back to New York City now."

"I gotta go," I say, and I'm out of my seat and across the room.

"Hi, Jack," the woman who's with Iris says. "I'm Stephanie."

Iris must have filled Stephanie in, and they both must have been expecting to see me here. That's a good sign, right?

My gaze flits between Iris and Stephanie. Iris doesn't look surprised to see me and her smile only fades slightly.

"Hi, Jack," Iris says.

"You can buy us a drink," Stephanie says.

"Sure," I say. "What can I get you both?"

The women exchange a look. "Tequila!" they both say in unison.

I order the tequila—the same bottle that Byron ordered.

Stephanie turns to me. "And now you have to introduce me to your friends, so I have something to do while you two catch up."

Iris wrinkles her nose. "Tonight was meant to be about you and me catching up," she says.

Stephanie puts her hand on Iris's shoulder. "I know. And we can do that. But these opportunities don't come along very often. The two of you should talk." She swipes the tequila bottle and two shot glasses from the bar and heads over to Bennett, Worth, and Byron.

"She's a woman who knows what she wants," I say.

"She's been like that since she was sixteen."

"It's impressive." I'm also grateful that she's left Iris and me alone.

"I told her I thought you'd be here. I filled in a few blanks for her."

"You thought I'd be here, yet you still came. You can't want to avoid me that much."

She sighs, her shoulders dropping, like she's disappointed or something. "Now you're here..."

I don't want her to finish her thought. I don't want her to say how we can be friends, or something that's not about the two of us spending time together and exploring the connection we so obviously have. "You want to go somewhere and talk?"

She pulls in a breath and immediately I know she's not going to say yes. What can I do to convince her? I can't just let her walk away.

"I think we should stay here," she says.

A speaker squeals from somewhere and then a guitar starts to play.

I watch Iris as she turns her head to see where the noise is coming from.

"It's Eva. I didn't realize she was singing today."

I follow Iris's gaze and see a woman sitting on a stool at the opposite corner of the bar. She has a guitar on her lap and there's a microphone stand in front of her. I've never been here when they've had live music.

The song the woman starts to sing is familiar, but I don't know the name.

"I love this one," Iris says, turning a little. I've lost part of her attention and it's like an arctic breeze tumbles in and blows down my spine.

I've lost this girl once. I don't want to again.

She turns back to me, her gaze snagging on something behind me. "We have an audience," she says, lifting her chin.

I turn and Worth is looking over. He's just worried

about me. Just trying to see if he can figure out if Iris and I are as connected as I think we are. He wants to be able to warn me if I'm going to get hurt, if this thing Iris and I share's just in my head.

"Worth," I say, a smile nudging the corners of my mouth up. "He's like the dad of our group."

"Like fatherly? To you?" she asks.

"Sensible and empathetic," I reply. "But yes, he's definitely watching us."

The door to Grizzly's opens and in walk two guys in jeans and baseball caps. One of them sees Iris and his entire face lights up. I can't blame him, but a surge of jealousy hits my bloodstream, and I want to know exactly who this guy is and what he is to Iris.

"That's Jason," Iris says, like she's reading my mind.

"The one who asks you out every year?"

She glances up at me. Her gaze hits me like an electrical current, and I have to fight the urge to snake my arm around her waist and pull her closer to me—away from everyone else. She looks away quickly. Has she been avoiding looking at me so she didn't have to feel this tangible chemistry we have?

"You have a good memory," she says.

"I've tried to memorize everything about you."

She sighs. "Jack."

"Wanna get away from these prying eyes? I feel like we have the entire town watching."

She lets out a small laugh. "That's because we do have the entire town watching."

I'm still waiting for her answer. I want us to get out of here and go somewhere we can be on our own.

"A walk?" she asks.

"Anything, anywhere," I reply.

"Let's go."

I don't have to be asked twice. I follow her out of Grizzly's. I don't even glance over my shoulder to wave goodbye to my friends—my friends who have all made the trip to Colorado for me. All I can think about is Iris.

THIRTEEN

Iris

I reverse out of my parking spot outside Grizzly's and turn right onto the main road. I don't know where I'm headed. If I was thinking straight, I wouldn't have come out tonight. I knew Jack would be at Grizzly's. He was waiting for me, I just knew it. Stephanie and I could have stayed on the farm and drunk moonshine and caught up. We didn't need to go out.

Except I did. I had to.

I couldn't know where Jack was going to be and not be there too.

I'm hoping that under the Colorado sky, he's going to hit different. I've convinced myself that if I can just see him again, the intensity I feel when I'm with him will fade. The way I can feel his gaze on me like he's skimming my body with his fingertips will disappear. I'm desperate to confirm that it all ebbs away when I'm not thousands of miles away from real life. In Star Falls, it has to be impossible for me to having feelings for a guy I barely know.

It has to be.

Because I can't let myself fall for a man like Jack.

"Where do you want to go?" I ask from the driver's seat.

"Let's go up the mountain," he says. "To the Club."

As soon as he says it, I know I should say no. The Colorado Club isn't home. It's too easy to believe I'm still in a fantasy if I'm not down in Star Falls.

Maybe that's where I want to stay for now. Anything to be with Jack.

I don't understand the pull I feel to him. All I can do is act on it.

"I never thought I'd see you again," Jack says.

"I didn't think so either."

"We came because my friends thought I needed a change of scene," he says. "Back in New York, I keep thinking I see you—the back of your head, the curve of your neck. Of course, it never is you."

I snap my head to glance at him while he talks. "That's what used to happen to me when my mom died. I kept thinking I saw her places."

He sighs. "I know for sure you're not dead."

"Different but not dead," I say.

"Different how?" he asks.

I sigh. The muscles that have been tense since I laid eyes on him in Grizzly's finally relent, and my body sinks back into the seat of the car. "Different because this is real-life Iris. Iris who doesn't go to the ballet or walk for hours with strangers in Central Park."

"You're just describing where you are. Not who you are."

"Maybe," I say. But it doesn't feel like I'm the same person as the one who's in New York. The one who steals away for the weekend is full of hope. Full of excitement for what she's going to do, what she's going to experience. Star Falls Iris knows exactly what each day brings.

"You look beautiful with your hair down."

Despite my attempts not to feel the flattery, it curls under the collar of my shirt and covers my entire body. I flush with embarrassment. "You prefer it?"

"I like it both ways," he says.

"I never wear it in a bun when I'm in Star Falls."

He nods. "I figured."

We pull up to the gates of the Club and we get let through. Jack directs me through the network of tiny roads and I pull up in front of one of the lodges.

"There's no point in swapping one set of prying eyes for another. I thought you could come to my lodge."

I pull in a breath. My answer should be no. I don't know if I'll be able to say no to Jack if we're alone together—in fact, I know I won't.

"Sounds good," I answer. Maybe this is what we need. Both of us. Maybe the pining for each other will fade if we're together—if we get to know each other better.

"Good," he says.

He leads me inside. The lodge is huge—open plan, but I'll bet it's bigger than our family home. I kick off my shoes and follow him.

"Are you staying here on your own?" I ask. "Or are you sharing with your friends?"

He shakes his head as he switches on the lights. I glance up. It doesn't bring the overhead lights on. But all the table lamps and floor lamps in the room come on all at once.

The place looks like something you'd see on Instagram. Except bigger and more expensive-looking. It looks like a place that would be much more in keeping with New York than Star Falls. The rug bounces beneath my feet it's so thick. I turn, taking the room in. Nothing in here was bought locally. I've never seen any furniture like this in any store I've ever been to. The couches are so huge it looks like you could get lost in them. The walls seem to be papered in fabric or something.

"Oh, you have one of Juniper's paintings in here. I heard she had some stuff up here." At least the paintings are local.

"You know that Juniper and my friend Fisher are together now?"

I nod but glance anywhere but at his face. I don't want to see what he's thinking. Because he can't be suggesting that because it worked out for Juniper and Fisher, it could work out for us.

We barely know each other.

We're not Juniper and Fisher.

From what I've heard, Fisher's family isn't involved in their relationship. There is no family legacy to worry about.

"Can I get you a drink?" Jack asks.

"Sure. Water would be great."

I slide onto one of the barstools by the kitchen counter and watch Jack grab a pitcher from the cupboard and fill it with water and ice. He grabs something from the freezer and I realize it's sliced lemon rounds. He slips a handful into the pitcher and puts the pitcher in front of me, alongside a glass.

All I wanted was a glass of water.

I got a pitcher with lemon too.

I wonder how often Jack prepares his own drinks. "Do you have servants?" I ask him.

He takes another glass from the cupboard and turns. His eyes are narrowed. "No one I call a servant, no."

"Staff, then. Is that what you call them?" If I lived in New York, I'd probably work for a man like Jack.

"I have a housekeeper who also cooks," he says.

"And when you say housekeeper...?"

He pulls in a breath. "Are you looking for differences between us? Because you won't have to look very hard."

"I'm just trying to imagine what your life is like in New York."

He glances down at the floor. "I like you. I think you like me." He pauses, his stare so intense I feel like I might burst into shards of light under his inspection. "I've never felt this connection. I think you feel it too." He rounds the counter and my heart rate ramps up with every step closer he gets.

I nod. There's no point in denying it. "Yeah, I feel it. But that doesn't mean... it doesn't mean..."

"What?" Jack asks. "You can tell me anything. You know that."

I *did* know that. I'm not afraid of Jack. "I suppose that there doesn't seem much point in pursuing something that's doomed to fail."

He takes a step back. "Wow. *Doomed to fail* Come on, Iris. That seems a little dramatic."

My mouth curls into a grin. "But seriously, it's not like this can ever turn into anything, is it?"

"You could make that case for any relationship. Maybe after spending some time together, we'll realize this chemistry is... not what we thought it was. Or that we don't want to pursue it. But to give up before we've even explored our connection..." He shakes his head. "That feels like the easy route. The safe thing to do."

He steps toward me again. I know it's useless to keep protesting. Despite knowing that I'm likely to end up hurt—

or simply wanting more than I can have—I can't say no to him.

I don't want to.

His fingers slide down my arm and my entire body shivers at his touch. Just the memory of his kiss in New York has me squeezing my thighs together and squirming. He grins as if he knows exactly what he's doing to me, exactly what I'm thinking about.

Him.

More of him.

All of him.

FOURTEEN

Jack

I've always known I was spoiled. I've never wanted for anything materially. I've been successful academically and in business.

But right now, body to body with Iris, I feel like I might just be the luckiest man alive.

How did I end up meeting this woman in the first place, let alone losing her and then finding her again? I can't help but think Iris and I are fated. I'm too cynical to believe in things like destiny. I'm used to scoffing at my friends as one by one they told me they've met the woman they're *meant to be* with. I certainly don't believe in fate.

Except I'm in Star Falls now.

And I think it's turned me into a believer.

She sighs, and the movement of her body makes me groan. I dip my head and sweep my lips over hers. I've waited so long for this moment. I've wanted it so badly that I'm concerned that now that I'm touching Iris, I might combust. She might be too much for me to handle.

"You smell the same," she whispers as I drop a kiss at the edge of her jaw.

Her hands slide tentatively over my shoulders. Her touch feels so good, I go dizzy and the room sways for a second. I pull in a breath and try to steady myself.

"You smell like heaven."

She smiles against my mouth as I press my lips to hers. We slide together perfectly, like we're used to kissing each other, like we've been kissing for the last decade, like we're made for kissing each other.

I slide my tongue into her mouth and the huff of breath she lets out travels straight to my balls. If I hadn't been hard the moment I touched her, that small sigh of air would have done it.

I deepen our kiss and she pushes her fingers into my hair. Her hands on me feel so perfect. And I feel like the luckiest guy on earth.

My hands cup her ass, and she writhes against them, like she wants more.

She keeps telling me that being together is impossible, but anything feels possible right now. Her fingers leave my hair and push down my shirt front, her hands shaking, trying to find the buttons.

For a second I want to stop her, ask her if she's sure, but I know it's useless. I don't have the strength to resist this woman. I don't want to resist her. I want as much of her as she'll give me.

Her hands press against my hot skin and it's blissful. I break our kiss with my moan.

"Jack," she says. "You feel as good as I knew you would." She pulls my shirt from my pants.

"You thought about this?" I ask.

She pauses and narrows her eyes. "I haven't thought about anything but you since we met."

Relief runs through me like a burst dam. Thank god she's had some of the longing that I've experienced the last few weeks. Even if she feels a fraction of what I do, I know pursuing this is the right thing to do.

I glance between her eyes and her mouth, then cup her face and claim her with another kiss. This time it's less controlled. Something inside me has shifted, and now that I know she wants this, I feel free. Like what's deep down inside me can finally see sunlight.

I pull at her shirt, finger the waist of her jeans. She grabs my shirt and pushes it over my shoulders. I don't know how but we both end up naked, grabbing each other, needing more of whatever this is that we have together.

I lift her and she wraps her legs around my waist. Her bare pussy against me makes me groan. Her heat around me has me needing more, wanting everything.

I walk us both into the bedroom—not because I'm against kitchen fucking. But because I want her comfortable. I want her spread out, so I can lick every inch of her. I want to see my come on her perfect skin.

I lean over the bed but she doesn't let go of me, so I crawl over her, kissing and kissing as I lower myself down. My erection presses into her thigh and she shifts so I'm between her legs.

Fuck.

We're naked. Bare. Together. I'm so close to sliding inside of her. Will I be able to survive this? Survive *her*?

"Jack?" Her voice trembles. But I know what she's thinking. She's wondering if she'll survive this too.

"I'm here," I say, pressing a kiss on her neck and then

pushing up so I can get a better look at her, naked in bed. With me. "It's going to be good." I drop a kiss between her breasts, rolling her nipples between my thumbs and forefingers.

She sighs. "You're really pretty."

I grin and drop a kiss on her lips as I acquaint myself with her body. I want to take it all in and savor every second. I want every touch to last a day and a half. Every part of her is desperately erotic. Her breasts are tight and round and perfect. I lick the jut of her hip bones. I drag my hands down her and press my palm on the bump of flesh under her belly button, edging lower, my fingers desperate for her heat.

I reach between her thighs, my palm sliding between them. She's wet... so wet, my fingers catch her juices as they skirt down her thigh.

I pause and take a second, trying to calm my racing heartbeat. Fuck. "That all for me?"

Her cheeks pink, and she gives a small nod before opening her legs wider.

I groan at the access I now have to her. My cock throbs in anticipation. I want to bury myself in her, slam right into her core.

But I want to taste her more.

I arrange myself between her thighs. When she realizes what I'm doing, she tries to close her legs.

"No, Iris," I say.

"But I..." She shakes her head.

"You don't want my tongue in your pussy?"

Her face flushes red, like she can't believe what she's hearing. Then I realize, she's not had a proper boyfriend since high school. Maybe he didn't go down on her. She needs reassurance from me. She needs to know I want this as much as she needs it.

"It's going to be great, Iris. They're going to hear your screams in Grizzly's."

I grin at her panic-stricken face. She reaches behind her, grabs a pillow, then opens her legs.

Victory: it's about to taste so good.

I pull her closer to me, my breath heating her. She's glistening, even in the dimly lit bedroom. Her need for me is right there for me to see. I nestle my tongue between her folds, and she groans and puts the pillow over her face.

Fuck, if I wasn't turned on to all holy hell before, I am now.

I work my tongue over and around her clit, flicking and sucking as she whimpers into the pillow.

Her wetness drips down my chin as I explore her, but I can't get enough. I want more. I push my tongue down and deep. Circling and pressing, over and over. Feeling her shudder under me. Her moans vibrate along her body, creating a buzz in me, and it feels like we're both floating. We're here, together, but we're not in Star Falls. We're not in Colorado. We're just together.

She calls my name into the pillow, and her fist grasps the bed cover.

There's no way I don't want to hear her come.

I take the pillow and toss it across the room. "Let me hear how much you love the way I touch you. How my tongue feels."

I dive back down, drawing circles down and around, and her back arches and her body goes rigid and she comes on my tongue, her legs vibrating around me.

I'm panting. Watching Iris, her hazy eyes try to focus, her hot skin, her soaked pussy—watching Iris come might just be the most satisfying, most fulfilling thing that I've ever experienced.

I crawl up her body and she slings her arm over her face, so I can't see her.

"Oh my god," she says as I lie next to her. "Who are you?"

I chuckle. "I'm still Jack."

"Wanna marry me, Jack?"

I burst out laughing. I remove her arm from her face and press a kiss to her mouth. "Yeah, I think I do. But I don't accept proposals within thirty minutes of an orgasm. So let's table that."

I pull her into my arms and revel in the way her legs slide against mine, her palm smooths over my chest. "I'm so glad I found you," I say.

Her hand dips to my rigid cock, and I groan as she grasps my length. But it's not her palm I want to feel around me.

"I'm not sure if you'll fit," she says breathily.

I groan again. I'm not sure I'll survive tonight without trying. "Wanna try?"

Our eyes meet and she nods. "More than anything."

I pull in a breath. There's nothing I want more right now, but at the same time, it feels like I've been wanting this so badly, I've been wanting her from the moment I saw her, that I'm hesitant. What if the physical connection isn't as combustible as I expect. And if it is, how will I ever leave Star Falls?

"I'm nervous," Iris says, putting words around my own thoughts.

"I know," I reply. "You're safe with me."

It's not like I have any choice but to find out. This moment has been written since the first time we met. It's as if we were careening toward a certain point, and now that we're here, there's nothing to do but give ourselves up to inevitability.

I reach for a condom and slide it on. I try and steady my breathing. This is what I've been waiting for. I maneuver so I'm above her, and she cups my face in her hands as she opens her legs. Her expression is one of surrender. She knows that this moment is more than about sex. About fucking. About climax. She's giving herself to me and I'm giving myself to her. We're at a fork in the road. She's come from one direction, I've come from another, but now our paths join and we'll go forward together. I feel it deep inside, like it's a part of my DNA.

My cock connects with the heat of her pussy, and my eyes flicker shut and Iris gasps. Her hands slide to my shoulders and she grips on to me, like she's preparing herself.

I circle my crown around her clit and down, right at her entrance.

She looks concerned, but it's not because I'm about to fuck her, it's because I might not.

"Please, Jack," she says. "This feels like torture."

"You're right," I say. "After tonight, not being inside you will be forever my own personal torture."

I slide in, slowly.

Gently.

Pushing into her.

Making her mine.

Her expression cycles, from relief, to bliss, to joy, and then back to relief again.

I keep sliding into her until I'm buried deep, deep, deep.

I take some steadying breaths so I don't boil over and empty myself into her right there and then.

Her fingernails bite into my skin. "I can't breathe. I'm going to come. Jack! I'm going to come!"

Fuck. We've not started anything yet and she's already coming on my cock.

"Jack," she calls out again. "Jack!"

"It's okay, Iris. Come. Come for me. Come again."

She sighs and convulses around my cock, still buried deep within her. Her back arches, her body pressing against me, heat against heat.

I press kisses against her neck, as her entire body shakes. She feels so good. So perfect. So mine.

"Jack," she whispers. "What are you doing to me?"

I pull in a breath. That's exactly the question I have for her.

"I'm going to move now," I say. "I'm going to fuck you. And you're going to come again. And I'm going to memorize every single one of your orgasms. I want to learn how your body works so I can make you come over and over and over."

"I think you already know my body," she says.

I want more, I think to myself. I want *everything*.

I start to move. It feels dangerous somehow. Maybe important is a better description. Fucking her for this first time feels like I'm crossing a threshold. Not just physically with Iris, but in terms of my life.

After tonight, it feels like nothing will ever be the same. Everything will be different.

My orgasm rumbles inside me, like the warning of a storm coming. I want to keep it at bay for as long as possible. I want us to savor these moments together before we both explode again into the next phase of our lives together. Our roads have joined and we're standing looking at the road ahead and everything is full of promise.

Her fingers slide across my bottom lip. She's gorgeous,

underneath me. Bright. Kind. Brave. But oh so beautiful. And responsive. And warm and so very fucking tight.

"You're fucking perfect." I grunt, as I shove up into her.

"Jack," she chokes out. I love the way she says my name. It's like no one has ever quite said it like she has. "I'm so full of you."

I groan at her words. That's what I want. I want her to be full of me.

She tightens around me. "I don't know how long I can last," she says, her eyebrows pulling together in concern, her nails sinking into the flesh of my arms.

"It's okay. I have you. Fall as hard as you like. I'm here to catch you." I take her leg under her knee and lift, getting a little deeper into her.

She lets out a scream.

Fuck. Making Iris scream might just be my life's work.

The slap of flesh against flesh becomes more urgent. It's like I'm racing to the finish line, and I'm desperate to take Iris with me. I need her with me. I want to see what I can do to her. What we can do together.

Her eyes are glassy, and I press my forehead to hers as she begins to dissolve around me. Our breaths mix, our skin slides against each other.

The final tether of her orgasm snaps and I can't hold back any longer. My muscles tense, my vision blurs, and I erupt inside her, shouting her name.

"Iris. Iris. Iris."

She's a prayer. My future. The beginning and the end of everything.

WE'RE a tangle of sheets and limbs. I don't know where I end and she begins and that's just perfect as far as I'm concerned.

"What time is it?" she asks from where she lies, spread across my chest.

"Four thirty."

She groans and rolls to her back and then she sits up. "I need to leave."

"Leave?" I say. "Where are you going?"

"Home, Jack. I need to shower and get to work."

"At four thirty in the morning?"

"No, but I need to be at my desk before seven. The pickers start at seven. That's when things start to heat up. My brother's broken his leg, so now I have to do some deliveries too." She raises her eyebrows, like she's daring me to say something. I'm not quite sure what.

"Okay, so I'll take you back."

She narrows her eyes. "I drove."

I can't remember much before the bits where we were naked. If she said she drove, then she drove. "Can I see you tonight?"

A smile tugs on the corner of her lips and I lean forward and press a kiss to her mouth.

"I have plans tonight."

"To be in bed with me?" I ask.

She shakes her head. "Spending time with you is far too dangerous. Before you know it, you'll be back in New York and you'll leave me here in Star Falls with nothing but memories and a broken heart. Last night was... we both needed it. And now we don't have to wonder what it might be like between us. Hopefully it gives us the closure we both need."

My insides swoop and my muscles tense. I sit up, mirroring her position. What is she talking about?

Closure?

That was the start of something, not the end of anything.

"That's what last night was about for you? Closure?"

She pulls in a breath, like she's trying to find the answer. "I can't deny there's something between us, Jack—"

"Good," I say. "Because if you did, you'd be lying to yourself."

Her eyes lower to her fingers, linked together in front of her. "We needed to follow it through. Get it out of our system or something."

"How's that working for you?" I ask. "Am I out of your system?"

She shrugs. "I don't know." She pauses. "But honestly, I don't want to get hurt. Life... life in Star Falls is easy. Kinda. There are no big ups and downs. Yeah, the margins at the farm are constantly under pressure and I'm not a member of the Colorado Club, but life is... okay. I'm not sure..." Her gaze flickers to me and then back to her hands. "I'm not sure I would be able to take it if..."

My heart aches at Iris even imagining life becoming difficult for her. I slide my hand around her waist. She flinches and then sinks into my touch.

"I can't get attached—any *more* attached, Jack."

I lean us back so I'm resting against the headboard and she's leaning against my chest.

"When I walked away from dance, I locked it away in a box. I couldn't even think about it for a long time. It was the only way I could survive. And I did survive. And every year, I let it out, but it goes back in the box as soon as I take off back to Star Falls.

"With you... I don't think I could ever... I'd have to live with the loss. I don't think I'm strong enough."

How can I argue against her logic?

"But—"

"Don't say what if it works out. Because you know it's impossible. I *know* you know that."

"It's not impossible."

"Liar," she says.

My chest rises as I pull in a breath. She's convinced. How could I ever change her mind?

"Our worlds are so different," she says. "Like just our day-to-day is so incredibly incompatible. Like tonight, what did you have in mind? Dinner at one of the fancy restaurants at this private resort that your friend owns?" She laughs, like the idea is just too wild to fathom. "A fancy date night for me is Pizza Meet Ya." She shrugs. "To be fair, it's great pizza. But there's nothing fancy about it."

"Fisher and—"

"Fisher isn't an Alden," she cuts me off.

She's right. He's not. "But he had a very different life to Juniper. Juniper is a mother. Unless you've forgotten to tell me, there aren't children in the mix. Or an ex who's hanging around."

"Right," she says. "But I've made commitments to my family in Star Falls and you've made commitments to your family in New York. They're not the same as the obstacles that Fisher and Juniper had. Theirs are surmountable."

"Let me take you to dinner," I say. "Tonight. Pizza Meet Ya."

"Haven't you heard anything I've just been saying?" she asks. "If I get in any deeper with you, I won't survive you leaving."

I close my eyes at her confession. It seems so unfair. We know what we have is rare and precious, but the stakes are too high to see this out, to see where this goes.

"Then marry me," I say. I check my watch. "It's been at least forty-five minutes since either of us orgasmed. I can ask you for real." A grin unfurls on my face. I'm joking, but if she said yes, I'd buy her the biggest diamond ring.

She sits up, putting distance between us, and she rolls her eyes. "No, I'm not going to marry you, Jack Alden."

"Then share a pizza with me."

"I don't share my pizza," she replies. "Not even with you. But seriously, I need to leave."

We both get out of bed and pull on our clothes from the night before. I don't want to try to persuade her to stay. She'll accuse me of not appreciating that she has a job to do, a life that doesn't revolve around me. And I get it. I really do. If she says she needs to leave, then she needs to leave.

"Okay, then two pizzas?" I suggest. "You know what we have between us. You know you've never felt it before. I'm sure I haven't. And yeah, our situations make things look impossible at the moment. I get it. I really do. But there's a solution out there. I know there is. And maybe it will become more obvious if we just spend some time together. Maybe life will show us how we can be together if we just give it a chance."

She sighs and sits on the bed, pulling on her socks. "No more marriage proposals?" she asks.

"I think I can hold off for the evening."

"Okay. But not tonight. I have some making up to do with Stephanie after ditching her last night. You can take me out tomorrow. Pizza. But I'm not sharing." She shakes her head. "I just can't say no to you, Jack Alden."

I know that feeling. My stiff upper lip vibrates with the need to claim victory. I settle with a grin.

"Tomorrow night, then," she says again.

My pulse starts to race at the thought that I won't see her until tomorrow night. I don't have long until we're due back in New York. I don't want to waste time not being with her. "You talked about the fruit pickers arriving at seven."

She checks the time on her phone. "Yeah. I need to go. I have to grab a shower before work."

"They seasonal workers?" I ask, as I grab her keys and we head out.

"Yeah. That's right."

"You need an extra pair of hands?" I suggest. "I don't know much about fruit, but I don't have anything planned today. I could give you a hand."

She raises her eyebrows. "You want to come pick fruit at Wilde's?"

"Yeah," I say, a little uncertain. I don't want to embarrass myself. It's not like manual labor and I are closely associated, but I had a gap year I spent in South America, building pathways. Presumably someone will show me the ropes.

"I don't know," she says. "Bray always handles the seasonal recruitment."

"Great. So, I'll get a shower and I'll turn up around seven?"

"You know that I'm not going to be picking fruit, right? I'm in the office all day long. You won't see me at all."

Somehow that doesn't matter. I like the idea of meeting her brother and her father. Of seeing the family farm. And I can't get what she said about margins being squeezed out of my head. I wonder if there's something I could do to help.

"I know," I say.

"If you want to pick fruit all day, then who am I to stand in your way?"

"And for the record," I say. "I'm not sure my heart would make it if I get in any deeper with you."

FIFTEEN

Iris

Getting to my desk felt more difficult today. Not just because of my lack of sleep, but also today I'm so aware of why I'm here. I feel resentful. Resentful that Wilde's Farm is the reason I had to stay in Colorado.

Of course it wasn't the farm, it was my brother and father's need for the business side to be covered that was the problem. But still, this place represents an anchor. Something that's chained me to one way of life when I wanted another.

I don't want to have to make that same decision again—the farm over ballet. Star Falls over New York.

I did it before and I know what it cost me. I'm not sure if I'm strong enough to do it again.

"Iris, do you know anything about this Jack guy who just showed up?" my brother yells as he limps into the barn. My stomach flips at the mention of Jack's name, and I screw my eyes shut tight in a futile effort to stop pictures of naked Jack from last night filling my brain.

Why Bray can't wait until he gets into my office, I have no idea. My office has been carved out of the barn closest to the house. I like the fact I actually have to get off the couch to come to work. There's a work life and a home life. Yeah, I can see the barn—and my office—from my bedroom window, but there's some separation.

My brother puts his head around the door and looks at me like he's waiting for me to reply. "Iris. Who's this Jack?"

I shrug. "Some guy. Said he was looking to work for the day. Don't like him, then don't hire him." Some guy who made me come last night until my body shook and my mind was blown. But Bray doesn't need to know any of that. Not that there's much to know. I keep out of his romantic life and he keeps out of mine. That's how it's always been since high school. I guess that's why I never knew he and Stephanie kissed. For a split second, I think about asking him about it and then I change my mind. If I ask him about Stephanie, he might think he has free rein to ask me about Jack. And I don't want any more questions about Jack from my brother.

"He's not stalking you, is he?"

"No," I reply. If he was stalking me, he wouldn't have been so surprised to see me at the diner.

"He's not our normal fruit-picking type," Bray says.

"I'm busy, Bray. You need to leave me alone. If you don't want to hire him, don't."

"How do you know him?" he asks.

I sigh, my shoulders sagging. "He's a friend of Byron's. Lives in New York. I have no clue why he wants to pick fruit, but if you don't hire him and I hear you complaining that you don't have enough help again, I'm going to bury you six feet under."

"Jesus, Iris, you're touchy this morning. What crawled up your ass?"

I sigh and spin my chair so I'm facing my brother. "Why are you bothering me? I have things to do. Staffing is your job. Not mine."

Bray shrugs and heads out. He's right. It is a little strange that Jack wants to pick fruit, but I was a little short on sleep when he suggested the idea this morning. If Bray hires him, I might sneak out and see what JFK doppelganger, Jack Alden, looks like doing a little manual labor.

Plenty of people would pay good money to see his shirtsleeves rolled up.

I jump in my seat as Bray pops his head around the door again. "If he breaks your heart, I will kill him with my bare hands."

I grin as I roll my eyes. "Good to know."

"I'll tell him to his face. If he doesn't like it, he can go and wash some dishes at the diner if he needs a day's work."

I nod, hoping that's the end of our conversation. But Bray lingers. "I don't really know what his circumstances are and everything. But I think you deserve a guy who doesn't need a job from your brother."

I tilt my head and look at Bray. We get on each other's nerves a lot, and we bicker like teenage sisters, but it's good to be reminded that he loves me.

"Thanks, Bray," I say, resisting the urge I have to pull him into a hug. "You don't need to worry."

He mimes strangling someone, laughs, and then leaves.

By eleven, I'm caught up on all the most urgent things on my desk, and I can't stop wondering whether Bray actually gave Jack a job for the day.

I come out of the office to see who's about. Maybe I'll run into Jack.

Do I want to run into Jack?

Who am I kidding? Of course I want to run into Jack. Even though I've been busier than the devil himself, images from last night kept pushing into my brain anytime I wasn't one hundred percent committed to whatever I was doing. It was easier to pretend that Jack was just some good-looking guy from New York I had a walk with before last night—not that it had been easy. But I'd been able to tell myself that whatever we shared that evening wasn't anything out of the ordinary.

But last night?

Last night had been anything but ordinary.

He knew my body like he'd designed me himself.

Every touch seemed to bring with it meaning. Like he'd crawled inside my brain and seduced me and then did it all over again with my body.

And I yearned for him.

Yearned to have him in my mouth, to feel him deep within me. To feel his come on my skin. I'd never experienced what it was like to really *want* a man before Jack. I would have done anything he asked of me last night.

And now? I can feel him between my legs, his teeth on my skin. His mouth on mine.

And I just want more.

I never want to give him up.

It's stupid. I know it's a hopeless situation. I know I don't want to hope for more than I already have. Everything in my brain is telling me to stay as far away from Jack as I can.

But my brain doesn't have rank over my heart. Apparently.

The barn my office is carved out of is used for stock overflow and right now it's completely quiet. It's really only used at the peak of the season. So I head out to see what's going on.

There are people everywhere. Crates of packed fruit are piled up left and right, waiting to be put on a truck. And I can see pickers heading into the packing barn with the fruit that's just been picked. Different customers have different packing requirements. But most want the fruit divided into packs that can be taken directly off market shelves. The fruit needs to be sorted through and weighed and those boxes put into crates for shipping.

Everything is picked, packed, and shipped same day. There's no point in letting picked fruit sit around in the sun to go bad. It's better staying on the tree or plant.

I try to scan the workers to find Jack. But I don't see him. I don't really know what I'd be looking for. When he was at the ballet, Jack wore what looked like a custom navy suit. Even in Grizzly's last night he was wearing an expensive shirt and jeans that probably cost as much as a day's worth of fruit.

I hope he didn't turn up this morning in brogues and a Ralph Lauren polo shirt. My brother might have kicked his ass just for that.

Just before I'm about to turn to head into the house to get a beverage, I spot him.

I don't know why I thought he'd be missable. He stands tall—he must be at least six-two—and his wide smile is unmistakable. He's carrying a crate of just-picked fruit, so he can't wave, so I wave at him. He only hesitates to wink at me before heading into the packing barn.

I try to think of a reason why I'd need to be in the packing barn. But really, there isn't one other than to ogle the man I spent the night with last night.

"So how do you know this guy?" Bray makes me jump as he comes up behind me and catches me watching Jack.

"Bray!" I say, swiping him on the arm. "What guy?"

Bray chuckles. "The one you're staring at now. He's a good worker, I'll give you that. A little chatty, but he picks things up fast."

"You got him on the strawberries?" I ask.

"Yeah. We're nearly done now. Even with the polytunnels. But you didn't answer my question. How do you know him?"

"I told you, he's a friend of Byron's."

"Yeah, but you're not. So what gives?"

I shrug. "I just ran into him. We got to talking."

"So he lives nearby?"

I groan. It's so typical of Bray to be destroying my buzz. "Leave me alone, Bray. I don't question you on your love life."

"Oh, so you're admitting this guy is starring in your love life at the moment."

I narrow my eyes at him, sending him death stares.

He doesn't take the hint. "Well, let me do you a deal. When the woman I'm dating turns up asking you for a job, you can ask me all the questions you want. How about that?"

"You need to get back to work. Focus on the fruit. Not me." I pause. "What do you mean he's chatty? What did he say?"

Bray chuckles. "Nothing about you, if that's what you're thinking."

"You're annoying," I say, and I turn and head back into the safety of my office. If I can't ogle the beautiful New Yorker who's on Wilde's Farm for the day, without my brother giving a running commentary, there's no point in being out here.

SIXTEEN

Jack

Being out in the late September sun in Star Falls is very different to the end of the summer in New York. The sun here is gentler. The air easier to breathe. The people are just as busy, just as focused, but here on Wilde's Farm we're all working together—with the same aim. To get the fruit off the trees and shrubs, packed, and on the trucks.

If I wasn't busy today, I know my mind would be full of Iris. Full of everything that happened last night. I've known our connection was strong from that first night, strolling around Central Park. But last night sealed it.

Last night wasn't sex, it was a goddamn pledge. It felt like we were giving ourselves to each other. Describing it as intense isn't enough. It was big. I'm just not sure what it means or where it can go, so I need to be busy so I don't drive myself crazy. Leo, Worth, and Bennett have headed back to New York and I don't want to be a third wheel with Fisher or Byron, so I'm here to pick fruit.

Wilde's Farm is a big operation. Bigger than I expected.

And more complicated. There's a ton of staff—most of which must be seasonal. And different shipments to different places piled up everywhere. I haven't even been here a day, so I don't know the ins and outs, but there are a lot of moving parts.

Being here, working on a business, reminds me of when I first bought my hotel. After business school, Bennett, Leo, Worth, Byron, Fisher, and I decided we'd each buy a hotel with some of the proceeds of the business we'd founded while studying, which delivered prescription medicines. The business had made us all independently rich. But we all knew we'd been successful because we worked so well together. We wanted something that would force us to stay in contact, so we'd devised a competition where the owner of the most successful hotel each year would win.

Little did we know that we wouldn't need a competition to keep us close. Our bond has strengthened no matter the hotels and the competition, and our focus on them has ebbed and flowed. When I bought my hotel—a small boutique place opposite the Four Seasons on East 57th Street—the place had been run into the ground. It was about to lose its four-star rating and any good staff had left or were on their way out of the door.

For me, those early days of getting under the skin of the hotel and figuring out what was going to have to change and what needed to be built on—who needed to be fired, who needed to be hired—were some of the happiest days of my life. It was like taking a spoonful of Beluga right from the jar and feeling it pop on your tongue—pure heaven. I reveled in those days. It was like decluttering on a massive scale. I tossed out the things I had no use for and were just getting in the way, put in place new structures and methods of working, hired better people, refurbished, opened a new restaurant that put The Alden Hotel on the map.

I loved it.

Now it's a five-star hotel and occupancy rates are some of the best in Manhattan. The staff is incredible. Our reviews are outstanding, and I'm happy to say I have the best boutique hotel in Manhattan—although Worth would disagree.

Being at Wilde's Farm feels like those early days of being at The Alden. Not that Wilde's is on the brink of closure or anything. It's just a new business to me. It feels good to be learning how it works. And coming from outside, I always think you can see holes that other people have missed. That's how consultants make their money, after all.

At the moment, all I can see is how hard everyone is working, but Wilde's is beholden to the weather, the quality of the transportation, and the buyers of the fruit. There's a lot of things that can go wrong and no obvious way of de-risking the business. I want to know how long the contracts are for. Do they get buyers rejecting stock? Do they get into legal wrangling? Are they pushed on price? Recognized for their quality?

"Wanna grab some lunch?" a voice from behind me asks.

I turn and it's Bray. Iris's brother. I tamp down a smile. He's a smart guy. I don't fit the normal type of person who turns up on the farm looking for day work. When I told him that Iris suggested I come down if I was looking for work, I could see his mind working overtime. And rightly so.

"Sure," I say. "Would love that."

I didn't bring any lunch, but Bray leads us into the back room of the largest of the sheds. I wasn't expecting what I see—a staff cafeteria.

"It's no fancy New York restaurant. There's soup, sandwiches, and veggies. And fruit."

"Sounds good," I say and pull off a tray from the pile. I end up with pea and ham soup, a chicken burrito, and a pear. There's more of a selection than Bray made out at first. There are chips, snacks, nuts. It's not some makeshift operation.

"I can get this," I say. "Where do we pay?"

Bray chuckles and rolls his eyes. "It's on me." He leads us out of the barn on the other side, where there're some picnic tables set out. He chooses one that's empty and I sit across from him.

"You don't charge any of the staff?" I ask as I open my water.

"I need them well fed. They all do very physical work. They don't eat properly at lunchtime and it means they're not as productive in the afternoon."

Smart, I think to myself. "I bet there are plenty of employers that wouldn't think that way."

"What can I say? There are a lot of dumbasses out there. But also, we're paying minimum wage to a lot of the staff. Some of them aren't going to have the money to have a good, healthy meal. It's the right thing to do."

The right thing to do. Feed your employees. Treat them right. I like the Wilde's Farm philosophy.

"So business is good?" I ask.

"Business is fine," he says dismissively. "Tell me how you know my sister."

I pull in a breath. Iris and I haven't discussed what we tell people about how we met. I'm pretty sure she's not going to want me to tell her brother I met her at the ballet in New York, seeing as she goes to great lengths to hide the fact that she goes off to Manhattan once a year.

"I'm friends with Byron Miller. You know him?"

"Kinda," Bray says. "But Iris doesn't really know him."

"I think we were in Grizzly's the first time... Was that it? Then we ran into each other in the diner and—"

I have to stop myself from laughing. How ironic that I came here to get away from New York because I was seeing Iris everywhere. And now here I am, with Iris.

"So you're staying up the mountain at the Colorado Club?" he asks.

"Yeah. I get a good deal there." I grin, but Bray doesn't seem amused.

"Not many people from up there come down the mountain looking for work."

"No, I guess not." There's not much I can say to that. He's asking why I'm here and I'm not sure I have the answer. I had nothing much else to do and I'd rather be near Iris than anywhere else.

"So, you're dating Iris or what?" he asks. He's straight to the point. I can't do anything but respect that about him.

"I'd *like* to be dating your sister," I say honestly. I'm not sure if what Iris and I are doing counts as dating? I'm trying to spend as much time as possible with her.

"She's not so keen?" Bray asks.

"I think she's... she's good at seeing the downside."

"What does that mean?"

I pull in a breath. "She's looking ahead, and because I live in New York and she lives here, she assumes it's not going to work."

"She's finding obstacles," Bray says. "And you don't think that's because she doesn't like you? Or doesn't like you *enough*?"

I chuckle at his honest question. "I've definitely considered that as a possibility, but no, I think she likes me. I think she's scared of what that means for her."

"She drives me bananas on a regular basis," Bray says. "But she's the most loyal, caring, thoughtful human on the planet."

I nod in agreement. "I know that. She's very special."

He looks me dead in the eye. "If you hurt her, I'll kill you."

I get his concern. I'm some guy from New York, staying up the mountain at the fancy private members resort, who's slumming it for a day picking fruit. I probably seem like a spoiled creep. And I'm definitely spoiled.

"I will do everything I can not to hurt Iris. I think a great deal of her."

Bray takes a bite of his sandwich and nods. After he swallows, he says, "So when are you going back to New York?" he asks.

"I'm not sure. The initial plan was to stay a few days." I've skipped a few meetings already. My father has asked his assistant where I am, but other than that, I've not been missed. I've had over thirty years learning how to be my father. I'm done with the training. There's no need to rush back to New York. "I might stick around for a little while longer."

I've not talked about my plans with Iris. Me staying might be the last thing she wants.

But it's what I want. I'm clear about that.

I was serious when I said to her that if we give what we have some time to simmer, we'll be able to figure out how we make things work or decide that we don't want to.

Except, I don't think I'll ever decide that I don't want to spend time with Iris. Something changed that evening in New York, walking the sidewalks in Central Park. Something in me shifted. Now I'm not sure if I work properly without Iris.

"You looking for a permanent job here at Wilde's?" He looks concerned. I'm not sure if it's because he doesn't have a job to give me or because he's worried that I can't support myself without Iris's family's help. He must know that if I'm staying at the Club, I'm doing okay? Maybe he thinks Byron's giving handouts.

I shake my head. "I thought it would be fun to come and see the farm she talks about. She told me if I wanted to work, I'd have to come to you. She wasn't going to put a good word in for me."

Bray chuckles. "She can be a hard-ass."

"She's been through a lot."

Bray's face darkens and he nods. "Yeah. So, you like the farm?" he asks.

I finish my soup and place the empty bowl back on the tray. "Yeah. It's great. It's hard to describe, but the atmosphere, the feel of the place—it's calm. Peaceful. Not sure if that's Wilde's Farm or just Star Falls in general."

"Well, the same could be said for both."

"I was wondering if you sell any of your fruit direct?" I ask.

"Oh, we just started doing that." He shrugs. "Really because the Club asked us to supply them. We've started doing it with a few other local businesses as well."

"Are the margins better?"

He narrows his eyes at me, suspicious. I get it. Who the hell am I to him? "I'm not after your money. I'm not a competitor. I'm just... I think I like getting under the skin of businesses and figuring out what works and what doesn't work. I like uncovering the holes and opportunities."

"You sound like some kind of business consultant or something."

I shrug. "Yeah. I went to business school with Byron, and we did a lot of that kind of thing and I really enjoyed it."

"What do you do for work now?" he asks.

Inwardly, I wince a little. I never want anyone to think that I'm bragging or showing off, but I also want to be honest with Bray. "I work in my family business," I say. "I manage our finances."

He pauses, waiting for me to say more, but I'm not sure what else I can say without coming across like a dick.

"What kind of business is it?"

He's pushing for more and I can't blame him. I'd want to know more if I was him. "We have investments in various smaller businesses."

He looks at me like he's examining me. "So your job is to keep track of your family's money." He's no dummy.

"Pretty much."

"So you must have a lot of it."

I nod.

Bray narrows his eyes. "So you're not wanting a day's work to take my sister to Pizza Meet Ya tonight?"

I start to laugh. "Irony is, I *am* taking your sister to Pizza Meet Ya tomorrow night, but no, I don't need a day's salary from you to make that happen."

"You have your own place in New York City?"

"I do."

"No mortgage I'm guessing."

I stay silent.

"You have your own plane? Yacht? Baseball team."

"No plane since my grandfather died. No yacht. And no baseball team."

"But not because you can't afford it, right?"

"Right."

We eat in silence for a few minutes.

"I noticed the Wilde's Farm brand isn't on any of the packaging that gets sent to customers."

"They want to use their brand names."

"That makes sense. It gives them more power."

"I guess," he says. "We just do what the customers want. I think we did offer them Wilde's Farm fruit at one point, but that's not what they want."

"And it puts the risk on you, because if you don't sell Wilde's Farm fruit, you can't easily repackage because the fruit will go bad." I think to myself. "What about freezing?" I ask.

"The bigger crates go to companies that freeze the food."

"Oh, I see. So some of it goes to be frozen, but you don't do that?"

"We don't have the equipment. We'd need an entirely new setup. Fast freezers. Trucks to carry that stuff. And then all the packaging for it would be different."

My mind starts whirring at all the possibilities. "Yeah. It would be a complete shift in the way you did business." I frown, trying to think through the implications for Iris. "And what about organic stuff? You do much of that?"

"We looked into it a while back. I can't remember what happened about that." He pushes his tray away from him. "You're really interested in fruit, huh?" he asks.

"I like hearing about other people's businesses. New businesses. And what are the margins like in the fruit business?"

"They're okay. Every year feels a little tighter than the last, but we get by. We had to change the menu in the lunch room," he says. "We've had to change the supplier of our boxes and the haulage company. We're always making savings."

"Being on top of your costs is always a good thing."

"Iris's really good at that," he says, clearly a proud brother.

She would be. She's smart. But cost control can only go so far.

I take a bite out of my burrito, the cogs in my brain turning. Iris's priority is her family and Wilde's Farm. The reason she stayed here and didn't go to New York was because she was worried things couldn't survive without her. But what if Wilde's Farm was in such a strong financial position that they didn't have to rely on Iris anymore? Wouldn't that give her freedom? Freedom to leave the farm and live anywhere?

Maybe even New York.

SEVENTEEN

Iris

Why did I suggest Pizza Meet Ya?

Jack is used to fine dining. If we find an artichoke on a pizza, it will be as exciting as it gets here. Although the pizza is the best I've ever had. But maybe I'm biased.

"What do you recommend?" Jack asks, his eyebrows pulled together like he's reading important financial statements rather than a pizza menu.

He looks gorgeous tonight. He's caught a bit of the sun and some freckles have come out across his nose. His shirt-sleeves are rolled up, in the way that people with money do when they want to look casual. His forearms are corded with muscle, and I have to stop myself from reaching for him and tracing the lines with my fingers. He looks so boyish. So carefree. So far away from the serious, intense man who sat next to me at the ballet all those weeks ago.

"It's all good," I say. "Best pizza in America."

Jack laughs. "I live in New York."

"So?"

"So obviously we have the best pizza."

I shake my head, half horrified by his arrogance, half ready for him to taste the pizza at Pizza Meet Ya. "You're about to have your mind blown."

"That's for *after* the pizza," he says, his eyebrows pulsing up, a grin spreading across his face.

I swear I never knew it was possible to blush all over before I met Jack.

"Trust me. It starts with the pizza tonight," I tell him.

"Challenge accepted," he says. "You've raised my expectations now, so this place better be good."

I order the four cheeses, because too much cheese isn't a thing.

"I think I'm going to have the pepperoni," Jack says. "That's what I'd have in New York, so it seems only fair that I'll compare like with like."

I laugh as Akira, the waitress, approaches our table.

Her eyes go wide when she sees Jack. Panic in her expression, she turns to me. "I don't do this very often. Just when I'm saving up for something," she blurts.

Jack looks as confused as I feel.

"And it's not like I've ever turned down a shift at the Club because of a shift here," she splutters.

"Okay," Jack says. "You don't need to worry."

"You won't say anything?" Akira asks.

I shake my head, unsure of what I'm not supposed to be saying to whom.

"Of course not," Jack says. "If it makes you feel any better, Byron doesn't even know I'm here."

Akira's shoulders drop, and she sighs. "I love that job. I would hate to lose it. I just need a little extra money, and they are very strict about the shifts they offer us."

Suddenly everything slots into place. "I didn't realize

you weren't allowed to work other jobs if you were at the Club." I remember Akira starting at Pizza Meet Ya. She said she worked at the Club and would only be working the odd few days here. It never struck me as strange or in the slightest bit inappropriate.

"Oh, that's not a rule. But the Club is so exclusive and... I don't know of anyone else having a second job. I just don't want to get into trouble."

Jack mimes pulling a zipper across his mouth. "Your secret is safe with us."

"But I know you're friends with Mr. Miller," she says to Jack. "I don't want you to have to keep a secret from your friend. Or from Rosey. I started at the same time as Rosey. She's lovely, and it's bad enough that *I* have to keep secrets from her."

"She doesn't seem like the type to be concerned," I say, not that I know Rosey. I've spoken to her a couple of times. Star Falls is a small town. If you live here, then everyone is going to bump into everyone.

"It's fine," Jack says. His tone is reassuring. Akira is overreacting, but Jack isn't dismissive of her or taking what she's saying as a joke. He's being really empathetic. It's kinda lovely. And kinda hot. "I have a terrible memory anyway. I'll probably forget all about tonight by tomorrow morning."

Akira sighs, but her expression is still slightly pained. "Okay, I'm so sorry to have hijacked your date. I'm Akira, and I'll be your server tonight. What can I get for you? The barbeque chicken special is my favorite."

We order beers and pizza, and as Akira heads back to the kitchen, I turn back to Jack. "How often do you eat pizza and drink beer?"

"I'm not an alien," he says. "I'm a New Yorker. I eat

pizza almost weekly. Or at least monthly. And if I eat pizza, I'm drinking beer."

"Weekly?" I ask.

"Probably less, now that Byron has met Rosey and Worth has met Sophia and Leo has Jules and Fisher has Juniper and Bennett has Efa."

"All five of your friends have girlfriends?"

"Fiancées or wives," he says.

"You're the only one left?"

"Oh, I'm not so sure about that," he says.

He sounds like he's saying that he's no longer the one without a fiancée or a wife. But he can't be saying that, right? I mean, we've known each other two minutes, and yes it feels like I've known him my entire life. It feels like he knows what I'm thinking. Yes, he can do things to my body that no man ever has. He's kind and patient and...

"So tell me about the wife your mom wants for you?" I ask, trying to bring us back to reality.

He flashes me a cheeky, sexy grin that has me squeezing my legs together. "Wow, you really know how to destroy the vibe, don't you?"

I laugh. "My specialty. But seriously, it's weird for me that she'd be so involved in your love life."

"She's not. But not because she doesn't want to be."

"I've heard about arranged marriages back in the olden days or in other cultures. But in America, it seems so strange to me. Is it normal for... people like you? Families like yours?"

Jack glances down at the table, a gloomy expression on his face. "I don't think anyone sees it as arranged marriage. There are expectations that people are consciously and subconsciously aware of. And then most people hang out with people who are similar to them, so bonds naturally form with acceptable people."

"Acceptable," I repeat. I definitely wouldn't qualify as far as Jack's mother's concerned.

"It's stupid," Jack says. "And my mother knows that's not how I think. That's probably why she's more invested than she should be."

"She's probably just looking out for you. Probably doesn't want you marrying a gold-digger or something."

Our eyes meet and things pass unsaid between us:

I'm not after your money.

I know you're not.

"My father's getting older. He and my mother want to see me settled. And..."

Jack doesn't normally hold back with me, so his hesitation intrigues me. "And?"

"Well, I haven't been so settled."

Realization dawns. He's a player.

"Right," I say.

"I want to be honest with you. I don't want there to be any surprises for you when you come to New York."

It's only Akira interrupting us with our pizzas that stops me shrieking. When have we ever talked about me going to New York?

"Smells good," Jack says.

"It's the best pizza in America," Akira says, before she heads back to the kitchen.

I raise my eyebrows as if to say, *I told you so.*

"I'm ready to be impressed." Jack pulls out a slice, the stringy cheese holding on to the other slices like the arms of babies being pulled from their mother. I watch as Jack takes a bite. His eyes go wide in shock as he chews, and then they close on a moan. Finally he swallows.

He's speechless.

I pick up my slice. "Told ya." I take a bite and grin at him.

"I'll never doubt another word you say," he says, taking a second bite.

"Let's rewind to the bit where you talked about surprises when I go back to New York. I have no plans to visit the Big Apple again until next September."

Jack chews as he looks at me. Then he swallows. "Because you don't want to? Because it's too painful?"

I pull in a breath and think. "I hadn't thought about it. But maybe because of the memories. Maybe because..." I don't say because I can't afford another trip, because I know Jack will just dismiss that particular obstacle. But that's what I'm thinking. The fact is, I don't want someone who pays for everything. It's another reason we're entirely incompatible and last night was just... and tonight is just... we're just getting this out of our systems.

Or something.

"I want you to come and see where I live. Meet my mother. I want to take you out to restaurants and to the ballet—every ballet in New York."

My insides seize up as he talks. Doesn't he realize he's being ridiculous? There's no way I can just take off. "I have work," I say.

"Okay, let's take New York off the table for now. You're going to need to show me around Star Falls. I want to see it all. Your high school. The first tree you climbed. Is there a lake nearby?"

"You want me to show you the sights of Star Falls?" I ask.

"Seems only fair after my tour of Central Park," Jack says.

He smiles, and I feel my resolve melt. I wonder if there's anything Jack couldn't get me to do.

Apart from go to New York.

"I'm going to stick around for a bit," he says. "I'm enjoying being at the farm. I had lunch with Bray and we were talking about the business."

"You and Bray had lunch?" I ask, heat chasing up my face. Oh god, the last thing I want is Bray and Jack getting cozy.

"Yeah, he's a good guy. Protective of you." He smiles. "It's good. Anyway, he was saying you never use the Wilde's Farm brand on anything."

"No, because the customers want their own brand on the packaging. But it's more than that. I'd like to be using the Wilde's Farm brand. It makes sense. Branding our fruit, making it a sought-after brand, it's the dream. But we're a small farm. And we're dependent on the crops. What crops we get depends on a lot of things, but the biggest variable is weather. We can't control that. We can't create a brand that people rely on and then be hit and miss with what we produce. That's why the big, branded producers have farms in different locations—to hedge the weather risk."

He leans back in his chair and nods. "You're smart. And I'm turned all the way on right now."

I roll my eyes, but squeeze my thighs together at his confession.

"You're right. It's a big obstacle. If you could control the supply better—hedge bad weather. You could do that by having farms in various locations—"

"Jack! You think we're going to start opening farms across America? You've lost your mind!"

"I'm not suggesting anything. I'm thinking aloud. There

are obstacles, and I want to see how to knock them down. That's all."

"You're going to ride in on your white horse and solve all our problems?" I ask him. Is he trying to fix me?

He shrugs. "Maybe I'm just looking at things with an outsider's perspective. If I can help improve things a little, that would be amazing, but I'm not going to interfere. You don't need to be worried."

"I'm not worried. Not about you interfering, anyway."

"What are you worried about, then?"

I sigh, wondering whether I should tell him the truth. "I'm worried I'll never be able to let you go."

He holds my gaze for a beat, a smile turning up the corners of his lips. "Maybe you'll never have to."

My heart inches higher in my chest. It's stupid, because I know Jack and I are impossible together, but I can't help but feel hopeful. It's like buying a lottery ticket—you know you're never going to win, but sometimes it's fun to let yourself indulge your fantasy about winning.

Akira comes over to check on us just as my phone buzzes. I reach for it to turn it to silent, but my reminder about applying to the course at community college flashes on my phone. My stomach falls through the bottom of my chair and hits the floor.

I push my chair out from the table. Jack has me so distracted, I'm forgetting about real life. I've been thinking about this course since I enrolled to get my high school diploma. This was always going to be my next step. I've only recently graduated high school, and the idea that I might get a college degree is exciting. I can't throw that away to get pizza. However good it is.

"Everything okay?" Jack asks.

I'm still scanning the email. The course is weirdly oversubscribed because one of the professors is a minor celebrity so the application process included an essay about why I wanted to enroll on the course. I've not even thought about it.

"Not really," I say. "I have to finish an application for a course I want to get into." What am I thinking, getting caught up in fantasies about a life with Jack? I need to keep my feet on Star Falls soil. Panic rockets through me, and I jump up.

"What's the matter?" Jack asks.

"The deadline is tomorrow morning, six a.m. I need to go."

"I'll take you," Jack says. He stands and pulls out his wallet.

"I can pay," I say.

He fixes me with a look. "Please, Iris. I'm not trying to buy you, but let me get this without you feeling like you owe me or something." He puts some cash—way too much cash, from what I can see with a casual glance—on the table and guides me out and into the SUV he brought us here in.

"Is there anything I can do to help?" Jack asks as we pull out onto the road. "Maybe it's stupid, but I'm happy to proofread stuff or act as a sounding board."

I shake my head. "I just need to get to my computer. I've been..." I shake my head. I can't blame Jack. The application was my responsibility. I'm not used to my head being taken up with anything other than work and my high school diploma.

We get back to the farm and I reach for the door handle of the SUV, and then turn back to Jack. "I'm sorry I ruined our evening."

He shakes his head. "Don't be. I want you to finish your

application. We'll catch up when you're done and you can tell me about the course."

"I'm going to be up all night." I slide out of the seat and turn to face him.

He winces. "Plenty of coffee. You want me to make you some?"

I smile. "Thanks, but I'm good." If Jack came inside, my dad and my brother would have something to say, and I wouldn't get anything done.

"Good luck," he says. "I believe in you."

My heart squeezes at his words. The idea that Jack believes in me brings me great comfort, I'm just not quite sure why. He's an almost stranger. A stranger from New York who I'm way too comfortable with. Way too attached. Way too attracted.

He blows me a kiss, and instead of shutting the door like I should, I clamber across the seat and kiss him squarely on the mouth.

"Thank you," I say as I pull back. My face goes up in flames, and I bite back a smile before turning and racing back to the house and my application.

EIGHTEEN

Jack

If Iris has been up most of the night, she's going to be exhausted. Which is why I pull up at seven at Wilde's Farm.

I'm not looking to pick fruit particularly today, but if that's what they need, I'm happy to do it. I want to be an extra pair of hands in case Iris doesn't make it to her desk on time.

I wave as I get out of the car and spot Bray.

"Morning," he says, his tone gruff. "Wasn't expecting to see you today. Thought the day before yesterday scared you off."

"I've got more time today." I had a few conference calls yesterday, but I would have preferred to be picking fruit. "If I'm in the way, just say."

"I'm about to get my sister out of bed. She never sleeps in, but I've just been to get some haulage lists from her and she's not in the office."

"What are the haulage lists?" I ask.

Bray shakes his head. "Don't worry about it. I'm going to ask Iris."

If she's sleeping, it's because she's tired. "I don't mind having a look around and seeing what I can find," I say. "And if I can't find it, and Iris hasn't appeared, I'll go and find her. I'm sure you've got things to be doing."

Bray shrugs. "That would work. I need to get out to the far south fields to check on the crops. The lists we're looking for are the ones for the deliveries that will go out today."

"I'll take a look." I head into the barn where Iris's office is, to see what I can find. It's not a big office. There's a window. And packing boxes seems to have sprouted up in various places, behind the door and under the window, but other than that the place is very neat. Filing cabinets form a wall behind the desk. But there's nothing on the top of them. There are no piles of papers or knitted strawberries or toy bananas with legs and a smile. I don't know if I'm slightly disappointed I don't immediately find something I can tease Iris about.

I round the desk to find her laptop missing. That makes sense. She probably brings it back up to the house every evening. But that's also probably where the haulage lists are.

I look around and tucked under a separate keyboard are three sheets of paper. I know before I see what they are that they'll be the haulage lists. I bet she prints them off every evening, just in case anyone needs them in the morning and she's not at her desk. Even though she's always at her desk.

Except for today.

I check the date. It's today's and it's divided between customers. Each line underneath each customer has the fruit and the amount to be shipped. This is just what we need.

As I come out of the barn, there's a truck backing into the loading bay.

Perfect timing.

What surprised me before was how efficient the farm was. They are constantly bringing fruit up from the fields, so it's packed within minutes of it being picked. And then deliveries are collected throughout the day. No hour is wasted.

"Hey, man," I greet the truck driver.

He nods at me. "Not seen you before," he says, tugging on his faded red cap.

"Helping out Bray," I say with a smile.

He nods suspiciously. "We're from Maxwell Food Distribution."

I look down at my list. Maxwell has one of the longest lists beneath their name. "Be right with you," I say. I head into the packing barn, tucking the haulage lists that don't concern Maxwell into the back pocket of my jeans. I'm not quite sure who's responsible for loading trucks, and does the fruit go out in order of priority? I have no clue.

A woman with curly brown hair and a Snoopy t-shirt is checking through the boxes of raspberries as they are stacked on the table by the door. She looks like she's in charge.

"Hey, I'm Jack. I'm helping out Bray and Iris. I have Maxwell Food Distribution who just arrived."

"Hey, Jack," she says, taking the piece of paper I'm holding. "I'm Marnie, and yup, this is for me." She glances up, spots someone and hollers, "Gabriel? Can you bring Frenchie and come and load up Maxwell?"

The guy she's yelling at raises his hand and nods, and yells to someone coming through the barn from the other side. They both head over.

"Can I help?" I ask.

Before she can answer, an older man in a black cap charges toward us, his expression like he's about to kill someone. "Who the hell are you?" he asks as he approaches me.

"I'm Jack," I say.

"He's dating Iris," Marnie says

Word travels fast around here. Seems like Marnie knows exactly who I am.

Then she turns to me. "This is my boss. Iris's dad."

"I'm here to help out, Mr. Wilde," I say offering my hand to shake.

"Yeah, okay," Mr. Wilde says, shaking my hand. "You can help out. And then you can drop by the house after hours and I can get the measure of you some more." He narrows his eyes, as if he's inspecting me.

I nod. "Absolutely. I'll drop by later."

Mr. Wilde just turns and heads back into the barn.

"Grab a couple of boxes from that pile there and stick 'em in the truck," Marnie says. "And don't try and bullshit that man. He can smell it a mile away."

"Thanks for the tip." I take a stack of boxes from where she's pointing and head out to find the Maxwell driver.

"Hey, Jack," Marnie calls, just before I hit daylight. "You got my other haulage lists there?" She nods at my ass.

I set down the boxes I'm carrying. "You want these?" I ask her, pulling the rest of the lists from my pocket.

"Have been waiting for Iris to get them. Not like her to be late."

It doesn't take long to load up the Maxwell truck. The operation runs efficiently and no one panics. The driver with the red cap seems happy and starts back up the road he came from.

"Who's next?" I ask Marnie, as we watch the Maxwell truck disappear.

"Now we keep packing and we get ready for Loopin. They usually pull up second."

"Can I help?" I ask again.

"Honestly, you're more of a hindrance than a help until the trucks arrive. These guys have been weighing and boxing fruit for years. They do it quicker than you ever could."

I nod in response. I appreciate the honesty. "How long have you worked here?" I ask.

She laughs. "Too long. Since before Bray had finished high school."

"You must like it," I say.

"I complain, but of course I enjoy it. Surrounded by hard workers and the Star Falls air. What's not to like?"

"Is everything I can see Wilde's Farm?" I ask.

"Everything. The west barn, where Iris's office is, isn't in use at the moment, but at peak times, we open that barn up."

There's a stretch of land behind the barns, the other side of the tractor trail, that looks like it might have had a building on it at one point. "What was that over there?" I ask.

"Oh, the old red barn. Or at least it used to be. It was a wreck. Got pulled down when they built this one. This one isn't quite as pretty, but it's watertight. And that counts for a lot."

I can't help but think that land is crying out for another barn. Another barn that could be the start of a shift in the direction of Wilde's Farm. But I'm not going to tell Marnie that. I'm not even going to tell Iris. I'm going to crunch some numbers. Get some of the people back in the Alden family office to crunch some numbers. One of them has an intern. They can do some desktop research for me.

I have an idea for Wilde's Farm. It could make the family a lot of money. But it would also bring change, and although I feel like I've known Iris my entire life, I don't know her brother and her father well at all. I have no idea if they would embrace the kind of change I'm thinking about. They've been operating successfully for years now without my help.

Just as another truck approaches Marnie and me, I see Iris come flying out of the house, holding one sneaker, with the laces undone on the one on her foot.

"I'm so sorry," she yells. "Marnie, I'm going to get you the haulage lists right now."

Marnie laughs. "No need," she yells back. "Jack's got it covered."

I can't help but laugh at the expression on Iris's face. She looks half shocked, half horrified. "Jack?" she asks, like I'm the last person she could fathom that would be able to help. She hobbles toward us, pausing for a second to pull on her missing sneaker.

"Did I see the Maxwell truck pull off?" she asks, looking between Marnie and me.

"Yup," Marnie says. "And Loopin's just arriving. We're all over this. You sleep all you need."

"I didn't finish my application until five this morning. I thought a couple of hours' sleep would be a good idea. But I slept through my alarm."

"Why don't you go and get a few more hours?" I ask. "Everything will wait."

"Are you my knight in shining armor, Jack?" She tips her head back and squints from the sun.

I lift my sunglasses, so I can see her clearly, with no

filter. Then I drop a kiss on her lips. "Hashtag life goals. You look beautiful."

"Jack, I haven't even brushed my hair." She rolls her eyes. "I bet the women in New York roll out of bed wearing lace and silk and go straight to Pilates."

"I'm not thinking about any woman other than you when you're in a fifty-mile radius."

Her expression falls a little. "New York is a lot farther than fifty miles away," she says.

"I'm right here, looking at you." I'm trying to be reassuring, but I get it. It's not like I'm moving to Star Falls. Maybe if Wilde's Farm makes the changes I suggest, there'll come a point where they don't need Iris here and she can come back to New York. "And anyway, once you've finished that course you're applying for, who knows where you'll end up."

She laughs. "Like I'm going anywhere. My family needs me. So Star Falls is where I'll stay."

I try not to let the disappointment I feel show on my face. I wonder if she'll always feel like Star Falls is the place she'll stay.

Iris's good at finding obstacles. But I'm good at knocking them down. That's what I've got to focus on.

NINETEEN

Iris

I'm doing my best not to burst into laughter at the photograph I'm about to take. Jack is the most unlikely Star Falls tourist, I just can't help it.

"Maybe scooch in closer," I suggest. "Marvin likes a hug."

"Marvin is a fiberglass moose," Jack says. "He's just happy his paint isn't chipped."

I roll my lips together, trying not to laugh. Jack said he wanted to see all the sights of Star Falls, so after a couple of weeks of dinners, coffees, and a thorough interrogation from my father, here we are on our first official day date, outside Snail Trail. We're getting the obligatory photograph with Marvin the Moose.

"People come far and wide to have a hug with Marvin. Don't try and minimize his emotional needs."

Jack raises his eyebrows. "I would never. Fact is, Riley tells me she's too old to pose with Marvin. That means I definitively am."

"No one's too old for a picture with Marvin." I step toward him and slide a hand around his waist and hold my phone up for a selfie with the three of us. "Better than the top of the Empire State Building," I say.

Jack laughs. "Well, that just tells me you've never been to the top of the Empire State Building."

My mood dips slightly. He's right. I always saw myself in New York, against a skyline that included the Empire State Building. It just didn't happen for me. It wasn't meant to be.

"Was I being an ass?" he asks, clearly reading my shift in mood.

I shake my head resolutely. "Not at all. But I'm a little offended you don't appreciate Marvin."

"I'm sure what you next have in store for me will blow me away."

"It absolutely will," I say. "But first, coffee. Ever read *Twilight* or seen the movie?"

"I saw the movie," he says. "I'm pretty sure... the one with the vampires, right?"

"Yeah? Did you love it?"

"I only saw the first one, but actually I enjoyed it."

"Prepare to have your mind blown." I march us in the direction of Twilight Latte.

"How have I not been here?" he asks, gazing up around the store as we enter.

"Because you guys are obsessed with the wings at Grizzly's."

"Yeah, because who wouldn't be? I'm not a monster, Iris."

"Fair. But this place does the best coffee in America."

"I will try not to scoff. I've learned my lesson after having pizza in this town." Jack seems obsessed with the décor and keeps pointing out little details that have gone over *my* head. I'm used to the huge pine tree decals on the windows and the life-sized cardboard cutouts of Robert Pattinson and friends. But I've never noticed the graduation cap artwork behind the counter that Jack assures me is from the Cullens' house in the movie.

"Wait, no, it couldn't be—" He sees something on the counter and reaches for it. It's the cup sleeves that have caught his attention. They're covered in printed sheet music.

"What is it?"

"I'm not very good at reading music, but I think this is 'Clair du Lune.' You know, the music Edward plays for Bella when she goes to visit his family?"

I pause and regard him, slightly concerned. "Jack Alden, you're just a big geek, aren't you?"

He blushes and puts a finger over his lips. "Shhh, don't tell anyone."

I laugh. He's such a fish out of water here in Star Falls. I wish I could be a fly on the wall in his life in New York. I bet he has a butler and a driver and has tailors coming to his house to fit him for expensive suits. Here I am taking him to our local pizza restaurant and making him pose in front of Marvin the Moose.

"Where do you get your coffee in Manhattan?" I ask.

"There's a little Italian deli at the end of my block."

I laugh again. "You make it sound very humble. I bet it supplies the White House or something."

He shrugs. "Maybe. In New York, anything's possible."

We order our coffees to go and head out. Our tour of Star Falls isn't going to take long. But we might as well take in the falls next.

"Okay," Jack says. "I can't believe I've never actually been to the place that gives Star Falls its name."

"You spend too much time in your gilded cage, Jack. You're about to find out that the real world can be even better." We slide into Jack's SUV and begin the drive out of town to the falls.

"I've never heard New York referred to as a gilded cage," he says.

"Really?" I shift around in the passenger seat so I'm facing him. His profile is lit up by the sun and his features look like they're carved from marble. "I'm sure it isn't for most people, but for some people, most of life is a gilded cage, isn't it? For others it's the exact opposite."

"I never really thought about it like that. What I like about New York is that there's so much diversity. From the arts, to the food, to the people. Every day is different."

"Potentially," I say.

"What do you mean?"

"I mean, life is potentially different. But I bet most days look similar to most people. Even you, I imagine."

He stares straight ahead, taking the turns of the roads slowly, like someone who hasn't lived here his entire life. "You're right. I guess I haven't looked at it like that."

"I'm not saying that's a bad thing," I say. "It's the same for most people. You can tell that at the farm, most days follow a routine. Obviously things change depending on the season, but the core remains the same."

"That's true of my life in New York, too. I guess I just haven't seen it. In New York, I'm surrounded by the possibility of things being different, but they rarely are." He pulls his eyebrows together, like he's thinking really hard. "You're right. It's just perception."

I reach out and push my hand through the hair at the back of his neck. "Did I just destroy your vibe?"

He smiles and shoots me a look. "It's rare that anyone ever challenges me to look at things in a new way." He hums, like thoughts are racing around his head and he's trying to sort them into some kind of order. "But you always manage it."

"Here we are," I say. "Just turn in here."

We pull up in the parking area for the falls. There's just one other car here.

"Do you get many tourists?" Jack asks, as we get out of the car and make the short walk to the edge of the pool.

"We get some RVs passing through in the summer that stop off on the way to somewhere else. It's a steady trail that bolsters local business a little. But the falls still feel like they belong to the people of Star Falls. It's still the place where most of the town had their first picnic, their first kiss, recovered from their first heartbreak. There are far more spectacular falls in the state of Colorado, so people naturally gravitate to those. I'm kinda pleased we get to keep these for ourselves."

He turns to me, a warm smile on his face. "Sounds like these falls have seen plenty of stuff." He slips his hand around my waist.

"I'm sure of it." I toe off my shoes. "I'm not swimming, but we have to get our feet wet. I mean, it's the law around here."

"Wouldn't want to break the law, now, would I?"

Jack rolls up his jeans. I wore a skirt, knowing this is where we'd end up. Jack follows me as we round the edge of the pools that the falls create. "This is my favorite spot," I say, coming to the large, flat stone near the entrance to the creek. "It's the perfect position to take in the falls."

The surface of the stone is just big enough for us to both sit. So we sit down and put our legs into the water.

"Shit," Jack says. "The water is freezing!"

I can't help but laugh. "Gilded cage, Jack. Gilded cage. If you can't even endure the Star Falls pool in October, then I don't know what to do with you."

He dips his hand into the water and then flicks it at me, and I can't help but think how differently we grew up.

"I don't know what I would have done as a kid, if it wasn't playing in this pool and messing about in the creek. If I was at home, Dad would always rope me into something at the farm. Some of it, I didn't mind. Fruit picking can be fun." I laugh at the memories of those summers when Dad would send us off to pick. "Bray and I would always make ourselves sick eating strawberries at the beginning of each season. Dad would be furious that we were eating more than we picked, so he'd send us off to do something else. And then by the end of the season, you couldn't pay us to look at a strawberry."

"Strawberries are your favorites?" he asks.

"Yeah. Always. When I was a kid, I had strawberry-covered sheets and even a lamp shaped like a strawberry. For six years straight, I dressed as a strawberry for Halloween."

"That's adorable," he says.

"I was twelve the last time. My classmates didn't think it was so adorable, let me tell you."

Jack lets out a deep belly laugh. "An adorable little geek. I love it."

"Says the guy who knows the set of *Twilight* like he lives there. What about you?" I ask. "What was your go-to Halloween costume?"

"I'm not sure," he says. "Superheroes probably. My

parents always threw a huge party at the house. The nanny would take me trick-or-treating when I was little. And then I got too old—or too proud—to go with the nanny once I hit eleven or twelve. I wasn't allowed to go out on my own, so I just stopped going."

I lean my head on his shoulder. "That sounds so sad."

"I don't have a therapy bill for it. Life's different in New York for a kid. That's all."

I'd take another six years as a strawberry over staying in my bedroom on Halloween. "Halloween is huge in Star Falls. Everyone goes down to the park and the diner sets up a barbeque. Usually there's a band playing."

"What about trick-or-treating?" he asks.

"The kids do that first and then we all head down about six." I try to think if I've ever seen a flyer or any ad for it. "It's kinda just become a tradition."

"Sounds nice," he says.

I want to say he can come to this year's Halloween—it's only a couple of weeks away, but I don't want to dip my toe into talk about the future. If I do, I might burst this bubble that we're in.

"My toes are numb," Jack says grimly. "I actually think they might have fallen off."

I laugh. "Oh, Jack. You're such a New Yorker."

He pulls his legs out of the water and stands. "Guilty as charged." He pulls me up and I lead him over to the start of the creek, where the water from the pool gently runs over rocks and stones on its way to wherever it's going.

"You have to try and find the sparkly stones," I instruct him. "I actually have found some beautiful ones over the years. I have quite the collection. I even thought about doing a geology course there for a minute."

Jack follows me as I move from rock to rock, peering at the bed of the creek.

"I've got quite the eagle eye, or so I'm told," I say.

"Tell me about the course you applied for," he says.

"I get college credit for it," I say, and then I realize I'm being defensive. Jack's not asking me to justify why I'm taking it. He's interested. In me. "I got my high school diploma by correspondence. I didn't graduate with my class because of Mom." I spot a sparkle of something submerged in the silt of the creek bed and bend to uncover it. When I pull out the stone, I realize it must have been the glint of the sun making it appear nicer than it was, and I drop it back into the water with a plop.

"I'm sorry," Jack says.

"Don't be. I only graduated recently. I didn't bother for years, and then I did a short horticultural class and hated it, and sent it to Bray. He's the farmer. I'm not that girl. But I'd gotten an itch, so I decided I wanted to get my high school diploma. I finished that this summer. I found it nice to have something other than the farm. You know?"

He nods, listening intently, his expression serious.

"So I wanted to have something else. Study something else. So I'm starting an American History class. We'll see how that goes."

"That's amazing, Iris."

I turn to find Jack looking at me like he's just found one of the dazzling stones that hide in the creek bed under our feet.

"I'll probably fail it or scrape by, because of my responsibilities to the farm."

"I doubt you'll scrape by. I bet you fly." He grins at me, and I can't help but smile back. I step toward him onto the creek bed and he steps off the stones onto the shingle to stand opposite me. The cold water rushes around our feet as Jack wraps his arms around me and presses his lips to mine.

He pulls back and our foreheads rest against each other's. "You've dealt with so much in your life, yet you haven't let it tarnish your spirit. You're still marveling at the moonlight's reflection, searching for the sparkling rocks among the silt of the creek bed. You're such a special woman, Iris. I don't think you have any idea."

My cheeks heat, and Jack cups my face. I lift my head slightly, impatient for his kiss. I don't have to wait long. His soft lips press against me and his tongue pushes through to find mine. He kisses me like he can't *not* kiss me. Like kissing me gives him energy, life, purpose.

My body begins to buzz. I don't know what it is, but when Jack touches me, my entire body seems to change. Like he affects every cell. I've never known my body to react in the way it does when Jack's near me. I can't imagine it ever will again.

I know Jack's special. I know what we share together is more than anything I could have ever imagined. And even though I'm not sure how I'll exist without him, I'll be forever grateful that I've had the opportunity to know this special man.

TWENTY

Jack

I pull up in front of Wilde's Farm late on Saturday afternoon. I know that Iris, Bray, and their father finish at the farm at three on Saturdays. So by now, they should have finished up and have had time to decompress. I've got an idea, and I want them in the right frame of mind for it.

All my friends have been back in New York now for weeks. I don't think I've ever spent so long away from Manhattan. It's coming up on four weeks. Even Fisher and Byron aren't in town. It means I can spend all of my time with Iris now. Or working at the farm. Or back at the Club, taking business calls. Iris and I both work in the family business. We're both tied to them in ways that neither of us chose, but we can't walk away. Yesterday, my father actually called to ask me where I was and why I was blowing off meetings. I can't remember the last time he called me himself. He usually sends messages through his assistant. I've had plenty of those over the last few weeks.

New York is calling. I don't know how long I can avoid her.

I take the stairs to the two-story farmhouse two at a time and knock on the door. I have my laptop in the SUV. But I haven't told Iris any of my plans. I didn't want her to tell me all the ways it wouldn't work. And I didn't want Iris's father and Bray to feel like this was coming from Iris and me. If they don't like it, I don't want them to think any differently about Iris.

I'm ambushing all of them equally.

I've tried to be subtle in my questioning, but over the last weeks on the farm, I've been able to talk to lots of the workers about Wilde's Farm, including Bray and Iris. In between, I've also been doing research about the industry across America and globally. Basically, I've been an undercover business consultant for Wilde's Farm.

"Hey," Bray says when he opens the door. "You can just come right on in. No need to knock."

I chuckle. So completely not like New York. "Thanks."

Bray and Mr. Wilde have softened toward me since Mr. Wilde's interrogation. He asked me every question other than my inside leg measurement and my net worth. I was completely honest with him. I like that he's so careful with Iris's heart. I hope he realizes I am too.

"You want a drink?" Bray offers as we go into the kitchen.

"I'm good. Is your dad about?" I ask. "Your sister?"

Mr. Wilde's hand flies up from the couch and he waves. "I'm doing a crossword. You'll have to help me finish it if you want my attention. If you're asking me for permission to marry my daughter, come back in a year's time with a criminal record check and a printout of your bank balance."

I can't help but chuckle. "I'll take the crossword. For now."

I don't miss the way Bray's eyebrows shoot up into his hairline. I head to the couch and Mr. Wilde hands me the newspaper.

"Jeez. You didn't say it was *The New York Times*."

"Didn't realize you were going to take me up on the offer. Anyway, I've done all the hard ones. Only two clues left."

I grin. Yeah, because everyone leaves the easy questions until last. I scan the clues. Crosswords aren't really my thing, but I've been known to get a few right answers. I look to see what letters we already have. "Eight across. Lunacy."

Mr. Wilde sits up straight in his seat and takes the paper from my hand. "I think you might be right. I was thinking lupine, but it doesn't fit. Lunacy works."

I shrug. "Like you say, you saved the easy ones until last." I glance around, looking to see a sign that Iris's in the house. I really want to speak to all three of them together.

"Is Iris here?"

"Iris!" Bray shouts. "Your boyfriend's here!"

I grin at being called Iris's boyfriend. I can't remember the last time I was anyone's boyfriend. I can't remember the last time I wanted to be. But I definitely want to be Iris's boyfriend. I want to be her everything.

The creak of the floorboards tells me Iris's heard her brother. We're going to dinner this evening. This time at the Club. Not because I don't like Pizza Meet Ya, but because it's good to have a change sometimes. I think I've eaten just about everything on that menu twice over now.

Iris appears in a Vivian Cross t-shirt and leggings. Her wet hair is pulled back and piled on top of her head, and it reminds me of the first time I ever laid eyes on her at the theater. She's stunning. Effortlessly elegant.

But I know more about her now that makes her even more beautiful. She's kind and clever and makes me think. I knew she was special as soon as I saw her. I just didn't understand how special.

"Jack?" Iris asks. "What are you doing here?"

"I actually wanted to talk to all three of you about something. Before we go out to dinner. About the farm," I clarify, before Mr. Wilde gets out his shotgun. "Next time, I'll bring my bank balance printout," I say, directly to Mr. Wilde.

"What?" Iris asks. "What bank balance?"

"I'm kidding. Not kidding, but it's an inside joke. Or not a joke. Anyway, I have my laptop in my car. I've been researching a few things about the farm. If you all have time, I'd love to show you something."

"The farm?" Bray asks. "What kind of thing?"

"Just give me thirty minutes. That's all I ask."

"Sure," Mr. Wilde says, getting up from the couch.

Bray and Iris share a look. I'm pretty sure that Mr. Wilde isn't always so welcoming to people wanting to talk to him about his business.

I grab the laptop from the car, and when I come back inside, the three of them are at the kitchen table. I pull up the presentation. "I've really enjoyed working at the farm. It's a great, efficient operation you have. But Iris was telling me that margins are tight."

"That they are," Mr. Wilde says. "But that's business."

"Absolutely. I've been asking around. Everyone thinks very highly of you as employers. You have a great internal brand. I had an idea of how you can make that an external brand."

Mr. Wilde glances at his son and daughter, who are

sitting either side of him. I'm not sure if he's seeing if they also think I'm full of shit. But I need to cut to the chase.

"I think you could build Wilde's Farm into a national brand of organic frozen fruit."

I go through my presentation. I talk about the market and how organic produce is in increasing demand. How the freezing operation would take considerable capital investment, but how much could be charged for the fruit once frozen, bagged, and sold to supermarkets.

"You want us to take a partner?" Bray asks, sitting back in his chair. "To pay for the new equipment and everything?"

Iris's shaking her head before I even have a chance to respond.

"No," I say. "This is a family farm, and that's how it should stay. I know that's important to all of you. I'm suggesting you take out a loan. That way you get all the upside when the business does well. A partner would take a portion of the upside. The bank just wants its money back with interest."

Iris's expression is brighter, and she sits forward in her chair. "But we can't just start freezing all our fruit. We don't have contracts with supermarkets for frozen fruit."

"You're right. You'd have to start small. Build the brand. Prove the quality. But I really think it's a way to future-proof the business."

Mr. Wilde folds his arms. "It's not how we work. We don't have any knowledge about freezing. I bet it's not so easy as dumping it all in a chest freezer. There are probably regulations. And how would we get all the bags, and we'd have to have pictures on them and..." He shakes his head. "It's not going to work."

My heart sinks a little. I don't know Mr. Wilde or Bray

well enough to know how to appeal to them. Maybe I've come on too strong.

"We can source packaging, Dad," Iris says. "Getting a designer isn't difficult. I actually have some designs that I've been messing around with."

"You have?" I ask.

Iris shrugs. "But the money required. The investment. It's a lot."

"You have the space for all the freezing equipment. And I've looked into some places where you can lease the equipment." This is really doable. And the bank loan wouldn't be as big as they think. Especially with the amount of upside at stake.

"The problem is if it doesn't work, it's a lot of money wasted," Bray says. "And we don't have money to waste."

I wish I could offer to lend them the money. I'd be happy to. Iris is smart. I know she could make this happen.

"I think you've underestimated how the crop yields go down when you switch to organic," Bray says. "It makes it all so volatile."

"But the prices you can achieve." I flip to another slide on my laptop. "The difference is incredible."

Mr. Wilde grumbles underneath his breath. "That's gotten even more expensive."

"Demand for organic is growing," I try to reassure him. "But if the horticulture is too difficult, maybe you start with nonorganic," I suggest. "That would give you an opportunity to get the freezing operation in place."

"It's a good idea, Dad." Iris looks at her father. "You've seen the figures. Business isn't getting any easier. We're always under pressure to reduce prices. It's never-ending."

"I've also got some data on some less-traditional fruit and how demand is growing for them. You could also think about trialing some different fruit and freezing them. That gives you an advantage against other operations that are just freezing berries."

Mr. Wilde shakes his head. "It's a lot of money," he says. "Like Bray says, we don't have that money to lose."

"Think about it," I say. "We could talk again, and I'm happy to do anything I can. I know other people who might be helpful for you to talk to. Finance people who'd be able to get you the loan, for example."

"But the loan would be guaranteed on the land, right?" Mr. Wilde asks.

"Probably," I say.

He shakes his head. "You owe me a crossword clue," he says.

I nod, getting the message. Our discussion is over. Business is done for the day. All I can for hope is that the idea percolates. This is a risk, and a big one. Like they say, they don't have money to lose. But there's a massive upside here. I just want them all to think about it. I just want them all to know that how it's always been doesn't have to be how it always will be. If they do, maybe Mr. Wilde will have a change of heart.

TWENTY-ONE

Iris

This evening, I haven't felt as out of place as I expected. Maybe because I'm with Jack. The Colorado Club is beautiful. I've never seen the main building other than the door of the goods entrance, and the kitchen. It lives up to the hype. At the same time, it's not stuffy or snobby. Everyone's friendly and warm. But not overly familiar.

"Was it as bad as you thought?" Jack asks as we head out of the restaurant, Blossom.

Neither of us have talked about Jack's presentation earlier in the evening. "Your freezing idea?"

He chuckles. "I meant the restaurant, but you can tell me what you thought about my idea, too."

I sigh. "I thought it was good. It all makes sense. But... my dad... I'm not sure if he's willing to take such a big risk." Jack starts to say something, but I stop him. "It's not me who needs to be convinced. And there's no point in pushing Dad. He'll have to come around to the idea. Or not."

"Okay, so what about spending your evening at Blossom?"

"Jack Alden, how could I have a *bad* evening with you? I feel how much you care in every word. Every time you check in on me about the food and my beverage. The fact you've taken so much time to think about my family's business. The way you pick out the things on the menu that you think I'll like before even thinking about your own order. You're kind and caring and any evening with you would be one of the best evenings of my life."

His mouth twitches at the corners. "I was concerned you'd feel uncomfortable."

"The meal was lovely, the view spectacular, but I was always going to have a great evening, because I spent it with you."

Jack takes my hand and presses it to his lips. "I don't know how I got so lucky. I can't imagine..."

I let him leave his words unfinished. I don't want to imagine what life will be like when Jack goes back to New York. I know there will come a time when I don't know him anymore. I can't bear to think about Jack back in New York, dating some society girl. Getting married to a suitable woman from a good family.

It might just kill me.

We don't discuss it, but as we exit the Club, we get into one of the golf carts outside and head over to Jack's lodge. Our relationship isn't all about the sex, but I'd happily spend the rest of my life naked with Jack.

"I've been wanting to get you naked all evening," he says, as we pull up in front of his lodge.

"I thought you liked me for my witty conversation, Jack."

"That too," he says. "And your kindness, the way you

look after your family, your intelligence and creativity. But that dress?"

I splurged on this blue dress online and it only arrived this morning. It covers me neck to toe, but it fits close to my body.

His eyes grow hooded and he cups my face with his hand. "That dress is the kind of dress that needs to be taken off."

My nipples press tight against the lace of my bra and heat rises in my body, like I stepped into a sauna. I just nod at Jack. It's all I can do. My mouth is dry, my knees are weak, and everywhere he touches me, he sets alight.

I don't remember climbing the stairs to the lodge and getting inside. I don't know how we ended up in the bedroom. But now that we're here, I'm very aware of everything. The pulse in my neck, the shallow breaths that make my chest rise and fall, and Jack, kissing every inch of skin he uncovers as he peels off my dress.

His hair is silky between my fingers. I would kill for hair this soft.

"Jack," I say, as my dress pools at my feet.

"Like I said, the dress looks great on my bedroom floor. And now I'm going to devour you."

I step away from him and shake my head. "No," I say, and I slide to my knees. "I want to devour *you*."

He groans and shakes off his shirt as I unzip his pants. Jack is big. I'm not quite sure how this will work, but I want him in my mouth. I want him every way I can get him. He's already hard, straining against his stomach, and I can't help but smile to myself.

I'm just some small-town girl who works on a farm.

He's a man who could have any woman he wants.

But all his hardness is for me.

He steps out of his trousers and stands before me entirely naked. His body is muscular, but not bulky. His muscles shift under his skin, and I reach up to his chest and smooth my palms down his hard body, enjoying the ravines and lines, like they're my own personal map of the rivers of Colorado.

"Can I ask you to do something?" Jack asks.

"You going to give me direction?" I ask, smiling at him.

He shakes his head. "Not at all. But could you put your hair up? Like in a bun?"

I raise my eyebrows. "I can do that." I've been able to get my hair in a bun without any pins since I was six years old. I stand, step back, snap my bra undone and let it fall to the floor. If he wants a visual, he's going to get a visual.

I lift my hands up to my hair and scrape my fingers through, getting it into a ponytail before twisting it up and around, tucking in the ends.

"Fuck, I can die a happy man, now."

I smile and step back toward him.

"You're beautiful," he says.

"Back at you."

I lower myself to my knees, bracing my hands on his hard, muscular thighs. I press my tongue to the base of his erect cock and lick, dragging it slowly up his shaft.

He growls and wetness grows between my legs. I want his fingers there. His tongue. Already I crave release from all this need I have for the man in front of me.

I reach his crown, circle and suckle, and I can tell he's doing everything he can not to move. I start again at the base and lick upward.

I feel so powerful. So in control. Making the man in front of me weak is an aphrodisiac like I've never experienced. I open my mouth and do my best to take him as far as I can. He's too big to fit. But Jack doesn't seem to think so.

"Iris," he gasps out. "Iris."

I lick and suck, take him deep into my mouth. My eyes are watering as I try to angle him. I grip around his shaft, trying to get him deeper with each movement. I want more. I want his hands on me. In me. I want his tongue. I want to get fucked.

"Jesus, Iris." He steps away. "You're going to make me come."

I moan at the thought of him being so turned on. "I want you to come," I say. I tip my head back and open my mouth.

He groans and steps toward me. Our eyes are locked as Jack paints my lips with the crown of his cock, dipping it between my lips, and in seconds, his hot come is spurting onto my tongue.

I shiver at him losing control. He cups my face and I lick my lips, taking in anything that I missed.

"You're so fucking beautiful."

"Jack," I stutter, need rising in me, threatening to burst out. "I'm so wet."

He groans again, and his cock rears in front of me.

"I'm desperate for you," I whisper.

He scoops me up and places me gently on the bed. He crawls over me and I widen my legs, allowing him to settle between them. His cock is nestled into the folds of my pussy, throbbing on my clit.

"Jack," I say again. "You feel so good."

He dips to claim a kiss. His breaths are heavy, his chest moving with every inhale and exhale. The weight of his body pins me to the mattress—there's no escaping him.

I squirm underneath him, rocking my hips back and

forward. I'm impatient. I want to feel him as he pushes inside and it's almost too much—just on the edge of painful.

"You don't need to try to get me hard," he says. "I'm already there." He shakes his head. "You might just kill me."

"Can you feel how wet I am?" I ask, my voice breathy with lust.

"I can. I'm covered in you already."

My eyelids flutter shut as desperation takes hold. "Jack, please."

He growls at my begging and reaches over my head. I hope it's for a condom. Although, right at this moment, I'm incapable of making good decisions and I'd be happy to take him inside me without one. I'd like to know how it feels to have him inside me without any barriers between us.

But Jack has found a condom.

I'm so frenzied with lust, I can't think about anything but how he's taking too long to push inside me. Finally, after what seems like hours, his crown is nudging at my entrance. I spread my legs as wide as they will go.

"You ready?" His expression is serious. He knows he's big. He doesn't want to hurt me.

I nod. "More than ready."

His eyes flutter closed as he pushes his tip inside. I let out a moan that's so loud, they can probably hear it in Canada. He just feels so good. Not just because he's big, but because he's Jack. Because he's careful with me, thoughtful. Because he's trying to help, trying to do the best by me and my family.

He's just so perfect.

He pushes inside of me and my fingers dig into his shoulders in an effort to take more of him.

"Too much?" he asks.

I shake my head. But I can't breathe. He's pushed all the

breath from my body. There's no room inside me for anything else.

He pulls out completely and slides his shaft up and down my folds, rubbing against my clit. I shake my head. It's too much. I can't take more sensation from this man. Inside and out, he owns me.

"You don't like it, Iris?" he says on a growl. "You don't like how I feel all over you?"

I whimper and sling an arm across my face, embarrassed at how much power he has over my body.

He pushes my hand away and then slams into me.

I scream as sensation blooms across my body. I can barely catch my breath as he starts to move above me, pushing in over and over, deeper and deeper, and I don't know if I'm going to come or pass out. Both, maybe.

The start of my orgasm vibrates deep between my thighs. "Jack!" I gasp. I don't know if he doesn't hear me, but it doesn't stop him moving above me—relentless, powerful, determined.

My back arches, my body starts to shake. "Jack," I call again, and my climax erupts like a volcano, liquid heat spilling through me.

"I want more," he says, thrusting through my climax.

My body is Jell-O. I have no strength even to lift my arms. Even though I haven't recovered from my orgasm, another one, something bigger, is approaching.

Jack pulls out and I catch my breath, just before he flips me to my stomach. He maneuvers my exhausted limbs so I have one knee up, like I'm almost crawling up the mattress. Cold air hits my pussy, making me shudder, but immediately Jack is behind me, his body on mine, his mouth at my neck, kissing me. His fingers find my folds, and I whimper as he flicks and rubs, growling in my ear while whispering how wet I am. He thrusts into me again, and I scream. Every time, I forget how he stretches me, how big he is, how he's almost too much.

But he feels so good.

He lifts my knee higher up the mattress and pushes deeper. My body shifts up, up, up at the power of his movements and I reach my arms up, to stop myself from hitting the headboard. But even if I do, I wouldn't tell him to stop. There's no pain that could outstrip the pleasure of Jack fucking me.

He grips my shoulders and pounds into me, and I'm lost.

He's all I can feel. All I can hear. All I want. He's everything.

"I'm—" My scream cuts off my words and my orgasm races through me, pushing, pushing, pushing and roaring into existence.

Jack bellows behind me, thrusting up, up, up, and then collapsing on top of me.

"I'd do anything for you," I gasp out, as I try to catch my breath. I don't know why I say it, it just feels like I need to.

He rolls to the side, deals with the condom, and then pulls me onto his chest as he lies on his back. "I feel the same. I won't give you up. I can't."

We both know there are no solutions to all the obstacles to being together, but at this moment, we're very clear that what we have together is important. Too important to sacrifice. Whatever that involves.

"I have something for you," he says. "I don't know if you'll want to go, but I got the tickets anyway."

"What?" I say, pushing up so I can look at his face.

He reaches for his phone and pulls up a screenshot. "It's a gala night at the New York City Ballet. There are some ballet legends who will dance to raise money for the ballet company."

My stomach flips. Jack's so thoughtful. So kind. But I don't go to New York more than once a year. I take the phone from his hand to read the details of who will be dancing.

"Mariana Lopez," I say. "She's always been a favorite, but I've never seen her perform live. And Carlos Acoma. I cried when he retired."

"The current principals will dance too," he says.

But how can I go and leave the farm so soon after my last trip?

He must sense my reticence, because he adds, "It's a Saturday night. So, if you want to go, we can fly in on Saturday and back on Sunday. You wouldn't be away from Star Falls long."

I sigh. I'd love to go. I glance at Jack. "New York?" I'm not clarifying the location, I'm just asking Jack if he thinks I could do it. I'm asking myself.

"Would it be too difficult?" he asks. "We don't have to go." He pulls me closer, shielding me, keeping me safe from my own thoughts.

Although thoughts of going to the ballet aren't difficult. Not tonight, anyway. I don't allow myself to think about ballet much between visits because it's too painful, but lying here with Jack, talking about going to the ballet so soon after the last trip, seems exciting.

Maybe Jack is helping me leave my past in my past.

"I'd love to go to the ballet with you, Jack."

He grins, flips me to my back, and presses a kiss to my lips. It's like I've just done him a favor, rather than the other way around.

TWENTY-TWO

Iris

I couldn't say no to New York with Jack. I cling to the hope being with him will override any painful memories. So, a week after he presented me with the tickets, I glance around at the sleek walnut finishes and cream leather of not just the chairs but the walls too. This is no commercial airplane.

"You okay?" Jack asks from where he sits opposite me. "You want to sit next to me?"

I shake my head. "I'm fine. This is... different to how I normally fly."

"Yeah," he says. "But this will mean we can get there quicker. And come back quicker."

The helicopter ride from the Club to the airport—which, I never knew existed—started off our journey differently. I always knew that this wouldn't be an ordinary trip to New York, but this? It's just me and Jack on this plane. The plane wouldn't be flying at all if we weren't on it. It feels... a little uncomfortable, to be honest. I don't fit here.

My cheap suitcase got loaded into the plane alongside

Jack's leather weekender that looked like it was straight out of Milan, and Jack's denim jeans and t-shirt have been replaced with blue slacks and a crisp white shirt. I'm sitting opposite New York Jack now. We're still in Colorado but we're on different territory.

"Sure," I say.

"You seem jumpy," he says.

I pull in a breath. "I feel jumpy. Or out of place or something."

He nods and reaches for my hand. "Let me give you an insight into the people I grew up with. There's no doubt that many wealthy people are snobs. They like to pass judgment on others. But what's interesting is they don't care in the slightest what people think about them. That's what separates the wealthy from everyone else. When we went to the Club, you didn't feel out of place, did you?"

I shake my head. "It was very relaxed."

"Right. Everywhere you go is very relaxed if *you're* relaxed. If you don't care what people think of you."

The plane starts to move, and I reach to get my purse from where it's sitting beside me. I need to stow it away. And shouldn't someone have come around to check that we had our seat belts on?

"Your purse is fine there beside you," Jack says, reading my mind.

"Really? I could move it."

"You move it on a commercial airliner in case it stops other people getting out. It's just us. The purse is fine where it is." He smiles at me, trying to be reassuring, but I don't feel reassured. I don't move in these circles. This is not where I feel comfortable.

"I'm just a hick," I say. "Not used to private planes."

At that moment, the nose of the plane lifts and we're flying away from Star Falls and safe ground.

"Well, you'll be used to them after this. And you're not a hick. You're a beautiful, intelligent, graceful woman. And I'm..." He stops himself before he finishes the sentence, and something inside me tells me not to press him on what he was about to say. "We're going to have a wonderful evening at the ballet." His eyebrows pull tight together and he tries to take a breath.

"What?" I ask him, squeezing his hand.

"I have something to tell you and I don't want you to... I thought it would be a nice surprise, but now I'm thinking you might see it differently."

"What?" I ask him. "Tell me."

"I thought I'd surprise you before the gala. I bought you something and it's—they're back at my place but... I don't want you to think I have any motives other than I want to make you happy. I want to spoil you." He looks so pained, I want to slip off my seat belt and slide onto his lap. Maybe that would be fine on a private plane during takeoff, but maybe not and I'm not going to risk it.

"I know you only have good intentions," I say.

He nods. "It's true."

"Then tell me."

"I bought you something to wear tonight. And I've arranged for hair and makeup people to come to the house."

I swallow down the mix of emotions. I understand why he was doubting himself.

"I didn't do it because I thought you needed... dressing or fixing or because—"

"Because you didn't think I'd have anything appropriate to wear to a New York gala night, because I'm from Star Falls." A niggle of discomfort gnaws at me. We both know I don't fit in his world. But dresses and makeup aren't going to bridge the gap.

"That's really not what I was thinking."

Jack's not a liar. I believe that wasn't his conscious intention. But maybe there was a part of him, buried. Subconscious. That doesn't believe I'll fit in to his world unless I change.

I can't blame him for thinking that. Because honestly, sitting on this plane, flying to New York for twenty-four hours, that's exactly what I'm thinking.

"You have a picture of the dress?" I ask. I don't want to make this moment more uncomfortable than it already is. Jack has tried to do something nice. I don't want to throw that back in his face.

"You don't have to wear any of them," he says.

I tilt my head to the side. "Any of them? There are multiple outfits?"

"I wanted you to have a choice."

I roll my eyes, amused and I hold out my hand for his phone. "Show me."

He brings up some pictures. The first is a sugar-pink strapless dress with a fitted bodice and a full skirt that looks almost like a long tutu. It's beautiful. The next shot is the same dress from the back. It's elegant and pretty at the same time. There's no way anyone couldn't like it.

I glance up at Jack and he's looking at me, nervously. I swipe the image to the next dress. It's long and black, with a silver belt and a halter neck. The back shows that the ties from the halter fall down the back of the dress, which is backless. It's very elegant. Perhaps a little more sophisticated than the first. Then the third is strapless again. It's blue and ruched on the bodice, which comes down to just below the bottom, and then there's a full skirt. It looks like someone put a sweater over a prom dress. I don't like it.

I swipe to the next image and it's various bags and shoes. They are all beautiful and look way too expensive.

I slide the phone back toward Jack.

"Did you like any of them?" he asks.

Of course I like them. It would be impossible not to.

"They're all beautiful. Which one was your favorite?" I ask him. I have no idea what the right choice is. He's the best person to make the decision here.

"I think you'd look beautiful in all of them. But you'll look beautiful no matter what you wear."

"I'll wear what you want me to wear," I say without bitterness. I'll do anything Jack wants me to. I'll wear whatever he likes. I know he thinks I feel uncomfortable, but I wonder if he's just as uncomfortable taking a girl like me out in New York.

"I want you to wear what *you* want to wear. If you want to wear jeans and a Snoopy t-shirt, that's fine with me."

I pause for a beat. "But is it? Honestly? Presumably there will be people at this gala who you know. And I'll be there as your date. You surely want me to look a certain way. You don't want me to be wearing my Wilde's Farm baseball cap, do you?"

Jack scrunches up his face and presses the heels of his hands over his eyes. "This is exactly what I didn't want. I wanted to spoil you. And you see it as me being embarrassed by you. That's not true. I don't care what other people think of me. Or you. I know who I am and I know who you are. That's the important thing."

I want what he's saying to be true. I think he believes it is. I just don't think it's real life. "It's natural to want me to fit in. I get it. I did bring a dress, but it's not as beautiful as the ones in the pictures."

He shakes his head. "I really wish I'd never bought them. It was a stupid idea. I've never had a girlfriend who I wanted to spoil before. This is new territory for me. And I'm fucking it up. I'm sorry."

His eyes look so sorrowful, and it melts me. Have I got this all wrong? I glance around toward the front of the plane. "Can I take my seat belt off?" I whisper.

He nods. I take my belt off and slide into the chair next to him, but it's not close enough. I take his hand and pull us over to the couch at the back of the plane. I wait for him to sit and then put my arms around his neck and sit on his lap. "I'm sorry if I overreacted," I say.

"Don't you apologize. I should be the one to say sorry, and I'm *really* sorry. I would never want you to think you're not good enough as you are. You're better than anyone I've ever met."

I press a kiss to his jaw and snuggle into his neck. "It was kind of you. And thoughtful. I wouldn't want to turn up in something that wasn't right for the evening. It would be embarrassing, and you buying these dresses—well, it makes sure that doesn't happen." I rest my palm over his chest. "You're a good man, Jack. We're just from two different worlds. When you're in Star Falls, I can half forget that you grew up in some fancy New York house and went to some fancy school. You're just my kind, handsome, geeky-about-*Twilight* Jack. Being here..." I look all around the interior of the plane. "It's a lot. And it's a long way from Star Falls."

He nods and pulls me closer. "Just because we're from different places doesn't make this impossible."

"I think we might be in for some turbulence," I say, grinning up at him.

"That may be so, but talk to a pilot and they'll always tell you that turbulence will never be the reason for a crash."

Maybe not turbulence, but there're a lot of other things that can send a plane hurtling toward the ground. I don't want to think about all the things that could end us right now. This certainly shouldn't come close.

I pull in a breath and press my lips to his. "I like the pink one," I tell him in a whisper.

"That was my favorite too," he replies.

"Can I tell you something else?" I ask.

"You can always tell me anything."

"I want to do my own hair and makeup. Wearing a new dress is one thing, but I still want to feel like myself."

"I think that's a great idea," he says. "But can I make a request?"

"Jack Alden, I know you want my hair up in a bun." I grin at him.

"Guilty as charged."

TWENTY-THREE

Jack

As we enter the Alden family box, the orchestra is tuning up.

"I love the sound of the musicians," Iris whispers, beaming from ear to ear. Her dress looks incredible on her. It fit like a glove and any awkwardness about me buying her a dress for tonight seems to have been forgotten.

I've always known I've had more money than I could possibly ever need in my life, so I've never resented picking up the bill for dinner or paying for holidays. But the fact that Iris had to be persuaded to wear one of the dresses I bought her, tells me everything about her character. She loves me for me. She worries she's not enough when she's more than I could ever have hoped for. I particularly love that she decided she wanted to do her own hair and makeup. She has more confidence to navigate New York society than she thinks she does. She just needs to believe in herself.

"Wow, you can see everything up here," Iris says, scanning the audience. "This is where you were when you saw me?"

I wrap my arm around her waist, pulling her toward me, and point at where she was sitting that first night when I laid eyes on her. "You were right there. And your silhouette lit up when the principal dancers came to the front of the stage. You were enthralled. Completely mesmerized by the performance. And all I could see was you." She turns her head and kisses me on the cheek when someone clears their throat behind us.

I turn to find Greg looking furtive. Iris spins to face him, too, and he glances between the two of us.

"I know I said your mother wasn't attending tonight, but she had a last-minute change of heart."

I roll my eyes. "You should have texted me."

"I did. She decided twenty minutes ago."

"Does she know I'm here?"

Greg nods. "I've informed her."

I glance at Iris. I don't even want to know if my mother knows I've brought someone. It doesn't matter. I sigh. This just got more complicated.

"You're about to meet the matriarch of the Alden family," I say to Iris.

"Oh god," Iris says. "Really?"

"Sorry, I had no idea she'd be here."

Before I can say more, the curtains of the box part and my mother enters.

She sees me and smiles, then Iris, next to me, catches her attention. Her smile doesn't falter. "Jack, darling. It's been a while. Where have you been?"

"At Byron's Club," I say. "Mother, this is Iris Wilde. Iris, this is Mrs. Joan Alden, my mother."

Iris holds out her hand and my mother gives it a short,

cursory shake and her smile tightens. "Wilde. Wilde. Are you from New York?"

I roll my eyes at my mother's snobbery. If you live in New York and my mother doesn't recognize your surname, then you're not worth knowing. "Iris lives in Colorado."

"Oh, how delightful," my mother says.

"In the town nearest the Colorado Club," Iris clarifies.

"Your family are from there?" my mother asks.

"Yes. Our family has a fruit farm on the outskirts of Star Falls."

"A fruit farm. How sweet." My mother smiles tightly and shoots me a look that says I'm being ridiculous by bringing a woman from a fruit farm to the New York City Ballet.

"We actually met in New York," I say. "Here at the ballet, actually," I say to my mother. "Iris used to be a dancer."

Before anyone can say anything more, the lights of the auditorium dip and we have to take our seats. Greg steps in and rearranges the freestanding chairs so my mother's seat is nearest the stage with the best view. I guide Iris to the seat directly behind my mother and take a seat beside her.

Iris glances across at me and smiles, but it's a smile lacking in enthusiasm. I wanted Iris and I to enjoy the ballet together tonight. The last thing I wanted was my mother to be the judgmental third wheel. If I'd known she was coming, I would have gotten tickets somewhere else in the auditorium. I wouldn't have used the family box. It's not that I was embarrassed or ashamed to be with Iris, more that I didn't want Iris's night to be ruined by my mother.

I take Iris's hand and squeeze it. At least we will have after the ballet. And we can come and see another performance another time.

The curtains open and I try to focus on the dancers and the music rather than the irritation of my mother being so close. But it's difficult. I just want to sit here and watch Iris. She's so animated as the different ballet stars take to the stage to perform parts of well-known ballets and some more obscure ones. She's half out of her seat when Carlos Acoma dances. She feels the performances as if she's living them.

I want to do this every week with her. I want to buy her a pretty dress and take her to the ballet and watch her light up. I feel so privileged to see this side of Iris. I imagine most people, not even people she's known her entire life in Star Falls, have seen this side of her.

The current principal male of the New York City Ballet finishes a leap with a particularly dramatic flourish and the audience bursts into applause. Iris is out of her chair and clapping furiously. She's a joy to be close to.

Iris's applause captures my mother's attention, and she looks up and around from where she's sitting. Then her gaze slides to me.

The curtain comes down and my mother gets to her feet. Immediately, Greg is by her side. "Mrs. Alden, did you enjoy it?" he asks.

My mother glances at Iris, who's still staring at the stage, willing the dancers back. "Not as much as others, apparently," she says. "Jack. Come and have a drink."

It's a summons, not a suggestion.

I pull in a breath and remind myself that I don't care what my mother thinks. What I care about is Iris. I know how I feel about her. I don't need commentary from my mother.

I turn to Iris. "Shall we—"

My mother takes Iris's hand. "Come and have a drink."

Iris's gaze flickers to me, an expression of panic on her face. "Certainly, Mrs. Alden," she says.

I shrug. It's ten minutes that we have to endure dodging jabs from my mother. I hope the ballet's worth it in Iris's eyes.

"So, Iris," my mother says as we sit at a low table, reserved for the Aldens. Three glasses of champagne are being poured by a waiter. "What did you think of the first part of the performance?" It's a test with multiple elements. Most of the women my mother has suggested I might want to date would at least pass parts of the test. But they would know they were under pressure to say the right thing.

I'm not sure Iris does.

My mother is looking to see if Iris truly knows anything about dance. It's not an automatic fail if she doesn't, but she has to be able to have enough knowledge to make small talk. My mother is also looking at Iris's body language, posture, her turn of phrase, her vernacular. It's all under scrutiny.

Iris sits back and considers my mother's question. My mother's eyebrow inches towards her hairline as she waits for an answer.

"I really enjoyed it," Iris says finally. My mother barely hides her eye roll. But Iris's not done. "It's wonderful to see some of my favorite dancers sharing a stage."

My mother doesn't respond, she just looks at Iris as if she hasn't finished, putting pressure on her to say more. I hope Iris doesn't fall into the trap. My mother is looking for rope to hang her with. I don't want Iris to help her.

"Carlos Acoma is... tiring," Iris says. "But it's to be expected at his age. I believe he's forty-two. His leaps aren't what they once were. But he still has that magnetic stage presence that has made him world famous."

I can tell my mother wasn't expecting Iris's detailed response. She didn't think Iris would really know anything about dance.

"It's a bit of a strange evening, isn't it?" Iris says, lowering her voice conspiratorially. "Wonderful. But it's unusual to have all these titans of dance performing snippets. It's harder to lose yourself in the music and the story in the way I'm used to."

I push my lips together to stop myself from smiling. There's no way that Iris isn't acing this test.

"Jack said you used to dance. Was that professionally?" my mother asks.

Iris shakes her head. "No. Family commitments meant that wasn't possible." She glances at me. "We all make sacrifices for the people we love. And dance was mine."

My mother stays silent for a moment. Iris wasn't what she expected. She had thought she would test Iris and she'd come out failing. But Iris is holding her own with my mother. No mean feat for anyone, let alone a hick from Colorado, as Iris sees herself. It's just proof that she's so much more than she believes.

"Did you enjoy the performances, Mrs. Alden?" she asks, her manners perfect.

"Like you say, it's a strange evening, but it's quite pleasant."

"Jack?" Iris turns to me.

"I'm happy if you and my mother are happy."

The corners of my mother's mouth twitch at my statement. I'm sure she thinks that sometimes I deliberately set out to torture her. Disappearing to Colorado for weeks won't have gone down well. But what I'm saying is true— I'm happier if my mother's happy. But I won't do everything she says. I'm not some docile, compliant son. But I *am* her son. I want her to be happy. I just want me to be happy too.

And right now? With Iris holding her own and my mother being checkmated, I'm about as happy as I've ever been.

TWENTY-FOUR

Jack

We ride the elevator side by side up to my apartment. I know if I touch her here, alone, we won't get *out* of this elevator.

I'm shaking, I want this woman so much. Since the moment I laid eyes on her, I've felt a connection that I've never felt before. Every time we're together, that connection grows and deepens.

Tonight?

Tonight, everything was so goddamn perfect, I could shout out loud with joy.

There are few women who can stand their ground with my mother. Iris's one of them. What's more, she didn't know what she was doing. She didn't understand she was being tested and she passed with flying colors. Just by being herself. Don't get me wrong, my mother won't want me to marry a woman who works on the family farm in Colorado, whether or not she knows about ballet and can hold a conversation to my mother's standards. But it showed me how Iris is everything I want in a woman—sophisticated but authentic. Her feet are firmly on the ground. She's always one hundred percent herself.

"You okay?" she asks from beside me.

Thankfully the doors open to the penthouse.

"I am now," I say, and I pull her out of the elevator and flip her against the wall. "I hope you weren't planning to sleep tonight," I say against her neck. I pull up the skirt of her dress as I press kisses along her jaw. I want to find her heat, her core. I need to see if she's desperate for me.

My fingers find the edges of her underwear and I sigh with relief that I've found home.

Thank god.

I push underneath and my fingers meet wetness—hot, silky wetness.

"Jack," she whispers. "We can't. Not here. What if someone sees?"

No one comes up here. No one *can* come up here. Only I have the key to get to this floor. Mine is the only apartment on this floor. This is the foyer to my apartment. It looks like it's communal to the building and there's a locked door for security, but it's actually part of my apartment. I don't have time to explain and reassure. I just need to get inside her. I need every part of me inside her.

"Come with me."

I round the table in the center of the foyer, a chandelier above it, and push open the double doors into the living space of my apartment. I lift her and toss her over my shoulder.

"Jack?" she screams. "What are you doing?"

I march along the wide, marble-floored hallway to my bedroom. "Those shoes wouldn't get us where I want us to be quick enough."

"I thought we'd hang a little in your very grand apartment."

"You thought wrong." The high ceilings and ornate light fixtures do emphasize the grand nature of this apartment. It was left to me by my paternal grandmother, and I haven't really done much to it since she died. For the first time since I moved in, I wonder what it would look like if I redecorated.

If Iris helped me redecorate.

That thought is stricken from my brain as we reach my bedroom and I set Iris down by my bed.

"You're beautiful," I say, taking a step back. "Breathtaking."

"This dress is beautiful." She glances down.

I shake my head. "That dress is the least beautiful thing about you. And it needs to come off."

Her hair is up in a bun just as I requested and the curve of her neck is so tempting. I want to lick her everywhere, but especially there. Some tendrils of her hair caress her milky-white skin and I'm ridiculously jealous that they get to sweep over that smooth, perfect skin all the time, whereas I have to be patient.

No more.

I reach and pull her toward me, snaking my hand up her back, trying to find a zip.

"It's buttons," she says, smiling at me.

"Next time, I'll only buy dresses with zippers."

She reaches for the skirt of her dress, and ruches it up. "Impatient?"

Heat sweeps through my body and I finger the collar of my shirt.

"The dress might have buttons, but we don't have to wait."

I groan and reach between her legs, finding her still hot and wetter than she was before. "I'm not the only impatient one," I growl against her.

She shakes her head. "I want you, Jack."

There's a part of me that wants to take my time, revel in her, seduce her inch by inch, but the part of me that wins is the part that just wants to bury myself in her as quick as possible.

My fingers shake as I roll on the condom I retrieved from my wallet. Not from nerves, but from lust. From desire. I don't have control over my body when Iris's around. She makes me shake. She makes me hard. She makes me fucking howl.

She takes me by surprise when she turns away from me and bends over my mattress, her dress around her waist, her ass on full display.

"These need to go," I say and I pull at her panties, ripping the lace from between her legs. Her juices have soaked through the material and I make a mental note to retrieve them from the floor later and keep them somewhere safe.

I sweep my hand over her smooth ass, and steady her as I position my cock at her entrance. "You ready to get fucked hard?"

"Yes," she whispers.

"I can't hear you. Are you ready?"

"Yes," she whimpers. "Please."

I can't wait another second and I slide into her, deep, so deep, right up to the hilt.

Her breath hitches, like she's not sure she can take it, but she can. She does. And I know from the way her fingers curl around my bedcovers that it feels like home to her.

I feel like home to her.

I wrap my hands around her waist and hold her as I fuck her. It's hard and relentless. It's what we both need. Her tightness around me milks my cock, like it's trying to stop me leaving her every time I pull out. And I slam into her like if I don't, we'll both dissolve into nothing. It's urgent and frantic and desperate.

It's like I'm trying to mark her here in New York—to prove that we exist as well here as we do in Star Falls.

We're perfect together anywhere.

"I can't hold on," she cries out. "Jack. I can't..."

"Come for me," I say, wanting her to let go and let it overtake her.

But I'm not going to stop. I can't. I need everything she has to give me tonight.

Her body. Her soul. And every single one of her orgasms.

I won't stop until she's wrung out and boneless.

I'm going to fuck her like she's my legacy, because that's how she feels. Like she's my future. My entire reason for being.

"Jack," she calls out, as her orgasm courses through her body. "Jack."

I know I'm being rough. I know that I should give her time to recover, time to want me again like I want her.

But I can't.

I have to keep fucking her.

I *need* to make her come again.

Her next orgasm comes quickly, like she's tired of fighting it and she's just resigned herself to the fact that I'm going to make her come so often tonight that she's not going to remember her own name. She's going to understand that I own her.

That's how it should be. Because she owns me too.

I withdraw from her just as long as it takes me to turn her onto her back. I want her to see me when I come. I want her to understand what she does to me. There can be no doubt in her mind as to how I feel.

I sink into her again, the tulle bunched between us, me pushing her legs as wide as they will go. I want to be as deep as I can be in her.

She screams out and throws her head back. The vibrations travel to my balls and I know I have only got seconds until she takes everything I have.

My orgasm pushes from every cell of my body like it's threatening me, letting me know that this woman might just be the end of me.

Or the beginning.

I let out a roar as it rattles up my spine and through every atom of my being. And I fuck deeper and deeper and deeper until she's coming too. And we're shaking and chanting and fucking. The entire city of New York could be falling to the ground and neither of us would notice.

All that matters is Iris. Me. Us.

TWENTY-FIVE

Iris

Despite my lack of sleep—just as Jack had promised—I can't stop smiling. Maybe it's the DNA-altering sex. Maybe it's just being close to him. I'm putting on my makeup in the mirror above the sink while Jack brushes his teeth in the second sink next to me.

His and hers sinks.

It's nice.

I haven't known him long, but this very settled, couply thing—it's better than I could have imagined.

Jack rinses his mouth and grins at me. "You're smiling."

"You're smiling," I say.

"I'm smiling because I've had you in my bed all night and now I get to spend the day with you. What's your excuse?"

"I need an excuse?" I say through my grin. But I'm kidding. He knows that I'm smiling because of him. "It's nice," I say. "Being here with you. Brushing teeth. Getting ready."

Doing couple stuff, like we're a couple. Not just a love affair that has a time limit on it. This feels like we're really a couple.

"It's not just nice. It's perfect. And if you keep looking at me like that, we're never going to make brunch."

"Like what?" I ask, surprised at his reaction. "I'm not trying to be..."

"Alluring," he says. "You're not trying. But you definitely *are* alluring. You don't need to try. You take up all of my attention anytime you look at me. But I want to show you brunch in one of my favorite places."

I blush at the thought. I've never considered myself as the kind of woman who's alluring.

"We're going to your hotel?" I ask.

He pauses. "No, actually that wasn't my plan. Did you want to go there?"

"Did I just come off like a stalker?" I say on a laugh. "I don't mind where we go. If you want to take me to your favorite place, then I want to go there. If you want to take me to your hotel, then take me there. Either way, I'll learn more about you."

"I think you know everything there is to know." His expression is serious, and he's looking at me with such intensity, I can feel it pressing into my skin.

"Jack," I say.

He shakes his head. "I'm crazy about you."

I tilt my head. "Crazy about me or just crazy?"

He grins and places a kiss on the top of my head. "Let's go."

My lipstick rolls off the counter and onto the floor. Jack immediately bends to pick it up. "There's a dressing table in one of the walk in closets. I can clear it out for you."

I narrow my eyes in confusion. "We're leaving after brunch," I say, and then I follow his train of thought.

He means if I was to come again.

If I was to move to New York and live with him.

But he knows that's not going to happen, right? We agreed we'd hang out, spend time with each other and kinda wait for a miracle. I'm sure he didn't put it quite like that, but that was the general gist.

Thing is, I don't believe in miracles, but looking at Jack's expression, he just might.

He stands the lipstick on the counter. I pick it up, drop it into my makeup bag and zip it up. It's ready to pop into my suitcase.

"So which is it? My favorite brunch place or my hotel?" Jack asks, as we hit the heat of the city sidewalk. The doorman holds open the back door to a sedan. Jack nods, gesturing for me to go ahead and get in.

"I'm going to be controversial, Jack," I say, as he slides into the car next to me. "Have you ever thought that maybe your favorite brunch place *should* be your hotel?"

Jack laughs and asks the driver to take us to The Alden Hotel.

I guess I'm going to see the hotel that Jack made.

"You make a good point. Again," Jack says. "I don't think we really make brunch a thing at The Alden. And maybe we should. You have some good ideas."

"You're the one with all the good ideas," I say. "The stuff about the frozen organic fruit." I shake my head, remembering my brother's and dad's reactions. "I'm sorry you didn't get a more enthusiastic response."

He takes my hand and presses a kiss to my knuckles. "It's completely understandable. It's a fundamental shift in how you do business. It would take... a lot. It would be a lot of change. A lot of money at stake."

"Right," I say. "But I think we could start small. Like you said, maybe we don't start with berries. Maybe we look into freezing a different kind of fruit. Something more unusual. And then we just invest in a small way and see if it takes off."

I turn and he's looking at me like he thinks I'm the best thing he's ever seen.

"I'm going to speak to them when we get back. See if I can convince them that your idea could actually change our lives for the better. Dad might be able to retire." I pause. I'm not sure what it might mean for me. "It could give us choices."

He nods, almost carefully, like he's afraid he might break something if he reacts the wrong way. "I'm happy to help where I can," Jack says. "But I don't want to overstep."

I squeeze his hand and we pull up to the curb. I dip my head to take in the smart blue-and-gold flag outside the building that reads "The Alden Hotel."

"We couldn't have walked?" I ask.

"It's way too hot."

I laugh at Jack's response. I guess heat hits differently in the city.

Jack slides out of the car and interrupts the doorman who's about to open my door, so he can open it instead. He's so cute and sexy, makes me want to fall to my knees right here and now.

Jack takes my hand and helps me out of the car and we head inside.

"Good afternoon, Mr. Alden," I hear voices say all around us.

"I really should have warned them I was coming," he

mumbles under his breath. "They're probably scrambling. I'm not here to make their lives more difficult."

"You're the boss. They're always going to be scrambling when you're around. That's just life with a boss." I guess Jack doesn't know because he never had a boss. In a way, neither did I. Bray tries—and fails—to tell me what to do. And my dad just has certain expectations. I don't think he's ever asked me for anything. Ever.

The hostess looks stunned to see Jack and me arrive for brunch, but finds us a table by the window opposite an elaborate flower display full of flowers I don't know the names of. "Can I offer you some champagne to start?" the hostess says.

I shake my head. "Not for me, thank you."

Just then, I hear someone call Jack's name, and then a woman in one of those jackets that looks like the seams are on display appears at our table. "I haven't seen you in ages."

Jack stands and greets the woman, who's a couple of decades older than him. She's dressed in white trousers and is carrying a little dog that looks like it could be the cousin of a hamster, it's so small. Her hair looks like she just stepped out of a salon and her nails are perfect and she has a small scarf knotted around her neck, like I imagine women in the South of France do. Glossy is the best way to describe her.

Shiny and neat and rich.

There's no doubt—from her confidence to her handbag—that she's got money.

"Melanie, this is my friend Iris. Iris, this is Melanie Bellingham."

I don't know whether I should stand or not, but I stay seated and we smile at each other. "Nice to meet you," I say.

"And you." She looks between me and Jack, probably wondering where on earth the two of us met. She probably knows from my outfit that I'm not New York old money. I'm not from one of the "acceptable" families that Jack's mother has decreed he's to marry. I'm just Iris Wilde from Star Falls, Colorado.

"We should catch up and have lunch sometime. I was really hoping that you'd step into Lionel's shoes and take a spot on the board at the Hurst Museum."

Jack pulls in a breath. "I'm at capacity when it comes to my board commitments," he says.

Melanie tips her head back and laughs like Jack told the most hilarious joke she's ever heard. "That's why I need to take you to lunch. So I can charm you and convince you. Poor Lionel would love it if you could. And you know Phoebe helps me with all the fundraising, so it's not like you'll actually have to do anything. And to top it off, you'll know most of the people around the table anyway."

Jack smiles tightly, and Melanie takes his unspoken hint. She pats him on the arm. "Anyway, I'll let you get back to your brunch. I'll call you about Hurst. Just think about it. Nice to meet you," she says to me, smiling. She's not openly hostile. Not super friendly either. I suppose she doesn't feel she needs to be. Jack's a player. She's probably used to seeing him with lots of different women.

He takes his seat opposite me again and sighs.

"Did the dog have a place setting, do you think?"

"Knowing Melanie, he probably did."

"How do you know her?" I ask.

He shrugs. "How do any of us know anyone? She's always been in my parents' circle." His mood has shifted, and he's turned quite gloomy.

"Does she upset you?"

He pulls in a breath. "No, that's not it." He reaches for my hand across the table. "I suppose I was just mentally pulled back to my responsibilities here in New York. And I'd rather be all about you."

I smile. Jack's charming and it's a really nice thing to say. But it's also not realistic. The two of us can't survive in a bubble, shutting out the rest of the world. Life doesn't work like that.

"Jack Alden?"

A shrill voice comes from behind Jack, and he closes his eyes in a long blink. I glance up, and a woman is looking between me and him, a huge grin on her face. She's about my age. Maybe a little younger. And she is beautiful. Her glossy brown hair is up in a ponytail and her face doesn't look overly made up. She's got a hint of lip gloss and some blush, but if you didn't look too carefully, she could pass for just being super-healthy or maybe having just finished a light jog.

"Excuse me," Jack mumbles to me, and he stands as the woman gets to our table. "Pippa. How lovely to see you." He greets her with a kiss on the cheek.

She glances at me, obviously expecting an introduction.

"This is my girlfriend, Iris Wilde."

Pippa's smile falters, just as mine does.

Girlfriend? We hadn't discussed being each other's... I mean, we haven't discussed anything about labels. But Jack didn't introduce me to Melanie as his girlfriend. What's changed?

"How wonderful to meet you, Iris," Pippa says. "Are you from New York?"

I don't know much about New York society, but I've gathered enough from my limited encounters that she's not just asking about the geographic location of my birth.

"Colorado," I say.

"Fantastic." Her smile widens, like she's trying to make

sure she doesn't show what she's feeling. "Jack, we must grab a drink sometime. I can get you caught up on all the gossip."

"Any plans for today?" I ask her. I may not have known Jack long, but I know him well enough to understand that he doesn't want to get caught up on gossip. Maybe a drink with Pippa isn't out of the question, but gossip? It's really not how Jack rides. Is it?

"Just brunch with a girlfriend and then some shopping. What are your plans? Are you in New York long?"

"We're both going back to Colorado this afternoon," Jack answers.

Pippa lets out a half laugh. "Really, Jack. I never had you down for being outdoorsy." He just nods simply. "Anyway," Pippa says. "I can see Charlotte, so I must go. So lovely to meet you, Iris. And, Jack—let's catch up properly."

She waves and heads over to the other side of the restaurant.

Jack sits, and I can't help wonder how long it will be until we're interrupted again.

"Seems like New York is a small town," I say, grinning at him.

"I never thought about it, but I guess it is in a way. In lots of ways, actually. I went to school with Pippa's brother."

"Did you use to date?" I ask.

He shakes his head. "No." He pauses. "But..."

"You've slept with her. She wants to date you. But you're not that into her."

He picks up a menu. "Do you know what I'm about to order, or do your mind-reading capabilities only extend so far?"

I grin. "I think you're going to go for the schnitzel."

He's definitely not going to order the schnitzel.

He looks right at me, his eyes narrowed. He's trying to figure out whether I'm messing with him. Of course I'm messing with him.

"You're going to get the salmon," I concede. "I think I'll do the same."

He shakes his head. "Have we known each other our entire lives?"

"It feels like it," I reply.

He eyes me over the top of his menu, a smile flickering at the edges of his mouth, and he slides his leg between mine.

He's not the Jack that Pippa knows. Not really. Not deep down inside. He's the Jack who's with me now in this bubble—me, the girl from Star Falls, Colorado.

The problem is, bubbles burst, and I'm not sure we can exist outside it.

TWENTY-SIX

Iris

New York was a twenty-four-hour whirlwind that passed so fast it might have been a dream. Now it's back to the real world. Or *my* real world, at least. And that means early starts in a barn behind my computer.

Even though I manage all the financial and administrative parts of Wilde's Farm, it's my dad's farm. It's always going to be my dad's farm.

Until it's Bray's.

Even if the ownership deed says Bray and I own it fifty-fifty, I'm never going to see it as mine. That's just how it is. That doesn't mean I don't want it to succeed. I know my dad dismissed Jack's idea about freezing and branding fruit, but I can't just abandon the idea. It's bold and it's a risk, and the idea is a good one. But my dad has shut down the idea and Bray doesn't seem interested. But I still have hope that they'll understand it could be the best thing we ever did.

It's lunchtime, and the midday sun is unusually hot. I

shade my eyes, trying to spot Bray among the workers having their lunch at the picnic tables under the trees.

"Who you looking for?" Bray asks, as he comes up behind me, making me jump. "Your boyfriend's not working today."

"Ha," I say. "Come with me, baby brother."

"Baby?" he asks.

"Well, you are younger than me, aren't you?"

"By thirteen months."

"Right, so come with me."

We head back into my office and we both take our familiar seats. I've cleared out some of the packing boxes, and Bray can actually move the chair so he's facing me without developing a crick in his neck.

"Did you get lunch?" I ask. "I don't want to talk to you if you're hungry. You know what a monster you are on an empty stomach."

Bray sighs. "I ate already. What's eating you? You never want to talk to me."

I laugh. "Yeah, well, that's true. Mostly. How's your bruised leg?"

"Bruised? I didn't fucking bruise it. It's a broken fibula."

"That's a made-up bone." I'm an almost thirty-year-old woman. Why does it bring me so much pleasure to mess with my brother?

"It's not a made-up bone, Iris. It's—" He grabs his phone, presumably wanting to prove me wrong.

Except I don't care.

"Well, at least you can put weight on it now."

"It's not made up." He turns his phone toward me. "Fibula."

I shrug. "I do want to talk to you about what Jack said."

"Your boyfriend, Jack?"

I give him a don't-fuck-with-me stare. Bray rolls his eyes and leans back in the visitor chair. "About the freezing?"

"Yeah. What he said made sense, right? Creating a consumer-facing brand is the way to improve margins."

Bray laughs. "You sound like you just swallowed an MBA. What the fuck are you talking about?"

"If we create a brand that people on the street recognize, we can charge more for it because we're offering a guarantee of quality. Like Kellogg can charge more for cornflakes than Trader Joe's."

"Yeah, I get it. So you're saying, create a Wilde's Farm brand?"

"With the frozen fruit," I add. "We can't do it as easily with the fresh fruit. Our farm isn't big enough, or we'd have to have farms all over America or something. But with the frozen stuff? That could work."

"Except we don't know how to freeze stuff, and we don't have freezers. We don't have any grocery stores calling us telling us they want frozen fruit from us."

I glare at him some more. He must know he sounds ridiculous. Grocery stores aren't going to proactively ask for stuff. They have people knocking down their doors, trying to get on the shelves.

"I *have* been thinking about the idea Jack had about more unusual fruit being our focus," Bray says.

I pause. Did my brother just admit that he'd actually been thinking about Jack's idea? He'd seemed to dismiss it just the same way Dad had, but maybe he'd been a little more open than I thought.

"I think it's difficult to do that here on Wilde's Farm," he says. "But I was wondering..."

I hold my breath, waiting for him to speak.

"We could maybe visit some farms that are already

producing the more exotic fruits and maybe freeze *their* fruit. That way we can still continue what we've got here and we don't have to worry about weather changes or crop yields. We just buy what other farms have and freeze that. I haven't thought it all through. Would we have to set up some kind of freezing operation near them, or would we have the fruit shipped to us? I'm not sure. I guess we have to look into it. But it would be a way of having that unusual fruit under our brand without being restrained by the Colorado climate or the size of Wilde's Farm or... It means we could keep doing what we're doing. Because we know we're good at that. But this freezing thing? Jack's right. It could be a way of future-proofing stuff."

I swallow, because I'm not sure I'm processing what Bray's saying correctly. He seems all in. Like, he's really thought about this and actually has taken the idea even further than Jack had. Bray and I don't have deep, meaningful conversations very often. We talk every day...

Pass the butter...

Did you get that haulage list...

That plate is a foot from the dishwasher. Is it so hard to just open the door and put it in?

That kind of thing. Brother, sister stuff. But we don't talk about hopes and dreams. We don't talk about the future and how Dad is getting slower with every passing year. How Bray has picked up a lot of the slack when it comes to organizing the staff but still has to defer to Dad on a lot. It must be tough, and I don't give him credit for it. Honestly, I barely think about it.

"I agree," I manage to eke out.

"The thing is," Bray says. I knew there would be a catch. Now Bray's going to tell me all the reasons why any kind of change will be impossible. "It's going to take a lot of work. And focus. Dad is..."

"Not getting any younger," I say. It's all we need to say.

"Right, and we'd need to travel to visit with other farms. Plus potentially oversee a freezing operation here. Maybe."

"We could give Marnie more responsibility. If she wants it."

Bray nods. "Yeah, that's what I was thinking. She's capable. Worked this farm longer than me. I think she could take over some stuff, which would free me up a bit. And you could get someone in to help you with the admin. Most of what you do is way above your paygrade."

I narrow my eyes, waiting for Bray to tell me he's joking, but he doesn't. I'm not used to compliments from my brother. "You think we can afford to get someone in?"

"I think we can't afford not to if we want to level up." He looks me dead in the eye. "But is that what you want? Do you want to be supervising a freezing operation? Putting it all in place, while I travel to other farms to see if we can invest in them and make them part of the Wilde's Farm brand?"

"I think it's a great idea," I say, not able to get my words out fast enough. He doesn't need to doubt me.

"But really?" he asks. "Jack is based in New York. I've been trying to come up with a solution to losing you to the Big Apple. It's easier *now*, when everything is how it's been for years. If we're going to try something new, I have to know you're in. That we're in this together."

"New York?" I let out a half laugh. "I've never left Colorado." Bray's smart. I've always known that about him. But I've never given him credit for how astute he is. He takes in a lot that he never talks about. I've been a fool to underestimate him. "I'm in," I look him in the eye. "I mean it. I'm not going anywhere."

Yeah, Jack is the best thing that's happened to me in a long time, but this last weekend in New York has brought into sharp focus how we're from two completely different worlds. The space that Jack and I occupy is being squeezed. There's no way we can survive in the long run. What can survive, what *has* to survive, is our family and Wilde's Farm.

"But just because I'm on board doesn't mean everything's good. In case you hadn't noticed, Dad still owns this farm. And he's not interested in a freezing operation."

"Yeah," Bray says. "He likes the status quo."

"The problem is, the status quo has us on the downslide. If we keep going the way we're going, I don't know if Dad will have a business to retire from. Everything's getting more difficult. And even if we do get paid by Oxburg, buying new cherry pickers isn't going to help us with margins."

"We should talk to him," Bray says. "We don't need new cherry pickers, despite what he might think."

"You know what he's like—stubborn as a mule."

"We have to find a way to get through to him," Bray says. "But in the meantime, we can start preparing—researching the fruits, finding farms that produce. Do financial stuff... whatever it is you do."

"Right," I say, rolling my eyes. "Financial stuff."

Bray smiles. "I'm serious. You're good at that side of things. Then we can go to Dad with more information. More facts. Then if we can get everything prepared before the Oxburg invoices are paid, then maybe we can change his mind before he spends all the money on new cherry pickers."

Bray's right. We need to plan. Prepare. Focus on the future. A future here on Wilde's Farm.

A future without Jack.

TWENTY-SEVEN

Jack

Star Falls feels like safer ground than Manhattan. Pizza Meet Ya, even more so. New York wasn't a complete disaster, but I hadn't expected to feel as uncomfortable as I did. It's not that Iris doesn't fit in New York, but I'm not used to having her in my world there.

I thought we could recreate that first night we met, when it felt like the two of us were alone in the theater watching the ballet, or we were sharing our souls as we walked around Central Park. But it wasn't like that. Real life came roaring toward us—first my mother and then seeing everyone at my hotel.

Iris handled everything beautifully. But I didn't want her to *handle* things. I wanted to whisk her back to Star Falls, where she'd be comfortable and everyone loves her for who she is.

"You seem deep in thought," she says, as we take our seats opposite each other at our now regular table for two at Pizza Meet Ya. The mountain stretches up behind us out the window, so high we can't see the peak from where we're sitting. Just trees and the sparkle of lights.

I smile at her. "What am I thinking?" Iris seems to be able to read my mind at times. But really, I want to read hers. What's *she* thinking? How was New York for her? I know I've said that we should continue to date and we'll figure out how to get to where we want to go, but since coming back from New York last night, all I can think about is the obstacles.

She reaches for my hand across the table and links her fingers through mine. "I had a really good time in New York. It was so kind of you to arrange it. You don't need to worry."

I smile, but I know it's half-hearted. "It didn't go quite as I had planned."

"I know, but that's life, isn't it? Sometimes we have a bumper crop of strawberries and sometimes we can't get them off the plants before they rot. There's only so much you can control."

I nod. She's right. Of course she is. But it doesn't make it better. "Being with you in New York... it made me see my life there in a different way."

Iris laughs. "You've decided you like farm life? An existence of early mornings and stained fingers, away from brunches and ballet?"

The thought hits me like a bullet. Our worlds are so incredibly different. But worst of all—she doesn't see me here. With her. She can't picture it.

The realization sends panic slithering up my spine. Not because she's wrong. But because maybe she's right. Maybe I've been kidding myself that a solution is just going to land. She's tied to Star Falls. I'm tied to New York —waiting to take over the Alden family legacy. There's no middle ground here. We're not going to both move to Ohio.

"I think we should go to Grizzly's," she says.

I lower my voice, wanting to avoid a scandal. "You don't like the pizza here?"

She smiles at me, but it's not the full-throated laugh I expect. "I think we should stop not talking about what we're both thinking. We need to go and eat some wings, play some pool and maybe even dance. I think there's a band there tonight."

"A band?" I ask. "I'm not sure I'm a guy who really chases after a band."

"I'm not suggesting we chase after anyone." She pushes her seat away from the table. "But I want to get out of here."

I get it. She doesn't want to face the inevitable, the cold hard truth—there isn't any magic formula that will mean we can be together. There just isn't.

We're living on borrowed time. We both know it.

But for now I'm holding on for a miracle that will change both our paths.

THE MUSIC LEAKS out of Grizzly's like it can't be contained, a bubbling-over pot of guitar and a woman's vocals.

I open the door and Iris turns her head and grins at me, like she's so pleased we came. The jury's out for me. I just want to be with Iris and block the rest of the world out. I don't want to think about tomorrow or this time next year. I don't want to think about my mother and the hotel. I want everything to just disappear and leave Iris and me. And maybe Grizzly's wings.

Iris slips her hand into mine and pulls me inside and toward the back of the bar. Anyone would think an entire band was playing from outside, but it's just a piano player, a guitar player, and a singer on a stool.

"I can't believe it," Iris says. "She hasn't done this song in forever."

I refocus and realize the singer is the waitress from Grizzly's. My cell buzzes, and when I check it, the caller ID shows it's one of the trustees from the trust board. I silence the call and slip it back into my pocket. I don't want my worlds bleeding together. I just want to be here.

In Star Falls.

With Iris.

The singer has switched gears and she's singing a ballad. Something about *snow-covered hills* and *getting older*. Her voice is incredible. Husky and powerful but so pure. A bit like the mountains that surround us.

Iris stands in front of me and wraps my arms around her, then hooks her arms around me. She feels warm, like she's a part of the earth or something, and I'm aware of how happy I am right now. In this moment. I wish I could make it last.

I try to commit everything to memory. Every note of the song. Iris's fingers wrapped around me. The way she smells of wildflowers. And most of all, this feeling of contentment I have deep down inside, which I realize I've never experienced until I met Iris.

Then the music stops and Iris turns in my arms.

"Wings?" she asks.

I hold her gaze, wanting to tell her how much she means to me. How much being with her makes me feel like I'm exactly where I should be. But I keep my confession bottled up. There's no point, is there? There's no point getting in deeper. Not if there's no possibility that we can get our happy ending.

"Dance with me," I say instead.

"I thought you couldn't dance."

"I said I didn't dance." A smile tugs at the corners of my mouth. "There's a difference."

Her tongue darts out and wets her lips. "Show me what you got."

I circle my arm around her back and pull her against me. Any space between us has gone. Our legs intermingle as she slides her hands up my chest and around my neck.

The heat from her is dizzying. The look in her eye that tells me she's giving me everything. That she'd *do* anything for me. It's almost too much.

Almost.

I start to move, bringing her with me like we're one person. We sway in time to the music. At least I think it's in time. Now that we're like this, I'm not sure I'm capable of focusing on anything but Iris. Anything but us.

My phone vibrates in my jeans pocket, but I ignore it. Nothing can get between us in this moment.

Not if I don't let it.

TWENTY-EIGHT

Iris

I scramble out of the house. No one tells me I have to be at work at seven, but that's when the farm starts work, and it's only fair that I'm around. Apart from the haulage lists, most days people start with questions about PTO and salaries before my ass hits my chair.

But today, I would have loved to have stayed with Jack up at his lodge and let everything else go to hell.

But I didn't. Because everyone's depending on me.

"Iris," Bray calls, as I head into the barn. "Jimmy just called me to say he did something to his wrist. He's going to see the doc."

I don't know why he's telling me.

"Okay," I say.

Wheels on the dirt road behind me catch my attention, and I turn to see Jack's car driving toward us. What's he doing here? I'm partly delighted to see him, but it feels like something's off. When I left this morning, he didn't mention he'd be coming down.

Bray and I wait as Jack pulls up and gets out of the car.

"Need an extra pair of hands?" Jack asks, shooting me a grin.

Bray shakes his head. "The things you do for love."

It's like he's stolen the air from my lungs. Love?

I avoid Jack's face. I don't want to see his reaction. I don't want to see him agree with Bray that he loves me, because I don't know what that means for us. And I don't want to see that he doesn't love me. And I sure as hell don't want to think about how *I'm* feeling right now.

I just want to go into my office and hide.

"Have at it, boys," I say, waving my hand in the air as I head into the office, like Bray didn't just say that Jack was here offering his help because he loved me.

I busy myself all morning doing everything I can to stop the thoughts from coming. How did Jack and I get to a point where I don't feel myself unless I see him? How did we get to a point where I miss him if I haven't seen him for a few hours?

How did I get in this deep?

I try to push the thoughts away. I get up to date on my daily tasks, and I'm about to check the profit and loss account when my cell rings. It's Karen from Oxburg. I really hope she's not going to start disputing the invoice. It's been outstanding for months now.

"Hey, Iris," she says.

"Hey, Karen. How are you?" I brace myself for her to question the invoice I've sent, which I have double- and triple-checked because I didn't want them to have any way of disputing it. The problem is, business is tough for everyone these days. If they're having difficulty and they ask for an extension or a discount on the invoice, what am I supposed to say?

"All good here, I just wanted to tell you that I approved both your outstanding invoices for payment and they should have already appeared in your bank account. I wanted to thank you for your patience with the entire situation."

"Oh," I say, my chest expanding with relief. "That's fine. I know sometimes things get stuck in the system." I quickly log onto our bank accounts and start scrolling through the transactions.

"Yeah, we've had to swap over our software, so things have gotten into a bottleneck, but it should be better from now on."

"Thank you. Yes, I can see them," I say. "That was really nice of you to call."

When I hang up, I have an urge to high-five someone. I feel like I scored a victory. Dad's going to be so happy.

I get up from my desk and head out to find him. And maybe catch a glimpse of Jack, even though I know I shouldn't and the feelings there are far too complicated.

I almost run into Bray as I exit the barn.

"Your boyfriend's in the south fields."

"It was you and Dad I wanted to see. Oxburg paid their outstanding invoices. They're all up to date."

I expect Bray to give me a high five at least, but he doesn't. He just rolls his eyes.

"What?" I ask. "I thought you'd be happy. Those invoices have been outstanding for months."

"Dad will get his brand-new cherry pickers," he says.

"We can delay telling him a few days while we finish up our plans," I suggest.

"If we let him spend the money on cherry pickers, it's over. It's not like we have money lying around waiting to be used up."

Marnie heads toward us to meet the truck from Loopin.

We exchange smiles as Bray and I stand by the barn, watching the truck pull in.

Bray lowers his voice so no one else can hear. "The more I think about it, the more I think it's our only way to survive. And we might have a real shot at thriving. We could take this farm to the next level."

More people start to head toward us, to start loading the Loopin truck.

I nod toward my office. This conversation is one to have in private.

I shut the door when we're both inside. "You definitely don't think the two cherry pickers need to be replaced?"

Bray scoffs. "Not at all. Dad just likes shiny new toys. You know what he's like."

"I don't think I did know that about him."

Bray shrugs and slumps into my visitor chair.

"So how much would it be to service or refurbish the cherry pickers that Dad wants to replace?"

"Less than fifteen hundred dollars."

I almost choke. "Are you serious?" I ask. "And Dad wants to spend forty thousand dollars on new machines?"

Bray raises his eyebrows as if to say, I told you so. "This farm has always been run his way. And it's been fine because—"

"Margins haven't been as tight."

"Right. Things were easier."

The door to my office creaks open and Dad appears in the doorway. "What are you two in here gossiping about?"

My face flushes with heat. I feel like I've been caught stealing apples from the Miller orchard.

Bray sighs. "Nothing, Dad."

"So why am I the only one in this family working?" he snaps.

"We were working, Dad," I say, feeling more than a little defensive. "Or at least talking about work."

"Did Oxburg pay their invoices yet?" he asks.

I flush with heat. I've never been good at lying. As a family, we might not talk about everything but what we do say is the truth.

Bray sighs. "Yup. They paid."

Dad's frown softens a little and he tugs on his baseball cap. "Oh, that's good. We can get those new cherry pickers now."

Bray groans and gets up from his chair. He might complain, but he's not going to say anything to Dad. If anything's going to change around here, I'm going to have to be the one to tell Dad what we're thinking.

"Dad, did you ever think that we could use the money you have earmarked for the new cherry pickers for something else?"

Dad crosses his arms, and Bray shoots me a look that says, *What the fuck are you doing?*

"Like what?" Dad asks.

"Like investing in a small freezing operation. I know things look like they're okay now, but it gets more and more difficult every year. We're going to have to think about changing the menu of the cafeteria next year. Or shutting it down completely. And that's in the short term. In the long term, things could get worse. We might have to fire some full-timers. Maybe even try to apply for planning permits to develop some of the land into housing."

Dad snorts. "Over my dead body."

The room rattles with silence. The fact is, Dad isn't going to be around forever, and if this farm is to survive, we're going to have to make changes.

"You can do what you like when I'm gone," he says.

"But until then, no one is selling off bits and pieces of this farm."

"I'm not saying we *want* to do that," I say, in that same voice I used at fifteen when I wanted a sleepover. "But if we keep going the way we are, there will come a time where we're going to be forced into doing something we don't want to do."

"If we don't have cherry pickers, we can't pick the fruit." Dad raises his eyebrows, daring me to disagree with him.

"Dad," Bray says, his tone a warning. "You know we don't need brand-new cherry pickers."

"They're more reliable," Dad says.

"Getting a new truck every year would be more reliable, but that doesn't mean it's the right thing to do. We can get the cherry pickers properly serviced or refurbished and save a ton of money."

"And buy a freezer?" he asks, as if he thinks the idea's ridiculous.

"We could invest in a small freezing operation, yes," I reply. "We can rent some of the equipment. And I found logistics companies that can transport the stock to retailers. We wouldn't have to have our own trucks."

Dad shakes his head. "Our fruit is fresh. We've always prided ourselves on it."

"But we'd freeze stuff the day it was picked," Bray says. "People would actually be getting it fresher than if it was delivered fresh."

"He's right, Dad. And anyway, Bray had a good idea about approaching other farms who produce more exotic fruit and freezing that. We could buy it from them and then freeze it and sell it on."

"That's insane," Dad says. "We're a fruit farm. We want to be selling fruit, not buying it."

"But what if we could be both?" I ask. "Frozen exotic fruit would give us a chance to develop a brand so people on the street, in the grocery store, would know Wilde's Farm quality and could pick it for themselves."

Dad fiddles with his cap. "It's too risky," he says. "Bray needs to focus on business here, not be hightailing it to wherever the hell they grow exotic fruit. We need all hands on deck here."

Bray slumps his shoulders—defeated.

And any optimism I felt dives into my shoes. I hadn't realized it until just then, but the idea of the freezing business brought with it so much hope. Not because it was Jack's idea. Or because the freezing business would mean the end of any financial worries. It gave me hope that things could be different. That the future wouldn't be the same as my past. And maybe Jack could have been a part of that.

TWENTY-NINE

Jack

Most of the workers have headed out already, but I'm going to stick around until Iris is done for the day, so I take a seat on the Adirondack chair by the packing barn.

The day in the late-September sun was just what I needed. It doesn't hurt that I know Iris is in the office and I can picture her through the barn walls, studiously making sure every penny is counted and every spreadsheet perfected. Being close to her, even if I can't see her, is something I've come to crave.

I close my eyes and chuckle to myself at how alien my internal thoughts would be to New York Jack. The Jack who brunches and goes to the ballet.

My cell rings. It's my mother again. I don't want to speak to her. Not today. Not now in this perfect moment. I should change her ringtone so I don't even have to check caller ID.

While I have my phone in hand, I scroll through some emails. There's the usual stuff. Things I can deal with tomorrow. But nothing much is happening until the annual meeting of the trustees in two weeks. I'll have to go back to New York for that. During those couple of days, a full analysis of my family's money will take place. What's been earned compared to various other indices. What's been spent. What needs to be spent next year. Then we'll go through all the charities we're supporting and how we'll support them in the future.

My father will lead the meetings. I won't speak much. It's the same old, same old. I'm there to learn the ropes—even though I know the ropes inside out.

I'm pretty sure Iris and Bray work on margins that wouldn't make it onto the balance sheet in my family's business.

I scroll to an email from someone I haven't heard from for a long time. A corporate finance guy who used to be at Goldmans but looks like he's moved. I open it out of curiosity. I half expected him to invite me out to lunch or ask me if I knew someone he wanted an introduction to, but that's not what his email says. He wants to talk about The Alden. He knows someone who wants a Midtown hotel.

Most hotels lease their buildings, but I own the building The Alden Hotel occupies. I wonder if he knows that? He's suggesting a lunch to discuss. But I'm not in New York. I can't just arrange a lunch.

It's like someone's pressed a button and a thousand thoughts are released at once. New York. Iris. The hotel. My friendships. My job. My life.

I don't have a date for when I'm going back to New York. Yes, I'll go back for the trustees meeting. But should I have a longstop date? Am I just waiting for Iris and me to fall apart? Am I expecting to get bored? And if I'm just holding out for a miracle, am I being selfish. By still having hope, am I making us both miserable in the long run?

I'm usually more focused on solutions. More optimistic. But that's because I've had a lifetime of getting what I want. Things have come easily to me. Money solves a lot of problems. But now? Now I want something I can't have. Now I want a life in Colorado with Iris. But my entire life has been spent preparing to hold the Alden family torch in New York.

I suppose I could tell my family I was moving to Colorado. They couldn't technically stop me. I could attend meetings by Zoom or fly back and forth for gala dinners and charity luncheons.

But Iris couldn't come with me. She has a life here. If I thought they'd accept it, I would invest in the farm so she would be able to accompany me.

But the Wilde family is far too proud to accept money from me.

So we'd spend half our lives apart. How could we have a life like that? Raise a family? Half our history wouldn't be together.

Time and distance would eventually take its toll.

However hard I try, I can't see a solution.

But there must be one. There has to be. And I won't give up hope. I can't. Not yet.

Because Iris is... everything to me. I was meant to spot her at the ballet. I was meant to run into her in the diner.

Before meeting Iris, talk of destiny would have sounded ridiculous coming from someone else. But the way I feel about Iris isn't ridiculous.

Destiny is how Iris feels.

Manhattan is where the Alden family resides, does

business, and gives generously. It's the only place I ever saw myself.

Until Iris.

It's too much to think about. I should focus on my emails. On The Alden Hotel. I bought The Alden when my five closest friends bought their hotels. Our ownership of the hotels was meant to bind us together.

Except does it?

We thought we needed the hotels. But things change. Maybe it's different now. They've all found the women they're meant to be with and the bond between the six of us is still as strong as ever. If I sold the hotel, it wouldn't make any difference to our friendship. I know that as clearly as I know anything.

I don't have anything to do with the day-to-day operations of the business. There's a hotel manager and an overall CEO of my personal businesses who also deals with the hotel. I enjoyed getting it off the ground, but it doesn't really have any value to me anymore.

Things change.

I've changed.

All I can think about is Iris. Has she changed?

My phone starts to ring as I'm holding it. My mother. I ignore it again.

And then her assistant, Greg, calls. I groan, and even though I know he's calling on behalf of my mother, I answer it this time. At least he can't chastise me. He can't judge Iris or, if he does, he has to at least pretend he doesn't.

"Greg. How can I help?" I answer.

"Mr. Alden, there's been an incident. Your father's on the way to the hospital."

I go cold, like all the blood has left my body. I jump to my feet and push my hand through my hair.

"What kind of incident?" I ask, my blood back, my veins pulsing in my neck.

"Are you in New York? You need to come to Mount Sinai." There's an edge in his voice that I can't place. There's something he's not telling me.

"What happened. Is he conscious?" I pat down my jeans, trying to locate my keys. I find them and head toward the car.

"We won't know anything until he's seen by doctors."

"Is he conscious?" I bellow into the phone.

"Yes, I think we can say he's conscious. But you need to come as quickly as possible."

"I'm in Colorado," I say. "I'll be there as fast as I can."

He's not telling me something. Is he dead already? My mind goes blank at the thought and I head out of Wilde's Farm.

Back to Manhattan.

Back to being an Alden.

THIRTY

Jack

I head to the hospital straight from the helipad. It's already nine in the evening when I step out of the elevators into the hospital corridor. The smell of disinfectant hangs in the air, and all I can hear is the sound of machines beeping and clattering furniture.

I try to ready myself for what I'm going to find. Greg's not been very forthcoming about my father's condition and I don't know what to expect. Of course, my mother's not answering my calls. I don't know if I should take that as a good sign or a bad sign.

I told Iris to stay in Colorado when she offered to come with me. I told her that Wilde's Farm needed her and that I'd keep in touch and let her know how everything was.

My overriding reason for telling her to stay in Star Falls wasn't because she was needed on the farm, although that was technically true. I just knew it would be easier dealing with my mother on my own. Especially if my father was sick. I didn't want to make the situation more tense by bringing Iris with me.

And I didn't want Iris feeling uncomfortable. I didn't want her abandoning her family. Mine wouldn't be as welcoming to her as the Wildes have been to me.

She heard the whole truth in my voice. I know she did.

The half lie feels like a chink of distance between us that threatens to bottom out into the Grand Canyon. But I can't think about that now. I just need to deal with my mother and see my father.

"Mother?" I call out. Where is she?

"Jack," my mother says, her voice a little shakier than I'm used to hearing it. "Is that you?"

Greg appears in the corridor. "In here."

"Jack," my mother says as I enter the room. I glance around, expecting to see a bed, a patient—my father. Instead, there are four chairs around a low coffee table. A vase containing pink faux flowers sits in the middle on it.

"He's next door," my mother says, her voice wobbling. "On a ventilator."

"A ventilator?" That didn't sound good. "Is he going to be okay?"

My mother just stares into her lap, stifling a sob. My heart steps up, pounding against my rib cage, but I try to keep calm.

"What happened?" I ask. I've had no further information than when Greg first called me. "Is he okay?"

"Your father had a stroke," my mother says, her eyes glassy.

The room tilts and my vision blurs. I fist my hands, trying to resist the emotions that threaten to overwhelm me. "How is he?" I glance between Greg and my mother. Why isn't anyone saying anything? Were they keeping him alive until I got here?

My mother nods at Greg, giving him permission to speak. Usually my mother likes to control things. Things must be bad if she's letting Greg speak for her.

"The doctors are still assessing him," Greg says. "It was an acute ischemic stroke. They put him on a ventilator to..." He looks down at his phone. He's obviously taken notes, which normally I would think was ridiculous, but now I'm grateful for. "In case he suffered a fit, according to the doctor. But he was conscious after the stroke. That's a good sign."

I let myself breathe for the first time in what seems like hours. "Good. So, he'll recover."

Greg flashes a glance at my mother and then addresses me. "They don't have a prognosis at this time, but... the doctor did mention his age and said it would likely be a long road to recovery."

It's a fact that my father's seventy-four. But before today, I never really considered him old. His schedule was packed from morning until night. He went into the office every day. He was out in the evening three or four times a week.

I thought he'd live forever.

Many men my father's age are retired and spend their time playing golf and bridge. Not my father. He's dedicated his life to the Alden family legacy.

"The first twenty-four hours are the most crucial," Greg says. "The doctors want him off the ventilator after that. And they'll do additional assessments and start rehab."

"And obviously, he'll have round-the-clock care," I say. "The best that money can buy." I pull in a breath. What can I be doing? Our family foundation built the children's wing of this hospital. All the staff must know who he is. He's going to get the very best care. But will it be enough?

My mother stifles a sob, and I take her in properly for the first time since I arrived. She's pale, but then, she's not wearing any makeup... and I try to remember if I've ever seen her not wearing makeup.

I don't think I ever have.

Greg is staring at my mother, chewing on his lip. "I'll go and see if I can get an update." He excuses himself. I'm pretty sure he just wants to give my mother some time to compose herself and he's being polite.

As a child, I never saw my mother until she emerged from her bedroom hair and makeup in place. I'd usually been up with the nannies for a while by then. Or later, I'd come back from a piano lesson or a tennis lesson to find her having tea and reading the newspaper with Dad, like I'd walked into a Norman Rockwell painting.

My mother and father are inseparable when my father isn't at work.

I've never thought about it, but they must really love each other.

"Where have you been, Jack?" My mother looks up at me, her eyes red, an almost childlike expression on her face.

A wave of guilt travels through me. "I was in Colorado," I say, as I take a seat next to her and put my hand over hers. "I got here as fast as I could."

We're not a family who ever had a tremendous amount of physical affection between us. But I want to try to comfort her. I half expect her to push my hand away, but she doesn't.

Instead she places her other hand on top of mine. "I'm pleased you're back."

I pull in a breath. "I'm pleased I'm here too." I stand. "I

would like to see him," I say. Yes, he's on a ventilator, but I need to see him with my own eyes.

"And you'll stay?" It's half question, half command. She doesn't mean stay in the hospital. She means stay in Manhattan.

She means, no more working on a fruit farm and spending time with Iris.

I don't answer. My father's sick. My mother needs me.

"It's time," my mother says, looking me right in the eye.

Two words that say so much.

My father is seventy-four years old. I should have been prepared that this could happen at any time. In so many ways I am prepared. This moment is what my entire life has been about so far. Now my father is incapacitated, I'm expected to take over the Alden family. The foundations. The galas. The meetings. The investments.

I'm no longer the heir.

I've inherited.

My father's life is now mine.

Someone's reached inside me and their fist is clenching my guts, seizing any choices I had over my life.

This is it. I'm expected to step up.

Months-long trips to Colorado are in my past. I have to be in New York now. I don't have a choice about that. I'm de facto head of the Alden family.

And Iris? I'm not sure how she fits into any of this, however much I want her to. However much I *really* can't imagine my life without her.

"We need an engagement, Jack," my mother says.

It feels like she's slapped me and I withdraw my hands from hers and sit back in the chair. I don't know if she could have said anything more appalling. Her husband is lying in a hospital bed, unable to breathe by himself. Why is she so concerned about me being engaged? And not just engaged, but engaged to someone she approves of. "I'm not even thinking about any of that. Iris and—"

"No Iris," she hisses. "You need to stop being so selfish, let that girl go and find yourself someone suitable."

It's like she's struck a match down a lighting strip and I feel myself burst into flame. "Selfish? How is dating someone I care about selfish?"

She fixes me with a look that could penetrate marble. "You think it's okay to stand by while what generations of Aldens have built goes to waste?"

I fight the urge to roll my eyes. "Stop exaggerating, Mother. I'm fulfilling all my duties."

"Oh really. Is that why you keep missing board meetings and the trustees haven't seen you in months?"

"I've been video conferencing in to most things," I mumble. "And even if I hadn't, me spending a couple of months in Colorado isn't going to destroy generations of wealth and power."

"It's where the rot starts," she says simply like it's the answer to a basic math equation. "That's why you need to come back to New York and stop spending time in Colorado. The family needs you."

There's no point in having this conversation with my mother. She doesn't understand how technology means I can work from anywhere. I can videoconference into meetings and fly back for really important things. It's not like we're living in a time where it takes three weeks to get a letter across the country. Plenty of people work remotely now.

"Listen to me, Jack." My mother's voice drops and softens, like she knows that she hasn't won me over and she's changing tack. But her stare is still as steely. "You think it's fair to be making some small-town country girl fall for you when *you know* it would be impossible for the two of you to be together?"

"I don't know it's impossible," I say indignantly. If Wilde's Farm do start a frozen business, maybe Iris will have more time to come back to New York with me. Maybe she'll let me help financially with the business. I'm not prepared to walk away from her. She's too important. Too special. I knew it from the first moment I laid eyes on her.

"So what's your plan?" my mother asks. "You're going to marry her? You know very well that there's no hiding who she is or where's she's come from. What will you do? Dress her up like she's a doll in the right clothes and the right shoes and hope it's enough? Send her to etiquette classes, and parade her around New York society as your girlfriend or wife, hoping your wealth and power will cover up the cracks? And then what?" She pulls in a breath, like this speech has been a long time coming.

Dress her up like a doll?

I think back to the ballet and how it had been difficult for me to even buy her a dress without it becoming messy and complicated. I didn't want to dress her up like a doll, but maybe that's how she felt. It's not like I care what she wears, but I want her to feel comfortable?

But maybe it's not possible for Iris to feel comfortable in my world.

"She's never going to feel quite good enough," my mother continues as if she's reading my thoughts. "Someone's always going to want to bring her down. She's going to have to live with knowing that you could have married someone who would have understood the rules and navigated them expertly. That you could have married someone with connections who felt comfortable in the world in which we live, Jack. And you're expecting some farm girl from Colorado to give up her life, say goodbye to everything in her world that makes her happy apart from you. To give up everything to be thrust into a world she knows nothing about and might just eat her alive."

I try and swallow but my throat is dry and I have to strain to breathe. I want to respond. I want to fight back. Tell her she's wrong. That Iris would be comfortable. That she'd have my protection. That I'd never want Iris to be anyone but herself. That we would be happy.

Am I fooling myself?

My mother fiddles with the clasp of her handbag. Then she looks me dead in the eye. "That's what you want from her? To sacrifice everything?" She glances down into her lap.

I don't want Iris to sacrifice anything to be with me.

Is that what it would take?

"Do you really think hanging on to Iris is anything but selfish?" she asks in a whisper.

Being with Iris isn't selfish. Is it? Am I fooling myself? Playing with her?

"Jack," she says again. "You're an Alden. You know what you have to do."

It feels like I'm being pulled under the waves and I don't know if I'll be able to swim to the surface again. I know that I want to be happy, and I'm happy with Iris. But I don't want Iris to have to sacrifice anything to be with me. I don't want her to give up who she is to exist in my world.

THIRTY-ONE

Iris

I've had a few messages from Jack since he left yesterday, but I keep missing his phone calls, and when I call him back, I get his voicemail.

I'm in bed when my phone vibrates with Jack's call.

"Hey," I say, so relieved we've finally managed to connect. "How's your dad?"

"Iris," he says on an exhale. "I'm sorry I kept missing you."

"No need to apologize. How's your dad?"

"He had a stroke. He's on a ventilator."

I sit up. "Oh god. I'm so sorry." I want to ask him how bad it is, whether he's going to make a full recovery, but it feels insensitive, so I don't. "How's your mom holding up?"

He pauses. "She's shaken up." If he were here now, I'd be able to tell what he was thinking. Or at least I'd tell myself I could. At the other end of the phone, it's different.

"I'm sure. It's a big shock." I want to put my arms

around him and try to comfort him. "I wish I was there with you."

"I wish you were too." He doesn't miss a beat before he answers and somehow it makes me feel closer to him, even if he's not telling me the truth.

He tells me about seeing his dad and how frail he looked. He tells me word for word what the doctor said when he spoke to him, and how he's ensured he's got the right specialists on board to figure out the way forward. His words say he's in control but the tone of his voice tells me he's scared.

I want to be there for him.

I might be able to give Marnie some of my responsibilities and go to New York for a couple of days. But... I'm not sure that's what Jack wants. I know that his mother isn't my biggest fan. She wants Jack to settle down with a suitable wife, not... hanging out in Colorado with some farmer's daughter. If I'm in New York, I might just make things more difficult for Jack. I don't want to cause him more stress.

"You're doing everything you can," I tell him.

Silence.

I can tell his brain is ticking over, even from two thousand miles away. "What are you thinking but not saying?"

He sighs, and the sounds of him rearranging himself wherever he is, echo down the phone. "I don't know," he lies.

"Just talk, Jack. You don't need to filter things with me."

He huffs out a half laugh. "I know. I'm thinking that I don't like being here without you. And I'm feeling bad I wasn't in New York when my father had his stroke."

Silence tumbles between us, until I finally say, "I get it. I miss you too."

"It's been a day apart, but I don't feel myself when I'm not with you."

I grin. "I don't think anyone's paid me a nicer compliment." There's more he wants to say. I feel it. "You've got a lot on your mind."

He groans. "I can't deny that."

"Nothing you say can... I just want you to tell me what you're thinking."

"I'm thinking that I've never felt the way I feel about you about anyone else. And I can't imagine I ever will. I'm thinking I love being in Star Falls far more than I could have possibly imagined. I always thought small towns meant everything was small, but it's the exact opposite. It's made me see how small New York is. It's simpler. Fresher. It feels how life is meant to be."

I can feel the "but" before he even says it.

"But New York is where the Alden family is based. It's our kingdom. And I know I said to you, let's figure it out later. That problems will dissolve and we'll find a way to work around obstacles..."

I close my eyes and turn onto my back, so I'm ready.

He's breaking up with me. I can hear it in his voice.

"I don't want to think about any of it," he says. "It's too difficult."

"Yes," I say. "It is difficult. Impossible maybe." If he's going to end things, I want him to do it quickly. Maybe it will hurt less. Maybe I'll be able to stop the blood loss if it's short and sharp.

I'm not brave enough to inflict the knife on myself, even though it would be cleaner that way. If he's not ready to pull the trigger, I should.

But I'm weak. Weak for Jack. Weak for the possibility of an impossible relationship.

"Let's change the subject," I say quickly.

"Yes," Jack agrees, almost before I can get my words out. "Tell me your deepest darkest secrets."

"You know everything," I say, but as I'm talking, I know it feels too much like a declaration. "Let's play a game instead."

"A game? What kind of game? I suppose I have a chess app on my phone. I sometimes play with Bennett."

I laugh. "I'm not playing chess with you! Not unless it's strip chess."

It's Jack's turn to laugh, and the sound rumbles down my body, as if it's bringing it to life. It feels good to be able to make him feel a little better—to be able to distract him. I wish I could do more.

"Let's play I-Spy."

"Correct me if I'm wrong, but we're not in the same state, let alone the same room. How am I going to tell what you're looking at? You want to switch to video chat?"

"Absolutely not," I reply. "I-Spy in the same room is for kids. Amateurs. We're playing professional I-Spy."

"I've never been into your bedroom in Star Falls. You always stay with me."

"Right. So this makes it more interesting."

"Or more likely that you'll win, seeing as you've been in my bedroom here in New York." It's the first time he's mentioned where he is, and for some reason, it's comforting to know where he is and that I've been there too.

"Maybe," I tease. "I'll go first. I spy with my little eye, something beginning with..." I look around the room, trying to spot something interesting. I lean over and click on the lamp. "L!"

Jack groans. "I just heard you turn on your light. Light."

"Wrong." Okay, so he was right, but I'm not going to tell him that.

"I'm not wrong. Unless you're being pedantic, and you're saying lamp."

Damn him. "Maybe this was a bad idea," I say.

"Terrible," he says, and I laugh at how grumpy he sounds.

"Okay, so tell me what you're reading. What's beside your bed?"

"There are a few books," he says.

"Tell me all of them," I say.

"Promise not to laugh."

"No," I say.

He chuckles. "Okay. The first one is a book Fisher lent me called *Shadow State* by Andy McNab."

"Any good?"

"Not really started it. Fisher loved it, but I'm not sure it's my thing. Lots of beating up bad guys from what I can tell."

"Yeah, I can see why that wouldn't be your vibe. What else?"

"Okay," he says, his tone a little more reticent. "There's one on fly-fishing."

The corners of my mouth lift at the thought of Jack in plaid and wader pants. "I didn't know you fish."

"I don't." He takes a beat. "I figured your dad and your brother did, so... I picked this up at a bookstore on the corner."

Oh my, he might be the sweetest man I ever met. "Jack," I say. "If I was there right now, I would do very, very naughty things to you."

He groans. "You're into fishermen?"

"I'm into men who want to find things in common with

my father and brother because they know it will make me happy to see you all get along."

As I say the words, I realize how much him even thinking about my family makes me like him more. I fell for Jack a while ago, but with every conversation like this, I fall for him a little more. What a sweet, sexy, thoughtful man. "I wish I was with you in New York."

"I wish you were here too." He doesn't ask me to join him, and I won't offer.

"We'll figure this out," I say, as much to myself as to him. Isn't that what he said to me? That we'd figure things out.

"The last book is an old book I've had since college." His tone's changed. It's brighter. I can't tell if he's pleased that I've told him we'll figure stuff out or if he's faking it. Somehow it makes me feel farther away from him. "It's a book of poetry. I had it from the library for an assignment and I must have forgotten to return it."

"Jack!" I say, half shocked.

"I've paid the fine, you don't need to worry about that."

"How big was the fine? You've been out of college a long time."

He chuckles. "Yeah. Well, it might have been in the form of a donation. I'm pretty sure I have a building named after me on campus. I'm sure they're not worried about an overdue library book."

"You've only just found it?"

"I came across it on the bookshelves in my office earlier. It's a collection of poetry of the British romantics."

"Like Byron and stuff?"

"Yeah," he says. "Although Byron was never my favorite —don't tell his namesake. Coleridge is my favorite."

"Read me one," I say.

The sound of him turning the pages of the book between his fingers comforts me somehow. "'The Nightingale'?" he asks. "Or 'Frost at Midnight'? They're probably my two favorites."

I grin at the idea that Jack would have a favorite poem. My exposure to poetry stopped at Dr. Seuss. "Both of them."

My limbs sink into the mattress as I listen to him recite first "The Nightingale" and then "Frost at Midnight."

They're beautiful, atmospheric poems. I don't necessarily understand them, but I can appreciate how beautifully the words hang together and how Jack's voice somehow conveys meaning in the words.

The more of Jack I have, the more of him I want. Seeing the side of him that has a favorite Coleridge poem and wants to learn about fishing... it makes me feel like New York might as well be the moon, he's so far away. I want him back, here, next to me.

"The next time you read me those poems, I want us to be wrapped in blankets around a fire."

"That sounds nice," he says, and I recognize the sound of Jack closing the book and sliding it back onto his nightstand.

He doesn't tell me he's going to make that happen. He doesn't promise that when he gets back to Star Falls, we're going to drive out to the lake and he's going to read us poetry while I make us s'mores. He doesn't counter that he's going to read it to me in bed before he puts his head between my thighs and makes me come. He doesn't say anything else at all.

And I can't help but think that in that silence, he says so much more. The silence is full of doubt and impossibilities.

It's full of *I don't knows* and *ifs*. It feels dangerously like the beginning of the end.

THIRTY-TWO

Jack

I pull my collar tighter as I head up the steps of Worth's town house. It's good to get a break from being in the hospital all the time over the last two weeks. I need to recharge.

It's been a while since the six of us were all together. Through the course of this year, a lot has changed. Even Worth's town house is now Worth *and Sophia's* town house. But my friendships with my five best friends feel as steady as ever. Nothing can shake what the six of us have built together.

"It's really good to see you, my friend," Worth says as he opens the door. Alongside me, Worth is probably the most serious of the group. But he's also intuitive. And such an intense welcome is just what I need.

"It's good to see you too." I mean it. It's times like this that I realize how strong our bond is.

We bundle inside and the chatter of my friends' voices tells me I'm not the first to arrive.

"How is your father?" Worth asks.

"He's off the ventilator."

"Breathing by himself. That's good."

I'm not sure *good* is how I'd describe my father's condition. Bleak would be more accurate.

We step into the drawing room. Apparently everyone arrived before me. Being the last to arrive is usually Byron's role. We greet each other with hugs and handshakes, and people retake their seats on the dark red oversized couches either side of the fireplace.

Worth hands me a glass of red wine and gestures for me to sit opposite him. There's three of us on one couch, three on the other. Soft music plays in the background and all I register is that it's *not* Fleetwood Mac. It's not the song the woman was singing when Iris and I danced together.

I take a sniff of the wine. "Malbec?"

"That Argentinean one from one of Efa's brothers-in-law's vineyard" Bennett says.

"Have we met this brother-in-law?" Fisher asks Bennett.

"Honestly, I'm not sure," he replies. "Maybe—oh no, definitely, because this is the American one."

"Oh yeah, Vincent."

"Vincent Cove? That's Efa's brother-in-law?" I ask.

"One of them," Bennett says.

I sit back on the couch and feel my body unlock, as if it realizes it's out of danger and my adrenaline and cortisol can return to normal levels now that I'm here. Among friends.

"I've missed this," I say.

"We've missed *you*," Bennett says.

"Don't get soppy on me, Bennett," I say, and raise my glass.

"What's going on with your dad?"

I let out a long sigh. "He can't speak," I say. "Not really. He can't walk. He can't feed himself." Seeing him today was hard. Physically, he looked like my father—a little less put together and like he'd aged ten, twenty years. He still looked like Mr. Alden. But his spirit wasn't there. It was like there was a newborn baby occupying his body. It had been horrifying.

My mother fussed over him in a way I'd never seen before. She plumped his pillows and offered him spoonfuls of ice cream. She brought him his iPad and switched off the television, which must have been left on by one of the hospital staff. She talked to him like he was talking back to her. She told him about the weather and bits and pieces of gossip from her social circle.

It brought with it pieces of memories. Maybe they were like this with each other when I was younger? Recent memories are of my father and me talking about business and my mother chastising me for being single. It's as if my relationship with both of them has become more distant as I've gotten older.

"I'm so sorry, Jack," Worth says, and everyone else offers their support in their mutterings.

"They say he should make some quick gains in the next few weeks. More over the next few months." I don't mention what the doctors said about risks of a second stroke and how his age will make recovery a more difficult path.

"That's good," Byron says.

I nod, trying to seem positive.

"And so you're stepping in for your father in relation to..."

"Everything. The trust, the foundation, the charitable endeavors." The role I've been training for my entire life is mine. The sword of Damocles has not passed from above my father's head to mine. It feels like it has fallen.

The responsibility sits heavy inside me. Not because I'm not capable. I am. The apprenticeship has been long and thorough. But I'm not sure I want it. I wasn't ever sure I wanted it, and now that I have it, it feels like it weighs me down in every sense.

"How's Iris?" Leo asks.

"Where are all your lovely wives and girlfriends?" I ask, suddenly aware that it's just the six of us. It hasn't been the six of us for a while. Monday-night drinks have been replaced with a Sunday brunch with partners invited. Even though I've enjoyed the change in dynamic, I have to admit, the six of us are what I needed tonight.

"Out together," Worth says. "Sophia's idea."

"Does anyone mind if I sell The Alden Hotel?" I ask. I can't keep my mind going in one direction tonight. It's thinking about my father, then Iris, then my friends, back to my mother, then Iris. Then Iris again. Iris, Iris. Iris.

My five friends exchange looks, and it feels like silence is being passed around between them.

"Did the cat get your tongues? A simple yes or no would do. Or maybe a thumbs up or thumbs down."

"Did you get an offer for the hotel?" Worth asks.

"I did. Are you thinking of making me another?"

"I wasn't, but maybe I am now. If you're serious, I'll talk to Avril."

"None of you care? Or have I said the unspeakable?"

"Everyone cares," Fisher says. "But not about the hotel. Everyone cares about *you*."

I glance around at the circle of friends before me. "What?"

"We asked you about Iris. And you started talking about

everything but," Fisher says. "How are things between you two? Every time I see you in Colorado, you look like..."

"A fruit farmer?" I suggest, trying to bring some levity to the conversation.

"Like you had the stick removed from your ass," he replies.

I huff out a laugh. "Yeah. I like it in Colorado."

"It's like you're more the real Jack," Fisher says. "The one we get to see behind closed doors, rather than the one who attends the ballet with your mom or is on the board of every charity run out of New York City."

I nod, agreeing with my friend. I have nothing to add. Everyone knows me well in this room, but Fisher probably knows me the best.

"And now you're back," Byron says.

"As are you," I say.

"But Rosey's with me."

"So?"

"Are you and Iris still together?" he asks.

I shift in my seat and then take a sip of the wine. It gives me a beat to think. Even after some time, I don't know how to answer the question. "I haven't ended things." The word "yet" echoes in my brain. It's inevitable though. Isn't it? I'm the head of the Alden family with duties and responsibilities. This is where I have to be...

And the last thing I want to do is be selfish. I want to put Iris first.

"You're planning to?" Fisher asks. "You two are..."

"From different worlds," I say, finishing his sentence for him.

"Join the club," Bennett says. "Efa lived on a different continent."

"But there are expectations of me," I say. It's difficult for my friends to understand how bearing the Alden name means life's been planned out for me since before I was born.

"Have you ever considered that you don't need to *accept* anyone's expectations of you?" Fisher asks. "I get you come from a dynasty I can't possibly understand. But what's going to happen if you tell everyone that you want to tread a different path?"

As if I could do that. "You should have seen the reaction when I wanted to invest in our business. Or the hotel. My father came around to the idea that I have my own personal investments, but it took time."

"So you've already pushed the boundaries," Fisher says.

"Pushed. Not broken. I didn't float the idea of becoming a fruit farmer in Colorado." I expect grins and laughs but I don't get any. I was joking. Can't they see that?

"Is that what you want to do?" Bennett asks, his expression completely serious.

I narrow my eyes at him. "You mean if I had complete control of how to live my life?"

His expression morphs into pity. "Yeah. If you decided your own destiny."

I pull in a breath. I only allow thoughts of what I want to do with my life to creep in around the edges of my brain. I suppose I don't want to feel any more restless and unfulfilled than I already do. "I don't know."

"Don't you?" Fisher asks. "Really?"

I sigh. This feels like some kind of intervention or something. Last time I looked, I don't have a drug or alcohol problem.

I'm privileged. I have every opportunity—within certain carefully defined boundaries. I have everything money can buy, but being with Iris has showed me that there's plenty that money can't buy.

Plenty in Colorado that I can't get in New York City.

"I would like to do some kind of business consultancy," I say. "When I first bought The Alden Hotel, I enjoyed getting it off the ground. Solving problems and making sure everything fit together and was doing what it should. And then having success at the end of it." I shake my head, thinking back to that time. It was really rewarding. "It's not that I don't think I add value to the charities and foundations that I sit on, but it's different. A board role is so far removed from the day-to-day. And it's in the day-to-day that you can really make a difference. I like getting my hands dirty." I chuckle at the thought. It's the exact opposite of what my mother would want to hear. "So I'd like to focus on helping businesses in trouble or startups that are getting off the ground."

"You'd be great at that," Leo says.

I pull my mouth into a forced smile, because I don't want to hear how I'd be good at something I'm never going to be able to pursue. "It's never going to happen."

"Why not?" Fisher asks.

Of course, the question comes from Fisher. He's completely self-made in a creative industry. It's different for him.

"Because I'm an only child who has inherited a large fortune. That fortune needs to be managed."

"But you have people to do that," Byron says.

"Yes, but I have to oversee it all."

"Agreed, but is there no room for anything else? You seem to have spent a lot of time in Colorado over the past few months. Maybe there's some space there for you to do your own thing?"

"To spend this time in Colorado, I've blown off in-person board meetings and done things by videoconference. I haven't attended functions that I'm expected to. I've been MIA. It wasn't sustainable. And now? After my father's stroke? Now the game has changed. Now there's no disappearing and pretending to be someone else for a couple of months. Now I have my father's life. A life that's here in Manhattan."

"In a perfect world, would you want to base yourself in Colorado?" Byron asks.

"I don't live in a perfect world." Iris would say I live in a gilded cage. I sigh. "I was in Colorado for Iris, but I've really grown to love being out of the city."

"So if you had a blank sheet of paper, you'd base yourself in Colorado. You'd do business consultancy. You'd manage your mountain of money."

"I'd give more away," I blurt. I don't know where the thought comes from. It erupts out of me. "I know I'm spoiled and selfish to think so, but all the money, all the legacy—it's a lot of responsibility. If I have children, I wouldn't want to burden them with it. And you know what? No one needs all the money the Aldens have. The Aldens are just me and my parents. And there's so many who could benefit. Not just the museums and ballet companies of America."

"Who's stopping you doing all this?" Fisher asks.

Fisher and I couldn't have had more different upbringings. But that's what I like most about him. He comes at life from a different angle. He's creative. He's clever. He's a really good guy. He also knows the answer to the question he just asked.

"My parents. Maybe when they pass, things will be different."

"But now you've got legal control over the family trust, right?"

I shrug. "Technically, I suppose. But I've never gone against anything my father or any of the other trustees want."

"But that could change."

"Now's not the time," I say. "I've never seen her so vulnerable since my father's been in the hospital. And my father, despite his... condition. He's still alive. I couldn't change things so dramatically. I wouldn't want to challenge the status quo while he's..." I don't want to finish the thought.

"The thing you have to remember," Bennett says. "Some things you can't get back once you have let them go."

He's talking about Iris. But honestly, what choice do I have? I can't leave my responsibilities in New York. And Iris can't come here. After what my mother's said, I don't know if I could ask her to. I don't want her to be anyone but herself and I'm not sure she could be herself in New York. I wouldn't want her to be unhappy, and the way my mother described it, there isn't another option.

There are so many things that are different about Iris and me, but we also have a lot in common. We're both tied to our parts of the world. "Some things aren't meant to work out." I try to swallow past the lump in my throat and push down the panic that threatens to rise at the thought of not being with Iris.

"Jack," Fisher says. "I've seen you two together—in fact, I haven't seen that *much* of you together, because you're almost always one-on-one. I've never seen you like this with a woman."

"I've never been like this with a woman."

"Then you can't let her go," Worth says.

I owe Worth an apology. I thought he was crazy, when he fell for Sophia as hard and fast as he did. It's been exactly the same with Iris. Except I haven't married Iris. We're not going to get our happily-ever-after.

"It's not so easy for me, Worth," I say. "I have obligations and I won't put those on Iris."

The front of my cell lights up and then goes black. I check it. I've had a missed call from Iris. I've wanted to hear her voice all day. I've called her twice, but she hasn't picked up. We've exchanged a few messages to try to fix a time to speak. We've still not landed on a time.

Why am I dragging this out? I just need to get past this bit—rip the Band-Aid off and tell her I'm not coming back to Colorado. The thought makes my gut churn. The idea that Iris isn't going to be a part of my life is almost impossible to imagine. From the moment I laid eyes on the woman, I felt a connection to her that I've never experienced before. When I'm with her, it's like I'm the best version of myself. I'm lighter. Hopeful. More me.

Just the thought of giving her up cuts like a knife. But keeping her hanging on isn't fair. It will make things more painful for her in the long run. And Iris's happiness comes before my own. I need to tell her.

My friends might think I can change the life that I've been born to live, but none of them inherited the life I did.

THIRTY-THREE

Iris

It's not until this moment that I realize how completely and utterly I know Jack.

Down to his bones.

As soon as I answered his call, I felt him. He's sad. So sad. I hear it in his voice, so thick I can feel it between my fingers.

I know what's coming, and even though it's so devastating that I can't stop my eyes from overfilling, at the same time I want to comfort my Jack. I hate hearing him in such pain.

"It's important that I'm near the hospital," he says.

"Of course it is." I hope he can't hear my pain like I can hear his.

"And his recovery is going to be slow and..."

"You have to be in New York. I understand," I say. And I do. If I switch my heart off, everything makes logical sense to my brain. He has to be in New York. I have to be in Colorado.

But my heart isn't switched off. It's on full volume and it hurts like it's trapped under ten tons of rubble.

"And with all the additional responsibilities I have now, I don't know when I'll get the chance to come to Colorado again."

The knife sinks deeper and I close my eyes, trying to shut out some of the excruciating pain that comes with his words.

"Yes," I manage to whisper.

"I don't want to be selfish," he says.

I don't know if I imagine it, but it sounds like his voice is breaking as he speaks.

"You deserve to be happy. I want that for you. More than anything," he adds.

You make me happy, I want to say. *Any crumb or snatched moment I can get, I'll take.*

I want to assure him I'll wait as long as it takes for him to come back to Star Falls. That I'll call him five times a day and visit him as often as I can.

But I don't think that's what he wants.

And he's not invited me to New York.

I can't find the right words—any words—to say in return. What is there to say?

I'll miss you?

I'll never forget you?

I'll think of you every day for the rest of my life?

None of it seems enough.

"I want you to be happy too," I say.

More silence.

Silence that lets the terrifying reality seep in. I know now that I'll never know anyone like Jack again. From this moment on, there will be a gap in my heart where Jack is meant to fit.

He's still on the phone, I can hear his breaths against the handset, but I feel so empty.

I want *you.* I *want* you. *I want you.*

It's all I can think. All I can feel.

But why? We knew this is how we'd end up. It was always going to turn out like this. His life, his family, his business is all in New York.

What did I expect?

That he'd give it all up and come and live on a fruit farm in Colorado?

Now we're both hurting. Him in one time zone, me in another. So did we let it go so far? Why did I let myself fall in love with this man?

I never had a choice.

Not since that first night in New York. I think I fell in love with him that evening.

I'm an idiot. I should have run when I saw him again at the diner. As far away as possible. I should never have let myself get into something that was going to be so painful to get out of.

"You're probably busy," he says.

I shake my head, but don't say anything. I can't. He'll hear my tears if I do and I don't want him to hurt more than he does. I know this is as difficult for him as it is for me.

More silence. I gather myself. I need to be strong. "Be kind to yourself, Jack," I manage to say.

It's not any of the things I want to say. It's not any of the things I feel.

But he knows. He *must* know. There's no point in making this worse.

"You too," he says.

And then he's gone and I don't know if I'll be able to keep breathing.

I lie back on my bed, letting the conversation sink in, wondering if the weight of it will pull me through the floor of this house, down into the ground.

Into my grave.

"DINNER IN FIVE MINUTES," Bray shouts from downstairs.

Eating is the last thing I want to do. But we've had a rule since Mom died—if we're in the house, we all eat together. No taking it to our bedrooms or having it later because someone wants to watch the game. I guess it was Dad's way of keeping us from drifting apart. And it's worked pretty much. Okay, so I got my high school diploma and I haven't told Bray or my dad, but we share stuff around the dinner table.

I pull myself up from the bed, check my face in the mirror and head out. I can't let myself cry. I won't. Not until later.

"You okay?" Bray asks, as I get to the bottom of the stairs.

I smile and nod, trying to be as convincing as possible. I'm anything but okay, but I'm not about to admit it.

"What the hell are you working on that won't wait until tomorrow?" he asks.

I realize I'm carrying my laptop. I don't even remember picking it up. It was beside me on the bed, as I was going through my emails when Jack called. Ironically, I'd had good news today. I got notified that I'd been accepted into the American History course that I'd applied for. I'd been excited to tell Jack. I thought it would distract him from thoughts of his dad. And I knew he'd be happy for me. And proud.

He'll never know now.

Pain burrows deep into my stomach and I sit, trying to pretend I can't feel it.

"Just some stuff," I reply.

After dinner, I'll work through some financial projections. It'll distract me. It's nothing that couldn't wait until tomorrow, but what else am I going to do? Stare at my phone, hoping that Jack will call and tell me he's made a huge mistake and he's on his way to Colorado? Even though I don't want him to do that. It will just stretch out the torture of being with him, knowing it's going to end. It's better like this. Now I can start to get on with life.

Whatever that means.

"Jack not around? Not seen him for a few days."

It's been twelve days since he left town, but naively, I always assumed he'd come back. I knew when we started, we'd end. I just wasn't expecting the end to come so soon and I didn't expect it to hurt like this. Like someone carved a hole in my chest and ripped out my heart.

I feel hollow. Empty. And what's worse is that I know deep inside, this is it. Things aren't going to get better. They just won't. They can't.

Life will go back to how it was before Jack. Frankly, it already has, but things will be so much worse now. I've seen what life can be like. I've seen the possibility. It's like being with Jack showed me what color is, and I'll have to go back to a world in black and white. I think I'd rather not have known. At least I wouldn't feel the loss so deeply.

"Iris?" my dad asks from the couch, where he's watching football. "Bray asked you where Jack was."

"He's in New York."

"Why's he in New York? And when's he coming back?"

"His father had a stroke. And he's not coming back."

I stand, scoop up my laptop and head back upstairs. I don't care about our rules for dinnertime. I want to be alone. I just want to stop thinking about all the times we had together in Star Falls. They're rattling around my brain like they're trying to haunt me.

I close my bedroom door and close the drapes. I want to block everything out. All my thoughts. All my senses. I take a seat on my bed, propping myself up on my cushions and open my laptop. I just need to stay busy until this pain inside me lessens. I just need to feel better—to know that this ache inside me won't last forever.

His voice was so tender. So concerned. For *me*. When it's *his* father who's in the hospital.

Maybe it would have been better if he'd cheated on me or ghosted me or turned out to be a gigantic asshole. But he's staying in New York to look after his father and the family business. He hasn't drawn this out—let me come to my own conclusions. He's done everything right. That's who Jack is —honorable. Trustworthy. The best man I've ever known.

And now he's gone.

There's a knock on the door, and I want to scream at whoever's on the other side to go away and leave me alone. Unless they can make this feeling of loss and hopelessness chasing through my veins go away, then I just want them to disappear.

Even though I don't answer, my dad opens the door. I keep my eyes fixed on the screen. I'm tap, tap, tapping away, creating a chart to make things more efficient.

Dad clears his throat. "I'm sorry about Jack," he says, his voice stilted. He never was any good at the emotional stuff. Since Mom died, the hugs disappeared. I know my dad loves me. But I also know he doesn't show it through physical touch and sharing our feelings. Right now, I need my mom. I want to crawl into her lap and cry and rail that the world isn't fair. I want her to pull me into her arms and rock me until I have no more tears left.

But I can't have her back.

Just like I can't have Jack back.

"Your mom was always better at this stuff than me," Dad says.

"It's fine," I say. "It'll be fine," I correct myself. Because it has to be, doesn't it? If I can get over the death of my mother, I can get over a man I've only known a few months.

I *have* to be able to survive this.

"Heartbreak is a horrible thing," he says, shoving his hands in his pockets. "But you're doing the right thing by keeping busy."

I can't look at him. I just can't. I know he's never asked me to stay, but I'm here for him. And Bray.

I've given up so much.

Most of the time, I'd make the same choice over and over. But today? With the breakup with Jack so raw? I don't want to be in this house with my brother and dad. I'll probably still be here, living in my childhood bedroom, in twenty years. Hopefully any thoughts of the life I might have had outside this farm will have ebbed away. The memories of ballet and Jack will have faded into nothing.

"Do you mind if I just have some time by myself?" I manage to speak despite my throat tight with unwept tears.

"Yeah, no, of course," Dad says awkwardly.

But as he's leaving, Bray steps into the room. "Hey, this letter's for you. I opened it by mistake. You finally graduated high school, did you?"

I glance up at Bray and snatch the paper from his

hands. "Why are you opening my mail?" I snap indignantly. I don't dare look at the paper. I don't want to have a conversation about why I bothered getting my high school diploma. Bray and Dad aren't going to understand.

"Hey!" Bray says. "I told you I opened it by mistake."

"You didn't need to read it." I drop it on the bed next to me. They've already emailed me to tell me that I graduated. Why are they sending me stuff by snail mail? And why's Bray being an asshole by opening my mail? He never gets mail. It's not like he could have thought it was for him.

"Shouldn't we celebrate?" he says. "It's a pretty big deal, you finally getting through high school."

I keep my head down, focused on the screen. Why is everyone in my bedroom? I left the living room to avoid people.

"Why didn't you say that you were studying for your high school diploma?" Dad asks. Maybe I'm imagining it, but he sounds a little hurt.

I just shrug. "I did it on my own time. It didn't stop me doing my job." I know I sound defensive. I just can't help it.

"That's not what I meant, Iris. I'm your dad. We're your family. Why didn't you tell us? We could have..."

"What?" I ask, finally looking at Dad. There's nothing he could have done. There's nothing I need from him.

"Are you looking at going to college?" he asks.

Bray chuckles, and even I let out a cynical laugh.

"How on earth would I go to college?"

"I just never knew..." He trails off.

"Is that what you're doing on the laptop?" Bray asks. "Studying?"

How is it that my brother never grew out of the immensely irritating stage? I spin my laptop around. "No, asshole, I'm working on spreadsheets to try and make the business more efficient so we can put food on the table, so can you just leave me alone."

I pull my laptop back around and slouch down on the pillows behind me. Bray goes to respond, but out of the corner of my eye, I see Dad point at the door, indicating he needs to leave.

I just want to be on my own.

I want to stop thinking. Stop feeling. Stop *everything*.

THIRTY-FOUR

Jack

My legs feel heavy, like I'm carrying rocks on sand, as I take the stairs in the apartment to the drawing room. She summoned me to lunch. If there's an impromptu date with a so-called suitable woman, I can't be held responsible for what I'll do.

"Jack," she calls. "Is that you?"

I take a deep, steadying breath. I know this feeling pulling on every step isn't my mother's fault, but I can't help hating her at the moment. And it's not just my mother I'm resentful of. It's every trust meeting. Every investment meeting. Every communication from every board my father's on, which all now assume I'll take over. Worse, it's even the blare of the horns of the traffic and the crowded streets.

I hate everything about my life.

The last thing I want to do is sit opposite my mother for ninety minutes and make nice. I don't feel nice. I feel like I want to crawl out of my body and into the ocean or something.

Crawl back to Colorado.

I enter the drawing room, bracing myself for who I might find there. Luckily, my mother is on her own.

"Good morning, darling," she says, putting down the magazine she was reading.

I bend and press a kiss to her check. "Good morning, Mother. How are you?"

"We battle on. I saw your father this morning." She sighs. "They tell me he's making progress."

We both know that whatever progress he makes, life will never go back to normal.

"I'll see him this evening. I have a call at five. I'll leave after that."

"He gets very tired in the afternoons, Jack," Mother says. She lowers her eyes, like she doesn't want me to look at her.

"I won't stay long," I say.

There's a knock on the door and Greg enters. "Lunch is ready."

We stand and head through to the dining room, where two place settings have been made. Everything's the same as it always is when we have lunch midweek. Except my father isn't in the office, he's in the hospital.

"I had a call from Regina," she says, as we sit. "She's very disappointed that I'm not going to make it to their gala. You'll have to go in my place."

"Absolutely not," I say. "You know I can't stand that family. And why would I need to be there? You can't make it, but it's the donation they're really interested in. Just be generous."

"It's important that we're seen at these things," she says.

"Important to who?" I ask. "Not to me."

"It's important that Aldens are seen at all the big society events of the year. If we're not there, we lose power. With your father's... illness, people will be whispering. Wondering whether the Aldens will still have the same place in society as they always have." She must sense my disinterest. "Your father would want you to go."

I sigh. The ultimate trump card. She's right. My father would want me to go. And he's at his most vulnerable. Why would I let him down?

Images of Iris and me in Grizzly's, listening to the singing, dancing, having fun, float through my head. "Aren't evenings meant to be about enjoying life? Why spend time at a function for people I don't care about?"

Mother sighs like I'm an utter disappointment. "You are the only son of James John Alden. It is on your shoulders to maintain the family name, the family legacy."

I've heard this speech a thousand times. It usually starts off with stories about the wonderful work the Aldens have done over generations to encourage and promote the arts. How the family has established and supported various charities, with long monologues about various achievements by said charities. I know it's ungrateful and disrespectful, but I'm sick of hearing how my ancestors have helped shape America. Because the stories always end up the same way: a huge lecture on roles and responsibilities.

I'm here. I've accepted my fate. I don't want to hear it again.

Not today.

"This is why you need a wife," she says. "If you were married, your wife could step in."

I think of Iris in Colorado. There's no way I'd want to put her through an evening with most of the people at these dinners and galas.

"Have you had a chance to catch up with Penelope Althorp?" she asks.

I narrow my eyes, trying to remember if I was supposed to be catching up with Penelope.

"You two would make a very good match."

"You want me to marry a lesbian?"

"There are lots of ways to have a baby, Jack. Test tubes and things. You wouldn't have to be intimate."

Is that what she wants for me? A loveless marriage? An arrangement? I don't know whether to be hurt or angry. I study her, trying to figure out if she cares about me at all. Or my father. Shouldn't she be more concerned about her husband and getting him as well as he can be, rather than my marital status? Or maybe she doesn't care about him either. Maybe their marriage was an arrangement too.

"Or Gabriella Campbell?" she says.

"I'm not interested in Gabriella Campbell."

"You need to put your mind to it. It will ease your burden. You need a partnership. I know you think I just sit around all day and have lunch, but I'm an important member of the Alden family. Your father relies on me. You need someone to rely on."

I don't respond. There's no point going around and around in circles.

Greg enters with our appetizers. "I have your scallops." He places down my mother's plate and then mine.

"So along with scallops, what else are we having?" I ask, hoping to change the subject.

"Chicken salad," Greg says.

"The one Bridget likes," my mother says. "With the pomegranate."

I don't know who Bridget is, and I don't want to know.

"She was telling me that she hopes Richard Ives will resign at the end of the year."

I take my seat opposite my mother and we eat the scallops, making polite conversation. She talks about various rumors about changes on boards and her contemporaries' children flunking out of college or being fired from Goldmans.

I'm not interested in any of it.

Then I realize that *this* is what she means. She's telling me things she would normally tell my father. Things that might be useful to him. This is why I'm here at lunch. I thought I was having lunch, but I'm having a meeting. This is part of my job now.

"I could show her what's expected of her," she says out of the blue. "While I'm still well, I could act as a mentor of sorts. Of course, whoever you choose to marry has to have the requisite social skills and social standing. But there are nuances to being an Alden that I will be able to share."

I can't think about any of this now. All I can picture when she talks of me marrying is Iris. And I'm absolutely sure that Iris's not the woman she has in mind for me, even if she was prepared to give up her life in Colorado and come to New York.

"Jack? Are you listening to me? You need to take action. And I don't mean by falling for some farmer's daughter in Colorado who has an interest in ballet because she took a few classes."

Anger floods through me. How *dare* she speak like that about Iris. About the woman I love!

Love.

I *love* Iris. *She's* the woman I want to come home to, the woman I want to be my partner in everything. It's Iris.

My mother thinks I need to find a woman to be my wife. But I've already found her. We just can't be together.

I swallow down my fury at my mother's comments. I know she's concerned about my father and what's going to happen about the Alden family legacy. I get it.

"Leave Iris out of this," I say, through gritted teeth.

And then realization dawns again. She met Iris. She saw us together. Maybe she suspects how deep we were in, and she worries that it's Iris I'll choose to be my Mrs. Alden. And worse, that I might move to Colorado. My lifetime's preparation for legacy and duty would all be for nothing if I marry some fruit farmer's daughter and go live in Colorado.

My mother sighs. "I'm only having this conversation with you because your father can't. There must be no more procrastination, Jack. A Christmas engagement and a June wedding." She says it like it's a certainty. Like she can decide the dates of my engagement and marriage even before I've found the woman I want to marry.

Except I have found her. What I feel for Iris can't be replicated. I know in my bones that I'll never feel for anyone the way I feel about Iris.

The thought of being with anyone else makes me sick to my stomach.

My mother asks as she puts her cutlery down after finishing her scallops, "Did you enjoy your appetizer?"

I've barely touched my food. "I'm not particularly hungry, Mother."

"I'm sure you'll find the chicken salad delightful. I think I'll set up a dinner with the Campbells." She fixes me with a look. "You need to make a decision."

Panic circles my ankles, anchoring me to the floor.

I don't want to marry someone suitable. I want to marry the woman I love. I want Iris. The last few weeks without her have been empty and I miss her every second. I can't do this. I can't feel like this for the rest of my life. I certainly can't marry someone else.

I just need to get away. From my mother. From New York. Away from everything.

THIRTY-FIVE

Iris

I'm at the kitchen table, on my laptop, going through the expenses from this time last year and working out whether any of them could be reduced. I'll have to speak to Dad and Bray, obviously, but we need to do something if we're going to maintain margins.

My dad and Bray are watching football, although my dad is also doing a crossword. He rarely just watches TV. Says he wants to keep his brain sharp.

Out of nowhere, the TV switches off.

I lift my gaze to the living area. "Is the power out?" I ask.

Bray is looking at my dad like he's lost it. "No, Dad just turned it off."

Dad sets down his newspaper. "Yeah, I need to speak to the two of you about something."

"Can we finish the game first?" Bray asks.

"No," Dad replies simply. "Get over here. We need a family meeting."

"Family meeting?" That's not a thing around here. I can't ever remember a family meeting being called.

"We were watching the game," Bray says.

"The Broncos are going to lose," Dad says. "You don't need to see the end of the game to know that. Now, get your ass over here, Iris."

Bray groans. I snap my laptop shut and go over to the couch.

"I've been thinking about a few things," Dad says.

"Uh-oh," Bray says. "Thinking is overrated." He grins widely but my dad is unimpressed, and his mouth is set in a thin straight line.

I take a seat next to Dad.

Dad glances between the two of us, his gaze resting on Bray. "You're fired," he says.

Bray laughs and rolls his eyes.

"I'm serious, Bray. I'll give you three months to find something else to do with your life, but you're not around next season."

My stomach turns over at Dad's expression. He's completely calm, but I've seen his expression when he's playing a prank, and he's not wearing it.

What is going on?

"As if, Dad. I'm not going anywhere."

"That goes for you too," he says, nodding at me.

"Me?" I say, my voice verging on hysterical. "What did I do?"

"And you both need to think about getting your own places."

"Dad," Bray and I say in unison.

"What the hell's going on?" Bray asks.

Then it hits me. The business can't afford both of us

anymore. And he's probably going to take in boarders at the house to make it work financially.

"And I've taken out a loan," he says.

I'm on my feet before I've had a chance to digest what he's saying. "What kind of loan? How much for? We can't afford loan payments. What are you—"

"For the freezing operation. I think it's a good idea."

Bray and I exchange a glance. Has Dad got some kind of brain issue? Like, is he suffering from dementia? I half want to start looking up symptoms, but need to brace myself for the next bomb Dad is going to drop.

"So you need the money you'd normally pay us in salaries to make the loan payments?" I ask.

My dad shakes his head. "No. I've looked into it. I can get most of the equipment on lease. But I'll need some modifications to the barn."

"So why are we fired?" Bray asks. "We've been the ones who were pushing the freezing operation, and now that you're going ahead with it, you're going to fire us? What the fuck, Dad? And we're going to be homeless. Where are we supposed to live?"

Dad sighs and glances down into his lap. "I've done a terrible job at being a father to the two of you."

"No you haven't." I reach for Dad's arm and he covers it with his hand, patting me. "You're a terrific dad."

"Most of the time," Bray says. "When you're not firing us. Do you have our replacements lined up or what? I don't even know what I'm supposed to do. Get a bar job at Grizzly's? I don't think they need anyone. And anyway, I can't think of anything worse than being stuck inside pouring people drinks. I love being outside. I love working with the people we have, seeing all the fruit that we've grown piled into boxes, knowing that it's going to feed people—provide people with the nutrition they need to survive. I *love* my job."

Dad huffs out a laugh. "Son, I never knew you thought so deeply about it."

"I never had to until I was fired."

Dad shakes his head. "I've relied on the two of you far too heavily. Maybe that was okay in the beginning, after your mom died, but I should have let you both go a long time ago." He pulls in a breath. "I've prioritized the needs of the farm over the needs of my children." His voice wobbles as he finishes his sentence and I scoot closer to him.

"What are you talking about, Dad?"

"Neither of you went to college. You've never left this town. You've never experienced anything other than this farm. I want you both to experience the world. See what's out there. If then you want to come back to Wilde's Farm, that's another thing."

"Are you serious?" Bray asks. "I never wanted to go to college. I always loved the farm. It's where I've wanted to work since I've been five years old."

"You've never known anything else," Dad replies.

"Maybe I don't need to. I knew I didn't want to fight in the Army, even though I'd never done it. I know I don't ever want to own a fucking cat, even though I never have. I love this farm. I love my job and... yeah, well, maybe moving out might be a good idea. It might be nice to have a place of my own."

Bray gets up from his chair and comes to sit on the cushion the other side of Dad. He slings an arm around his shoulders. "But I wouldn't want to leave you."

"That's what kids are supposed to do," Dad says. "They leave the nest. And if they don't, then the parents haven't been doing their jobs properly. After Mom died, I wanted to keep you close. I wanted to protect you from everything. But now? Now I just want you to be happy."

"We are happy, right?" Bray asks, looking at me.

"Even if you don't want to, Iris needs to spread her wings," Dad says.

Tears gather in my eyes. Not because I've just been fired by my dad, but because he's saying things I haven't even allowed myself to think about.

"Iris never wanted to go to college, either."

I meet my dad's gaze. We both know that's not true.

"No," Dad says. "Iris couldn't go to ballet school because she dropped out of high school to make sure this family didn't go under."

I exhale. The time after Mom died is never something we discuss. It was so dark and felt so hopeless that we were all on autopilot. And the word ballet has never been uttered in this house since Mom died, either. It feels like we've been keeping all this in and holding it so tightly, that it's a relief to let go. Finally.

"Knowing that you've done your high school diploma without telling me..." My dad shakes his head. "I realized how blind and selfish I've been. Maybe that was forgivable just after your mom died. But I should have fired you a long time ago."

I nudge my dad. "You can't fire us, Dad. We're going to help you transform this business into a national frozen fruit brand."

Dad pats my arm again. "Maybe Bray is. But you're not, my darling. You are going to go and be with that man who looks at you like you just hung the moon."

I blink back my tears and shake my head. "No, Dad," I force out. "No, I'm not. Jack ended things and went back to New York."

Bray groans. "We need him to advise on the freezing business. He had some great ideas."

"Don't be an insensitive asshole, Bray," Dad growls. "Iris is upset. She's had her heart broken. Let me tell you, son. Broken hearts don't heal easily. But now you don't have a job. Maybe you can go to New York City and find him." He sighs. "I should probably tell you that I know you've been going there every year since forever."

I pull back. "What?"

Dad shrugs. "I should have said something. I wanted to respect your privacy. If I'd thought about it, I would have realized you were going to the ballet. Seeing what you missed out on."

It's almost too much to hear from him, and I cover my face, trying to stop my tears from falling. "It's where I met Jack," I blurt out. Loss envelops me. But not the loss of ballet from my life. Or even my mother. It's Jack I miss in that moment.

"You need to go and find him," Dad says.

"I don't want to leave you. Or this asshole here." I nod toward Bray.

"We're going to be just fine. And we'll always be here when you come back."

I shake my head. "I'm not going anywhere."

"Maybe not right away," Dad says. "But you need to figure out where your future lies."

Where would I go? Star Falls is all I've known. There's no possibility of me chasing after a dream of dancing. That dream is long dead. And Jack? He's gone. He has his hands full with his dad, and even if he didn't, I'm never going to fit into his world and he never asked me to try. He always said he was sure there was going to be a way through for us. But I wonder if he really believed it.

I'll never know. I need to move forward. Maybe I'll figure out a different dream for myself. Maybe I'll figure out that being in Star Falls is exactly what I want.

Dad hooks his arms around both of us and pulls us into a hug. I can't remember the last time he hugged me. "You're good kids. I'm a lucky man. Your mom would be so proud of you both."

I glance across at Bray and tears are gathering in his eyes. I grab his hand and squeeze, trying to breathe as my own tears fall. I miss her so much.

"This is what she'd want," Dad says, his voice tight. "I bet she's up there laughing now, telling me it's about freaking time I let y'all lead your own lives."

I lean my head on Dad's chest and let the warmth of him soak into me.

The idea of being free from Wilde's Farm is terrifying. But there's a glimmer of light, a star in a dark Colorado sky that whispers that it's exactly what I'm meant to be—free and in control of my own destiny.

THIRTY-SIX

Iris

When Dad fired me a couple of days ago, he also said that before I went anywhere, he wanted me to train up Marnie to do everything I do. She's more than capable, and a good choice as she gets older and less able to do the more physical sides of her current job.

But it will take a while. Especially when we've got the frozen side of the business to get off the ground. Dad also said I'd always have a job at Wilde's Farm, if that's what I choose. I've told him I'm not going to be making any quick decisions. The breakup with Jack has left me tired and emotional, and I don't want to make any rash choices that I'm going to regret later. I also need to figure out what to do with my life.

With the space to think about it, it's clear that my college course isn't exactly what I want to do. An online course was always going to be a compromise. I think I was just wanting something more and anything would do. But if I could actually do something in person, that would be better. But I don't know if that's what I ultimately want to do. There's so much to think about at the moment.

I step out of my office for some fresh air. The first of the deliveries will be loaded onto the trucks about to arrive. A pang of loss fills my chest. When Jack was here, it was so nice to see him on Wilde's Farm, getting his beautifully manicured fingernails dirty, laughing with the other farm workers, the sun shining on his already bronzed skin.

He seemed happy here.

And now he's back in New York. Even though it's where I met him, and I know it's where he grew up, it's so difficult to picture him there.

He seemed so at home in Star Falls. With me.

The sound of the first truck of the day's tires on the dirt entryway pulls me out of my thoughts. But when I look up, it's not a truck. It's a shiny black limo.

That's weird. We don't have anything that *isn't* a truck coming to the farm.

It parks in front of the barn, just a few feet away from me. The windows are blacked out, so I can't see anything. The driver steps out, but I don't recognize him. There're a few people milling around but the driver ignores me.

"Can I help you?" I ask. He heads to the back door of the limo and opens it.

I peer into the car, and it takes my brain a few seconds to realize that the person in the back, getting out of the car, is Jack's mother.

"Mrs. Alden?" I say.

"Iris," she says, offering me a little smile. "Is Jack here?"

My heart starts to pound. Why would she think he was here? Has something happened? My brain whirs through the possibilities of what might have happened to Jack to bring Mrs. Alden to my door.

I shake my head. "I haven't seen him since he went back after your husband's stroke." It's been nearly a month since Jack has been here. I'm not sure why she would come looking for him here.

"Can we go somewhere and talk privately?" she asks.

She must see the confusion on my face, but she doesn't offer me any explanation.

"Of course. Why don't you come up to the house?" I suggest. I can't imagine what she's going to say to me. My entire body tenses. I want to demand she tell me what's going on immediately, but I know it won't do any good. I have to be patient. Follow her timeline.

She nods very slightly and we walk silently up the path that joins the house to the rest of the farm.

Once we're inside, I offer her a beverage but she refuses everything.

"May I sit?" she asks, tilting her chin at the dining table.

"Of course." I just want her to tell me what's going on.

We both take seats at the table. I've never been very good at small talk—especially with a woman like Mrs. Alden. She's completely intimidating. I hope she cuts to the chase.

"I want to tell you how I came to marry Mr. Alden," she says. "Maybe your judgement of me will be less harsh when you hear my story."

"My judgement of you? I never..."

What's she talking about?

"If you would listen to me for just a few minutes, I would be very grateful."

She's firm, and I'm not going to mess with her. I give her a half shrug and she continues.

She sighs and places her hands in her lap. "No one

apart from my husband knows this. Not even Jack. But it's the truth."

I nod, not quite knowing what to say, other than why are you here? On Wilde's Farm? You look like a bumblebee on a glacier. Where's Jack? Is he okay?

"I met Mr. Alden when I worked at Saks." She pulls in a breath like she's just confessed to a murder and it's taking everything in her to say the words. "I sold small leather goods. Gloves. Wallets. Glasses cases. That sort of thing. He came in looking for a pair of gloves for his mother."

For some reason, I'd expected Mrs. Alden to have been from a wealthy New York family. But apparently she was a sales assistant.

"You have an excellent poker face," she says.

"I'm not trying to hide any reactions. I'm just trying to listen to your story."

She nods slowly. "Well, we were instantly taken with each other. James wined and dined me. Took me dancing. But always back where I lived in New Jersey. As our relationship progressed, I came to know who he was, and what the expectations of his family were for his future wife."

This sounds like a familiar story. If she was here to warn me not to get involved with her son, she's way too late. He's gone. "You know Jack and I are no longer together?" I ask her.

She ignores me. "But Mr. Alden and I were in love, and we wanted to be together. Back in those days, the people who fit into New York society were more easily identifiable. Deportment. Conversation. Clothes, hair, nails. Everything told a story."

I glance down self-consciously at my unmanicured nails.

"Things were less fluid then. People didn't cross the

class barrier so easily as they do now." She sighs. "Anyway, I knew I wanted to be with Mr. Alden—James. And he wanted to be with me. But we both knew his family wouldn't approve. So we concocted a story about my background. About how I was from an upper-class family in England, but I'd come to New York for summers and was living with some friends of the family.

"James arranged for a close friend of his to open their doors to me, and I moved from my parents' house in New Jersey to Manhattan. James taught me how to make small talk. How to walk. He even paid for some lessons to help me speak with a hint of a British accent. He taught me to dance, and we went to dinners that doubled as lessons in social etiquette. It was quite the marathon year of preparation."

"You spent a year doing all this?"

"A year of meeting in secret, preparing to be introduced to his family."

Jack has always described his mother as being a complete snob. How is that possible when she'd come from such humble beginnings? She's a total hypocrite. She must have suspected how Jack and I felt about each other, but it never mattered to her.

I press my lips into a thin line, not wanting to be rude to someone in my father's house. If this was *my* house, I would have asked her to leave already.

"We had a cover story for everything. And when we felt we'd covered every base, James arranged for me to meet his parents at a society wedding. Then again at a charity ball. And for a third time after he'd proposed."

"Did they approve of the marriage?"

She frowns slightly. "They had wanted him to marry someone else, but they accepted his choice."

"Good of them."

"It had taken a lot of work to turn me into a woman they would accept."

I sigh, irritation prickling at the back of my neck. Why is she telling me all of this? Did she miss the part where I told her Jack and I had broken up?

"Did they ever find out that you weren't who you said you were?" I ask a little provocatively. "That you're not who you say you are?" She'd just confessed to being a liar.

She shakes her head. "No. As I said, no one knows apart from me and James now that my parents have passed. And now you."

Jack doesn't know. "You lied to your own son?"

"To protect him." She pulls in a breath. "To protect the Alden name, the Alden legacy and Jack's future."

"You think anyone would care? Now? You talk as if the Aldens are royalty and you have to maintain some kind of bloodline."

Her expression remains neutral. Probably something she learned during that year of preparation.

"I love my husband very deeply and this is what he wanted. He wanted us to be married, and he knew his family would never accept who I really was. So we created someone."

I can't imagine the kind of pressure that would lead to two people lying to everyone they cared about in order to be together. It must have almost broken them. It's awful. And I know it's a pressure Jack also feels.

"But his parents are long dead." Couldn't the obsession with the Alden name, the power, and the legacy die with them. It seems to cause such unhappiness.

"But the Alden name is not."

"Okay," I say. "I guess that's your business. I'm not quite

sure why you're here in Star Falls making me the third person alive to know this about you."

"Jack's missing," she says. "I pressed him on his future plans a week ago and... I haven't seen him since."

Missing? I rub my hands over my face. "Could you repeat that, please? In English?"

"Jack's father will never make a full recovery. Jack is now the head of the Alden family trust and overseeing all the investments and charitable endeavors. He *is* the Alden family. And I told him he needed someone to share the burden with."

I stay silent, and Mrs. Alden shifts in her seat.

"I told Jack he needed to find a suitable wife," she says.

The words are like a red-hot poker straight through my heart. She's not telling me anything I didn't already know, but hearing it from his mother makes it sound more real. The room tilts as anger rises through my body, threatening to engulf me, but I push it away. This woman is ridiculous. This entire situation is ridiculous.

"Why are you here? I get that I'm unsuitable in your eyes, and you're desperate to maintain the precious Alden legacy over your own son's happiness."

"You might see that as me being hypocritical."

"That *is* you being hypocritical."

She nods. "I understand that. But I was trying to do what I thought was best for my son and the family legacy."

I roll my eyes. There's been far too much mention of the word legacy. "And you're here because?"

"Because after our conversation, Jack left, and I haven't been able to contact him since. I thought he might have come here."

I sigh. I wish he had. Even though it would have stung

all my fresh wounds, I want him to run to me when he's hurting.

"He's not here," I say. "I've not seen him since he left for New York after his dad's stroke."

She has the decency to look ashamed. "I'm worried about him."

Her expression sends a shot of concern into my bloodstream. "We need to find him. Have you tried Fisher? Or any of his friends?" I ask.

She shakes her head. "I thought this would be the first place he came."

It hurts more than it should that I *wasn't* the first person he came to. I pull out my phone and call Jack's number. I close my eyes as the phone rings. And rings. And rings.

Panic pushes at me. I hope he's okay. I hope he just ran from his controlling mother rather than had an accident. One of his friends is bound to know. But I don't have anyone's numbers. I scroll through my contacts. I have Juniper's number. Fisher should know something.

Juniper's number rings out. I know Byron isn't at the Club all the time, but if he's not up there, they must be able to reach him. I can tell them it's an emergency.

"I just hope he's safe," Mrs. Alden says.

I get to my feet. Of course he's safe. It's completely unacceptable to think that anything would have happened to him.

"And your assistant hasn't spoken to him?"

She shakes her head.

"Wait here. I'm going up to the Colorado Club. Byron might be there or at least they can get me a number for him. One of his friends should know where he is."

I head out of the house, grabbing my car keys on the way. On my way up to the Club, I'll check the falls. My head tells me Jack won't be in Colorado. It's far too far to come to just get some space. And he ended things between us. But I can't shake the niggling feeling that he's nearby.

I PULL up to the falls. There's just a gray truck parked. When Jack was here, he rented a black SUV. But they might have been out of SUVs.

I take the short path up to the falls. I hear the water over the stones just before they come into view.

As I walk further away from my car, my heart lifts in my chest at the hope I might find Jack here. It doesn't make much sense, but I really feel like he *could* be here.

I scan the area and spot one of the kids from the next town over with his girlfriend. The truck wasn't Jack's.

My heart sinks back down, deeper than before. I don't know why, but I thought he really might have come back to Star Falls.

I get back into my truck and head toward the Colorado Club. I just need to find Byron or get a number for him.

I turn onto the main road up the mountain. It's getting dark, even though it's only just past three. It's starting to drizzle. We've been told to prepare for heavy rain tonight. Everyone's been working really hard to get the farm as prepared as we can.

I flick on my headlights and reduce my speed. I'm not going to help Jack by racing and getting stuck in a ditch.

A truck comes toward me. I recognize it as Mike's, the man who used to own the cabins on this road that Byron bought. Then I pass the bus that brings staff up and down the mountain. The Club has definitely brought more people into Star Falls. But there's only one person I want to find right now.

Just before the incline starts to accelerate, another car approaches. I slow, wanting to see if it's Byron's car. Would he be coming down to check on the progress of his house?

As the vehicle comes closer, I can tell it's not Byron. It's a black SUV. I bring my speed down even slower. It's just like the one Jack drove when he was here before.

I'm doing about ten miles an hour as the car passes me. I check out the driver in the window and my heart soars, pressing hard against my rib cage like it's trying to break out and get to the passing car.

I'd know that profile anywhere.

Jack.

My Jack.

All the air disappears around me and I can't breathe. For a split second, I feel like I'm floating, suspended in this moment where Jack and I are in the same place at the same time. I want to hold on to it and savor it before the moment dissolves forever.

At the last second before he passes me, he catches my eye and brakes.

I catch my breath and press my foot down on the brake.

I come to a stop and open my car door, wanting to get to him, not even caring that we're blocking the entire road. The rain is coming heavier now, and it feels like the insides of me since Jack left.

"Jack!" I call.

He's out of the car, striding toward me like he's going to mow me down.

"Jack," I say, my voice soft. It's so good to see him, it feels like I'm going to erupt, with emotion. Anger that he left me. Relief that he's safe. Bliss that he's here.

All of it.

I can feel everything now that he's here.

He's so handsome, but he looks like he has the weight of the world on his shoulders.

He cups my face as he gets to me. Our faces are wet as we gaze at each other.

"You're here," he says.

"I was looking for you," I say, gazing up at him. Seeing him again doesn't hurt, it heals something in me. His jaw, his perfectly shiny hair, his now-sad eyes. I've missed him so much.

His eyes narrow in confusion. I press my hands on his chest, wanting to feel him, to make sure he's real, wanting him to understand that I'm right here, staring at him.

"Your mom's sitting at our kitchen table."

"She's in Star Falls?"

I nod. "She was worried about you."

His gaze hardens, but he doesn't say anything.

"And I was worried about you when I heard you were missing. I couldn't get hold of Juniper."

"I just wanted to get away," he says. "To think."

"Think?" I ask.

"About everything. About how I'm supposed to live the rest of my life miserable without you."

"Maybe you aren't," I say on a whisper.

"I don't want to live the life that my mother wants me to."

"What *do* you want?" I ask.

He blinks and then his eyes meet mine, and they're so sad. So hopeless. And the pull towards him is too strong. I can't help hold him. I want to make this better for him, even if in the long term, it makes my pain last longer.

"I love you," he chokes out.

The words chase my breath from my lungs. They're the last thing I expected him to say. But they hit like the Colorado rain—making everything fresh and green and perfect.

His confession brings me to life. It makes me believe that life can be good. That life is just about perfect. Jack being here means everything is where it should be.

It's like he's placed a glass slipper on my foot. And it fits.

Perfectly.

My prince came back.

"I love you too." I gaze up at him, not wanting the moment to end.

"I think I've loved you since the moment I saw you at the ballet."

It's like we're encircled in a warm blanket and immune to the freezing November rain. With Jack here, nothing can be anything but perfect.

My lips curve into a smile. "How could you love me when we hadn't even met?"

"I don't know, but I did. And now that I've been lucky enough to know you, everything has changed." He pauses. "Maybe it hasn't changed, maybe I've just seen things differently. I can't accept the things I thought I could. I don't want the destiny mapped out for me...

"I want more.

"I want you. I want to move to Colorado and help you and Bray with the farm. I don't want to have a life without you."

I close my eyes, trying to commit what he's saying to memory. Moments like these are the ones poets write about. The ones that live on forever when committed to paper and lovers read to each other for generations.

I open my eyes and smile. "Actually, I'm not going to be working on the farm for much longer. I'm showing Marnie my job, and she's going to be taking over. Dad wants to start the frozen fruit brand, and I think he and Bray are going to be working on that together."

His completely confused expression makes me laugh.

"You haven't been gone long, but you've missed a lot."

"So, what are *you* going to do?"

I shrug. "Dad wants me to figure out what I want to do."

"American History?"

"You know, I don't think so. But I'm not sure what's going to take its place. Oh, and Dad's throwing me out of our house. So I don't have anywhere to live either." I laugh to myself. I'm nearly thirty and about to have nowhere to live and no job.

Jack shifts so he's facing me. "You want to stay in Colorado?" he asks, urgency in his tone.

"I don't know. I haven't really had time to think about it." I sweep raindrops from his brows. "All I know is that I want you. Do you want to stay in New York?"

"I want to be anywhere you are."

His words melt in my chest like ice against a flame. I nod. "Same."

"I should have never ended things," Jack says. "I've been so stupid. I thought it was for the best. That I was being selfish by trying to figure out a life together. I thought I'd be asking you to make too many compromises. My mother said I was selfish, that you'd face too much nastiness back in New York. Too much gossip and sniping."

I shake my head. "You should have talked to me, Jack. I'm a fully grown adult and I get to decide the compromises I'm prepared to make. Not you."

He huffs out of half laugh. "Yes," he says. "You're right." His shoulders drop like he's just thrown off some of his burden. "It won't happen again. I'll never let you go. If you're unhappy, I'll do whatever it takes to make you happy."

I know Jack to his bones and I know he means what he's saying. I don't doubt him. I don't doubt us.

"So if you're not tied to Colorado... this means..." He takes my hand. "I'm not sure what this means."

"I'm not sure either. But even if I don't have to work on the farm, I'm still a small-town girl from Colorado who's never going to be from a family with the right connections."

"I don't care about any of that stuff, and now I don't care what my *mother* thinks about any of that stuff. Or any of New York society. None of it matters here in Colorado. We can stay protected from it all right here." He shifts closer to me. "I thought I could go back to New York and eventually forget you. I knew how I felt about you, but I thought I could get on with my life and I could get back to normal. One day. Now I know that's impossible.

"You've changed me.

"It's like I've been cracked open and reborn. There's no going back.

"I can't go back.

"I *won't* go back.

"Nothing my mother or New York society can say will change that. If New York doesn't want you, as perfect as you are, then I don't want New York. We'll build a life together in Colorado."

"Your mother said New York wouldn't want me?"

Jack shrugs. "She said a lot of things that don't matter." I think he might understand her concerns if he talks to her and she tells him the truth. "What does matter is *I want you*. Wherever you are. Whatever you're doing. If I'm with you, nothing else matters."

My heart feels so full that my entire chest might explode.

Jack came back to me.

And he's back for good.

He lifts me up and I wrap my legs around his waist, gazing down at him as he holds me. "I'll follow you wherever you want to go." I press a kiss to his lips.

His gaze darts from my eyes to my lips and back up again. "I'm so in love with you."

"The feeling's mutual."

Our lips crash together and finally I feel like I'm home.

I've lived in Star Falls, in the same family home, since I've been born... but I never feel more at home than I do when I'm with Jack.

We fit perfectly together. Soul mates. My entire heart. The love of my life.

"I love you," I say between breathy kisses.

"I love you too," he says on a groan. "Will you ever forgive me for letting you go?"

"Only completely and utterly," I say. I think I'd forgive the beautiful, gracious, sweet man in front of me anything. Absolutely anything. "As long as you don't do it again."

"Never." His words burrow into my heart and tattoo themselves deep in my chest.

A horn blares out of nowhere, and I'm brought back to the reality that we're reconciling in the middle of a road. There's the bus on its way back up the mountain. I'm blocking its path.

"Back to Wilde's Farm," I say as he releases me. "Be

careful," I add. "The roads are slippery." I want to keep him close to me. He doesn't know these roads like I do.

"I'll be fine," he says as I get back into my car. "U-turn here and follow me back."

"I'll follow you anywhere, Jack Alden," I call after him.

THIRTY-SEVEN

Jack

The last thing I want to do is see my mother right now, but Iris's asked me to speak to her, and I'll do anything for Iris, so we've come back to the house. As we head up the porch steps, I take her hand. I can't get close enough to her.

"Jack!"

I hear my mother's voice before I see her. I scan the room and see her standing at the kitchen table, a tissue in her hand. She brings it to her face and stifles a sob. "I thought something had happened to you." She shakes her head. "I would have never forgiven myself."

Iris slides her hand from mine and sweeps it across my back. "I'm going to make hot chocolate for everyone."

I just want to go up to the Colorado Club and get Iris naked, eat with her, drink with her, watch the valley and the town of Star Falls from halfway up the mountain with her.

The last thing I want to do is have hot chocolate with my mother.

But if that's what Iris wants, then that's what I'll do. I

want to make her happy, and I'm going to spend a lifetime making up for the fact I ever walked away from her.

"Mother," I say on a nod.

My mother steps toward me and pauses before patting me on the shoulder. It's the closest she's come to hugging me in years.

"I'm so relieved you're okay," she says, squeezing my hand.

It's comforting and uncomfortable at the same time. I don't know what to think. "I'm fine, Mother."

She frowns and takes a step back. "I'm so very sorry for pushing you about the December engagement."

"And the June wedding with someone I don't love?"

"I just wanted it to be easier for you," she says on a sigh, but I don't quite know what she means. "And Iris."

"Iris and I are together now," I say. "That's not going to change." I spot Iris's smile from where she's pouring milk into a pan.

"I understand," she says.

I'm not sure she does. But she needs to get on board because I'm going to make it work with Iris. If she's serious about no longer working on the farm, then maybe she'll be free to come to New York.

"I'm going to marry her, Mother," I say under my breath.

I glance up at Iris. I'm not sure if she heard me, but I swear her cheeks have flushed the most gorgeous shade of pink.

My mother nods. "Yes. And I know you don't need it, but the two of you have my blessing."

I freeze in shock at her words. Did I mishear her?

"You probably don't believe me." She sits on one of the farmhouse chairs around the dining table.

I glance at Iris, and she nods as if to say that I should sit too. So I do.

"I have some things to tell you," she says. "Things that might be difficult to hear. Things that might make you think very differently of me."

"Mrs. Alden, nothing you're going to tell Jack is going to make him think badly of you," Iris calls from where she's making us drinks.

My mother's expression says that she's not convinced by what Iris's saying.

"I want to talk to you about how I met your father."

I've heard this story. My mother was over from Europe, staying with distant family for the summer. What's there to tell?

Iris comes over carrying a tray holding two mugs of hot chocolate. I'm not sure my mother has ever drunk from a mug before. She sets one in front of Mom and one in front of me. She goes to leave, and I catch her hand. "Please stay."

"Jack, this is between you and your mother."

"Iris, I'd like you to stay," my mother says, her voice soft.

"Are you sure?" she asks.

My mother nods. "Yes. I'm sure."

Iris holds my hand as my mother then confesses her real background, and how she and my father lied to his family about where she came from.

I can't take it all in. My mother isn't who I've believed her to be my entire life. My mind is a tangle of thoughts and feelings. She always told me she had no living family when I was old enough to ask. Is that true? Do I have family nearby? In New Jersey?

Everything she's ever told me about her background and family has been a lie.

I don't know what's real about my life.

"I saw so many parallels between your father's and my story, and you and Iris," she continues. "I was worried. Life is different these days. The internet means you can never leave your past behind. You can't reinvent yourself in the same way I did. I remember how much effort the lying had been. How hard it's been to keep up pretenses at times." She pulls in a breath. "I didn't want it to be as hard on you as it has been on your father."

"It seems to me you were being a hypocrite," I say. How dare she criticize me for wanting Iris when she wasn't some English aristocrat's daughter as she alluded to, but born to a family in New Jersey she disowned. "You clearly think it was okay for my father to marry a woman who wasn't from the right social circles, but not for me."

"I wanted it to be easier for you," she says, her tone pleading. "I didn't want you to live a life worrying about being found out."

My mother's expression is usually completely unreadable. Today she looks bereft. Undone.

"Times have changed," Iris says. "I don't know life in New York high society, but from what I can see, I don't think the boundaries are as clearly defined as they once were."

My mother nods. "Maybe not. I know it's easier when people aren't gossiping and laughing about you, and you know they have reason to. I was lucky. I was with James and nothing else mattered."

Her words thaw my mood a little. I'm glad she and my father found a way to be together if that's how they felt for each other. They clearly loved each other a great deal. Back then the pressure on my father to marry someone suitable was probably far greater than I've been subjected to. It must have been a concern for them.

So I don't understand why she can't have more empathy for me wanting to be with Iris.

"I didn't want you to live your life in constant fear of being found out and being ridiculed."

She's talking about herself. That's how she's spent her life and pity settles in my stomach. The thought of my mother living her entire life worried that she could be found out that she wasn't who she said she was fills me with sadness and pity. What a horrible life she must have had full of fear and pressure and expectations. It's one I don't want for myself.

"It doesn't matter," I say. "Because I don't want to live my life in those circles anymore. I don't want to spend my life going to charity functions just to be seen. Or sitting on boards that don't really do anything. I want to live my life differently."

Iris reaches over and squeezes my hand.

My mother clears her throat and pulls back her shoulders, regaining some of her composure. "I don't know what that means."

I sigh. "No, I don't quite know what that means either. But I'm going to figure out how I want to live my life and do it exactly that way."

My mother's throat bobs as she swallows. "I would just ask that you try and see things from my perspective. I was trying to protect you, protect the name that your father and I spent our lives trying not to sully, so you wouldn't have to deal with the consequences of having a mother who wasn't... wasn't anyone."

Iris reaches for my mother's hand. "You're not no one. You never were. You're Jack's mom, and Jack turned out pretty great, so from where I sit, that's a legacy. And from what you told me, you were so completely and desperately in love with Jack's father that you would have done anything for him. That's not no one. That's someone who loves with their whole heart. Don't let yourself think you're no one."

I stare at Iris. How can she find so much compassion for my mother when she hasn't been treated well by her at all? But she does. Because *she's* kind and compassionate and understands the sacrifices we all make for our family.

"You are very kind, Iris," my mother says. "It's more than I deserve." She turns her attention to me. "When you disappeared after our argument... I understood for the first time that your happiness means more to me than the Alden name. More than the family legacy. All I want is for you to have a life you deserve and enjoy."

It hits me right then that I don't think my mother has ever talked about my happiness.

"I don't want to lose you, Jack," she says.

"Thank you, Mother. I don't want to lose you either. But things have to change."

She nods. "You get to decide, not the rules now. Not just live by them like I did. Your father and I weren't as brave as you. This is your life. Your legacy. I understand that now. And I'll do what I can to help you. Help you both. New York society is..." She sighs. "It's tough."

"I can do anything with Jack by my side," Iris says.

My mother smiles and it feels warm and more genuine than I can ever remember one of her smiles ever being. It feels like the beginning of something new. Like the shoots of a new relationship with my mother might be poking through the cold November dirt. We both need to nurture it going forward to make sure it doesn't wither and die.

I glance at Iris. The woman who changed the entire trajectory of my life. Even my mother can see how important she is to me. Iris's the woman I love. My future wife and the woman I'll be with forever. She smiles at me and it's like sunshine and I find myself softening under her gaze. I can only think the best of the world and everyone in it when she's next to me.

It's possible that my mother has been trying to protect me from the sacrifices she felt my father made. Time will tell whether she means what she says about the Alden name being my legacy now. But like she said, I get to decide my future. My future with Iris.

EPILOGUE

Iris

Jack has barely taken his eyes off me since we said goodbye to his mother as she headed off to the Snowdrop Inn. It's like he thinks I'm going to bolt or something. But I'm not going anywhere.

We pull up in front of his lodge and I put the car into park. I insisted on driving after the revelations from his mother.

"We need to talk," I say. We need to reestablish trust between us, but I know I'll do anything Jack wants me to do.

"I should never have ended things," he says.

"I understand why you did. You have a lot on your shoulders."

"That's all over now. I'm not going back to the life I had before. I know my dad's not going to be able to go back to his life before his stroke, but I can't just take over from him and continue things the way he's done everything. I won't do it."

I sigh, trying to think about how to move forward. "No

decisions need to be made today. But your family has a lot of money. That brings a lot of opportunity."

I shift in my seat and face him. "You know how you said you liked the idea of going into businesses and solving problems, helping them grow?"

"Yeah. Like I did in business school."

"Well, you might be able to combine that love with the resources your family have and really make a difference in the world."

He gazes at me like I'm the most fascinating person on the planet and I stifle a giggle at how adoring he looks. I smooth my hand over his face and he leans into it like a cat being stroked.

"Think about it. You could identify a global issue that needs to be addressed. Maybe it's the pollution of the oceans or microplastics or whatever. You could work to develop a plan to solve that problem and put Alden family resources behind it."

His eyes widen. "The Aldens are rich, but we can't single-handedly clean up our planet's oceans."

I smile at him. "No, but you know everyone there is worth knowing. You can form an alliance. Fundraise. You could create a global foundation. Maybe you just tackle one issue so you don't spread your resources too thinly. That way you could make a huge difference."

Jack furrows his brow like he's confused. "You're amazing."

"And this is a shock to you." I roll my eyes in mock irritation.

"I just don't know how I got so lucky to even meet you, let alone spend the rest of my life with you."

I blush. "Forever?"

He raises his eyebrows. "Forever. It's a non-negotiable for me. Take it or leave it."

I laugh. "I'll take forever with you, Jack Alden."

"I'm serious," he says. "I don't want to propose right here, but know that I want to marry you."

I swallow. It's not a shock. He said it before. But it's difficult to imagine what marriage with Jack would look like. But I know I want it.

"I want to marry you too."

He nods, like he knew exactly what I was going to say. "So that's settled."

"One thing though." I stroke along his furrowed brow. "No lies. Your mother has spent her entire life pretending to be someone she's not. I know you're angry with her and confused and I'm sure you feel betrayed. But make sure you keep in mind that at least part of the reason she did lie was for you—for her child and heir—so you could hold your head high."

He groans.

"I know the status doesn't matter to you. But we live in very different times, Jack. She and your father tried to do the right thing. They might have gotten it wrong, but they weren't out to betray you. They wanted to be together and they wouldn't let anything stand in their way. Sound familiar?"

He shakes his head like he can't believe what he's hearing. "You make me better. You show me the world differently. Even that first time I met you. The way you talked about the fountain and the moonlight? When I'm with you, the world is a better place. You're a happiness filter."

"Jack..." I'm not sure anyone has ever said anything nicer to me.

"It's true. Just being around you makes me feel better about everything."

I smile, tilting my head at his words. "We have a lot to figure out," I say.

He shakes his head. "I don't think so. We've done the big stuff. The rest will follow."

He's right. We will figure it all out, but I'm just not sure where the end point will be.

"I don't want you to worry," he says.

I nod, trying to reassure him. "I'm not worried exactly."

"We should have a base in Colorado. And New York."

I glance out of the windshield toward the lodge of the Colorado Club. I'm not sure I could ever feel comfortable living in a place like this. It feels more like a hotel than a home. And Jack's apartment? It's all gold and crystals. That wouldn't feel like home either. But it's not like Jack and I can move in with Dad and Bray.

"I don't mean the Colorado Club should be our base." It's like he can read my mind. "I want us to have a home here. Although I hope Byron still lets us use the restaurants."

"So in Colorado but not at the Colorado Club. You want to find a house?" I ask.

"Sure. Or we can build one."

I let out a laugh. "Just like that."

"Yes. Just like that. Your happiness is my priority. Everything starts there. And in New York, we can move if you want to. Or we can just redecorate. If a house is better, we do that. Although, because we'll spend so much time in Colorado, an apartment makes sense because of the security."

"You really want to spend time in Colorado?" I ask.

"Are you kidding?" Jack scowls, then laughs. "It's out of character, I admit. I always swore I only ever left Manhattan if I was going to Europe, but honestly, I love it here. I love the sky and the mountains and the people. I love it all."

"I love it too," I admit. "But New York is where I always saw myself. It might not be quite the way I planned, but I'm looking forward to making my dreams a reality and living there."

"We'll have the best of both worlds," he says.

"I'll have the best of all worlds if I'm with you," I say.

"I'll make sure of it." He opens his door and rounds the hood before pulling my door open. "Now we're going to go inside and we're going to get naked and start practicing for all those babies we're going to make."

I squeal. "Jack, we haven't talked about kids!"

"You want them?" he asks.

I only have to think for a second. I'd never really thought I'd find anyone to have children with, so it's never really been a consideration. "With you I do."

"Whatever you want," Jack says, lifting me out of the driver's seat.

"Jack, I can walk."

"I know, but I like carrying you."

I wrap my hands around his neck, relishing the feel of him beneath my fingers as we climb the stairs to the lodge.

Jack

My entire life has turned around today. I had no idea where I was heading when I landed in Star Falls. But once again this place has worked its magic and somehow everything has worked out in the best possible way.

I have the woman I love in my arms and I'm never letting her go again.

"What?" she asks as I set her down on her feet. She reaches up to her eye. "Has my mascara smudged?"

"You're beautiful," I say. "I can't stop looking at you."

"You don't ever have to."

I drink in her words. Thank god I don't have to let her go. I'm not sure I was going to make it without her.

I take a step toward her and wrap an arm around her waist. "A lifetime isn't going to be enough with you, Iris."

"We'll make every moment count," she says on a sigh.

I press kisses up her neck and along her jaw. I could do this forever and I wouldn't have done it enough. Already I'm irritated that I've arranged to meet my mother for lunch before she leaves Colorado tomorrow. I want every moment with Iris to be like this.

Iris slides her fingers into my hair and I feel the muscles in my body unlock. God, how did I ever think I was going to live without her touching me?

"I want you so much, Iris."

"You have me," she whispers.

I push the shoulders of her coat off and then tug on her top. She grins at my ineptitude and strips off her turtleneck. Thank god.

Her breasts look deliciously ripe pushing up over the lace of her bra like they're straining for my touch. I harden as I take her in, and when I glance up, she's watching me, watching her.

"You look like you want to eat me," she says.

I raise my eyebrows. "I have no poker face. Eat you is exactly what I want to do."

In seconds we're in the bedroom. All I've managed to take off is my sweater and shoes. But it's okay because Iris is completely naked. I circle my hands around her waist, my fingers pressing into her soft skin as I maneuver her to the bed.

"You're so fucking beautiful," I whisper.

She pulls her eyebrows together like she can't quite believe what I'm saying.

"I mean it," I reassure her. "I've never laid eyes on anyone so astonishing." I guide her so she's sitting on the bed. Then I reach for behind her thighs, pushing her back to the mattress while I kneel before her.

Her delicious scent ratchets up my desire for her. I can see how ready for me she is. Her slickness glistens under my gaze. I can't quite believe how lucky I am that I'm the man that gets to have this woman for the rest of my life.

I press her thighs wide and bring my lips as close as I can get to her pussy without touching her. I just want to breathe her in.

"Jack," she whimpers. "Please, Jack. Make me come."

I groan. She's never begged me like that. I've always known I was lucky, but now I'm sure I'm the luckiest man who ever lived.

"I'm not deliberately tormenting you. I just want it all to last forever."

She arches her back, pushing herself onto my tongue and she sighs with relief.

She's lush and ripe and wet and I bury myself in her, licking and sucking. I want to take all her sounds and bottle them so I can play them whenever I want, but then I realize, I don't have to. I don't have to think about not being with her, because I will always be with her. I'll always be able to taste her. I'm going to make her come on my tongue every fucking day for the rest of our lives.

She pulses against my tongue, her clit swollen and needy, her folds engorged and ready. It hasn't taken long to take her to the edge like this.

"I love you," she calls out and I growl into her pussy and her entire body vibrates as if my sounds are carried into her body, her soul and push her off the edge into bliss.

I lap at her softly as she floats back down to earth, wanting her clean. Wanting her fresh for what comes next.

I stand and strip off, but I can't take my eyes from her. She's splayed out across the mattress, her chest still heaving at the effort of orgasming on my tongue. She looks wonderous. A vision. A goddamn goddess.

I have to be inside her.

I glance around, trying to figure out where my wallet is.

"No," she whimpers from the bed. "No condom, Jack. I want you bare inside me. Nothing between us."

I have to steady my breathing. I have to try and block out what she's saying. If I don't, I'm going to come standing here in front of her.

I close my eyes. And block out the sounds of her. The slightest thing will push me over this cliff edge I find myself on.

I fist my hands and take a deep breath. My vision blurs. All I want to do is fuck this woman in front of me. Fuck her until neither of us have the energy to do anything but lie in each other's arms. Fuck until we're old and gray and the world has collapsed around us.

I open my eyes and she's propped up on her elbows looking at me.

She reaches out her hand. I step closer and crawl up her body. The heat of her skin makes me feel like I've come home.

She's home.

She's all I've ever wanted and I never knew it.

If all the money, my name, the status, the charities—if everything disappears tomorrow, it doesn't matter because I have Iris.

I cage her with my arms. We're face-to-face, body-to-body. She slides her legs wide, my erection pressing against her mound.

Her throat bobs, like she's anxious. But I don't want her to be.

"What's wrong?" I ask

She shakes her head. "Nothing... it's just..." She stops.

"What?"

"I know you'll propose and we'll get married in front of our family somewhere—"

"In Star Falls," I say. "It has to be here."

She smiles. "In Star Falls. And I know I'll have the best time and everyone else will think, oh they're married now. Now they're husband and wife... but—"

"But this, now, this is our ceremony." I finish her sentence for her. "This is our union."

She swallows again. "Yeah."

My love for the woman under me threatens to overwhelm me. I know exactly what she means. I feel the same way. We're bonded forever, not by legal document or official ceremony, but our commitment to each other.

I press at her entrance, our eyes locked.

She nods, urging me on. I push deeper, our bodies sliding together in a final act of giving ourselves to each other.

"I love you," I choke out.

"I love you too," she says, her fingertips pressing into my shoulders.

She feels like silk and velvet and exactly like heaven. As I withdraw, she grips me like I might never return, and I have to pause to make sure this isn't over before it's begun.

"It's better like this," she says, her voice breathy. "I can feel how hard you are."

I groan. This woman is trying to kill me.

Her hands skirt the sides of me and pull me closer to her. I push in again, harder this time and she cries out my name.

I slam into her deeper and deeper, pressing and pressing, wanting her to feel everything I can feel.

"You're perfect," I cry out, tensing my jaw, sweat sheening my body.

"Jack," she moans again.

My orgasm breaks from its leash and steals up my spine, sending blistering strikes of pleasure up every nerve ending, so deep inside me. If feels like I'm hurtling into a black hole, clinging on to Iris. She's the only thing I'm sure that exists in this moment. The rest of the world falls away and I don't care about anything else. I don't think I'll ever come back from the pleasure, the release, the feeling of pure bliss that fills every cell and the world goes black.

The next thing I'm aware of is Iris's fingers, trailing down my spine. I think I might have actually blacked out.

She's panting and hot and so fucking sexy, I have the urge to fuck her again instantly.

I roll to my back, bringing her with me, like we're stuck together.

"I think I passed out," I say.

She smiles at me. "I can't believe I get to have a life with you. Are you sure this is real? Am I dreaming?"

"You're not dreaming unless I am too. And if we're both dreaming, I hope neither of us every wake up."

A lazy smile curves around her lips and she rests her head on my chest.

I trace circles on her back and she shifts slightly on top of me. I try and ignore the blood rushing to my cock, every time her skin slides against mine, every time she breathes in and her body rises on mine.

"I can't imagine a life without you," I reply.

She lifts her head. "You don't have to. Right?"

"Right."

She pauses. "It might be a bumpy road here and there. I'm not used to your world."

"Life can be bumpy. As long as we're together."

"Right." She slides onto my cock, her eyelids fluttering closed.

"I'd give it all up if that's what it takes to be with you."

She gasps as she sinks down as deep as I will go. "I'd give up everything for you."

I slide my hands around her ass, my fingers tangling in her long hair. She tips her head back and sighs, then opens her eyes with a grin. "I forgot how you like my hair in a bun."

She gathers it up in her hands and twists and turns, and in the few seconds it takes, I get to enjoy the jut of her nipples and the bob of her breasts. I can't believe I get to have this woman forever.

"Better?" she asks, turning her head from side to side.

"You're always perfect."

She furrows her brow and leans forward, dragging herself off me and I don't know where her moans stop and my groans start. It's just so good.

I pull her back onto me, fast and hard and she cries out. "I'm so full of you," she whimpers.

I begin to lift and lower her, maneuvering her up and down my cock. Our eyes stay locked together as I plunge into her over and over and over.

Her cries get wilder, and I sit to be closer to her, and our movements become smaller but more intense. I'm deeper in her in every way.

"Marry me," she sighs in breathy moans. "Marry me."

We don't live by the rules anymore. Even the one that says we can't propose twenty minutes either side of an orgasm.

"Every day for the rest of my life."

It feels like both our bodies begin to vibrate. I'm not sure if it's the beginning of her orgasm or mine. I can see hers in her eyes and I'm sure she sees mine just as clearly.

"Iris," I groan as the waves of pleasure race toward us. "I love you."

Her fingers press into my shoulders and she drops her mouth to my ear. "I love you," she whispers.

Both our bodies go rigid at the same time, our orgasms mixing, enveloping us and binding us together.

Our bodies, minds, and souls forged together into one.

Forever.

Three weeks later

Iris

Being in New York with Jack this time—for the third time—is different. The first time we met, the second time, all I could see were the differences between us. But this time? This time we're here as a couple. A couple who are planning their future together.

Back at Wilde's Farm, I've been showing Marnie the ropes. She's picked everything up quickly and this five-day trip to New York is kind of a test for both of us. Can I let go and trust that Marnie and my brother and father have this. And is she okay without me hovering over her. Of course I know she'll be fine. So will Bray and my dad.

It's exciting and terrifying to be moving on to a new chapter. One that's going to involve more than Wilde's Farm and Star Falls. But at the same time, I don't want to leave either of them behind. There's magic in Star Falls. Both Jack and I know that.

After spending Thanksgiving in Star Falls, we arrived in New York this morning. I expected Mrs. Alden to resume some of her frosty demeanor she had the first time I met her, but she hadn't. I really think she accepts me as Jack's choice and wants to support me.

Mr. Alden is making good progress. His speech is improving and he's taken a few steps. But Jack is now in charge of the Alden family business. That brings responsibilities. But he's drawing boundaries and rearranging things to suit him. To suit us. After he resigned from three charities' boards in one day, I keep reminding him that it doesn't all have to happen overnight.

"Are you ready?" Jack asks as The Alden Hotel comes into view.

I nod, grinning at him. I'm ready for anything when I'm with him. He makes me feel like a blonde Jackie next to his handsome JFK.

"I love your smile," he says.

"I love *you*," I counter. "How do you feel now that you said no to the offer on the hotel?"

"Good," he says. "There's so much going on, I don't want to be making so many changes all at once. And my friendships with the guys are important. I know selling the hotel wouldn't have undermined those relationships, but I want to keep it. For now. Maybe I'm being sentimental, or maybe I just want to beat Bennett before I sell."

The car pulls to a stop and immediately my door is opened by the hotel doorman. We head inside to the private room Jack has arranged. We're having a second Thanksgiving dinner with his New York friends this evening. It will also be an introduction for me to most of them. I've met Fisher and Byron, and Juniper and Rosey, but I'm looking forward to getting to meet Bennett and Efa, Leo and Jules, and Worth and Sophia. They're all so important to Jack, so they're important to me.

Inside the private room, we're the first to arrive. There's a bar set up at one end and a bartender, organizing the bottles.

"Champagne?" Jack asks me.

"What are we celebrating?"

Jack grins, that boyish, hopeful grin that makes me so happy. "What aren't we celebrating?"

The bartender fixes us our drinks, but before I can take a sip, Jack produces an iPad. "I have something for you."

I narrow my eyes. "An iPad?"

Jack chuckles. "Sure, you can keep the iPad, but let's play the video on it."

He stands it up and presses start and the screen comes to life. It's a video of the road outside of Wilde's Farm. The camera sweeps down and it's as if a car is driving along the road with Wilde's Farm on the left.

"I don't know if I ever told you this, but I saw you here, outside the farm when I arrived in Star Falls after losing you in New York. I didn't realize it was you at the time. You were standing by the fence."

I reach up and stroke the side of his head and we both turn back to the screen. Is this going to be some kind of sentimental film of our history that he's had made?

The camera passes the farm and then turns right, down a driveway that I know for sure doesn't exist. "What's this?" The driveway is flanked by beautiful iris plants that lead up to a huge, two-story, stone-and-timber house. Or hotel maybe. It's huge.

I glance at Jack, wanting to understand what I'm looking at, but he's just staring at the screen, smiling. "Look," he urges me.

The camera is giving a bird's-eye view of the house, a pool behind it, and what looks like an ornamental pond, overlooked by various balconies and terraces at the back of the house. Then the camera sweeps down into the drive and it's as if a person enters the building. Inside is a huge entryway with thirty-foot ceilings and a stone fireplace.

"What is happening?" I ask. "What is this place?"

"It's just a suggestion of what we can build there. Obviously we can change whatever we like, but the land is ours."

"The land?"

"I bought the land opposite Wilde's Farm. I thought it would be a perfect place to build our home in Star Falls."

My heart soars in my chest. "You bought land—why didn't you tell me?"

"I probably should have. I just wanted to surprise you. Plus I didn't want you to tell me all the reasons we didn't need so much. If I could buy the entire goddamn town, I would. I have so much to be thankful to Star Falls for."

"Star Falls doesn't need you to buy it. You just need to believe in its magic."

"Oh, I do already." He grins at me. "So, you like it?" He lifts his chin at the iPad. "We can build whatever you want to build on there. I just wanted to get something together that looked like a home—"

"A mansion," I correct him.

He shrugs. "I know we'll also have a place in New York, but this is the place we're going to have everyone stay. Our kids are going to grow up here. We need the space. And then, if your father needs to move in later on—there's a guest cottage in these plans. I don't know if Bray will want to take over your family home one day. If he does, there's room for your dad to stay with us."

Jack has thought of everything and everyone. He's the most generous, thoughtful man I know. New York was lucky to have him as long as she did.

He's mine now.

I wrap my arms around his neck and lift myself up on tiptoes, pressing my lips to his, just as the doors to the dining room fly open and voices crash in, disturbing our moment. But they're more than welcome.

"I'm Sophia." A beautiful woman pulls me into a hug before Jack can start the introductions. "I'm Worth's wife. I'm so happy to meet you. I just knew Jack would fall hard when he found the right woman. Someone to make him believe in love."

My heart aches a little for the Jack before me. And for the me before Jack. We were both lost before we found each other. Together we're the best versions of ourselves. We're stronger. Happier. Better in every way.

"I've heard so much about you," I say. "And Worth. And all of you."

"I'm Jules." Another woman pulls me in for a hug. Then Juniper and Rosey and someone else who must have been Efa.

"I'm Leo, Jules's husband." A very handsome man grins

at me. "This must be overwhelming. I'm here to tell you it won't get any better." He chuckles and I'm not sure how to respond.

"Have you two set a date yet?" Sophia asks. "I guess it's not going to be a Vegas wedding?"

Everyone laughs and Jack catches my eye and then takes a couple of steps toward me. Somehow we've been separated as everyone descended on us. "Sophia and Worth got married in Vegas after drinking too much."

"It wasn't a mistake," Worth says. "Not for me."

"Best decision of my life," says Sophia.

"Yeah, they stole our thunder. We were the ones that were supposed to be getting married," Jules says, laughing. "So be careful, in this group of friends, you never know who's getting married."

Everyone's gaze turns to me and Jack.

"We haven't set a date," I say. "Oh and actually, we haven't actually decided to get married, have we?"

"Are you unclear that I love you, want to marry you and spend the rest of my life with you?" Jack asks and his friends ooh and aah.

I shake my head.

"Good." He slides his hand into his pocket. "I wasn't going to do this right now, but seeing as my friends have ruined the moment—"

He slides to one knee, right in the middle of all his friends, and stares up at me. "I have loved you since the moment I saw you across the theater. I knew you were the woman I wanted to make happy forever. I've never wavered in knowing that. I long to be your devoted husband. I love you, Iris Wilde. Will you marry me?"

He snaps open the ring box in his hands to reveal a beautiful emerald-cut diamond ring. "The stone is a

Colorado diamond, and the setting was made here in New York."

Tears gather at the back of my throat. He's thought of everything. It couldn't be more special.

I can't speak, and my gaze flits between Jack and the ring. I wasn't expecting him to formally propose. I knew we were going to get married, but I didn't expect this. I didn't expect the house. I didn't expect Jack on his knee in front of all his friends, declaring his love.

"I love you, Jack," I say, unable to put into words how lucky I feel every moment that I'm with the man in front of me. I've never felt safer, never felt more loved, never felt more hopeful about the future. The future together. "Of course I'll marry you."

Everyone starts cheering and Jack stands. I cup his face in my hands and press a kiss to his lips.

"I'm the luckiest man in entire fucking universe," he says.

Fisher slaps him on the back. "Nope, that's me."

"That's all of us," Worth says. "We've been lucky to find each other and then the women than make us better."

In all the chaos of the ten friends that surround us, offering congratulations, love, and laughter, Jack takes the ring from the box and slips it onto my left ring finger.

It fits perfectly.

Just like a glass slipper.

I've found my prince and my happily ever after.

MY NEXT BOOK **is The London Man**

He's London's coldest billionaire. She's the influencer setting his world on fire.

Read on for a sneak peak.

Missed any stories of the couples in this book? Read on for a complete list of couples.

FOR LOUISE BAY **news and releases, including bonus content, sign up to my newsletter at www.louisebay.com/newsletter**

BOOKS BY LOUISE BAY

Each book is a stand alone

Don't know where to start? Try **Mr. Mayfair**

The Hart Family Billionaires

The London Man

The Colorado Club Billionaires

Love Fast - Byron & Rosey

Love Deep - Fisher & Juniper

Love Hard - Jack & Iris

The New York City Billionaires

The Boss + The Maid = Chemistry - Bennett & Efa

The Player + The Pact = I Do - Leo & Jules

The Hero + Vegas = No Regrets - Worth & Sophia

The Doctors Series

Dr. Off Limits - Jacob & Sutton

Dr. Perfect - Zach & Ellie

Dr. CEO - Vincent & Kate

Dr. Fake Fiancé - Beau & Vivian

Dr. Single Dad - Dax & Eira

Related to the Doctors Series

Private Player - Nathan & Madison & Nathan

The Mister Series

Mr. Mayfair - Beck & Stella

Mr. Knightsbridge - Dexter & Hollie

Mr. Smithfield - Gabriel & Autumn

Mr. Park Lane - Joshua & Hartford

Mr. Bloomsbury - Andrew & Sophia

Mr. Notting Hill - Tristan & Parker

The Player Series

International Player - Noah & Truly

Private Player - Nathan & Madison

The Gentleman Series

The Ruthless Gentleman

The Wrong Gentleman

The Royals Series

King of Wall Street - Max & Harper

Park Avenue Prince - Sam & Grace

Duke of Manhattan - Ryder & Scarlett

The British Knight - Alexander & Violet

The Earl of London - Logan & Darcy

The Nights Series

Parisian Nights - Jake & Haven

Indigo Nights - Dylan & Beth

Promised Nights - Luke & Ash

Standalones

The Deal Maker - Hunter & Lucy

An American in London - Tuesday & Ben

14 Days of Christmas - Celia & Sebastian

Hollywood Scandal - Matt & Lana

Love Unexpected - Blake & Mackenzie

Hopeful - Joel & Ava

The Empire State Series - Ethan & Anna

Sign up to the Louise Bay mailing list at www.louisebay.com

What kind of books do you like?

Fake relationship (marriage of convenience)

Duke of Manhattan

Mr. Mayfair

Mr. Notting Hill

Dr. Fake Fiancé

Dr. Single Dad

The Play + The Pact = I Do

An American in London

Enemies to Lovers

The London Man

King of Wall Street

The British Knight

The Earl of London

Hollywood Scandal

Parisian Nights

14 Days of Christmas

Mr. Bloomsbury

The Play + The Pact = I Do

Small Town

Love Fast

Love Deep

Love More

14 Days of Christmas

Hollywood Scandal

Friends to lovers

Mr. Mayfair

Promised Nights

International Player

Office Romance/ Workplace romance

The London Man

Mr. Knightsbridge

King of Wall Street

The British Knight

The Ruthless Gentleman

Mr. Bloomsbury

Dr. Off Limits

The Boss + The Maid = Chemistry

The Play + The Pact = I Do

Second Chance

International Player

Hopeful

Best Friend's Brother

Promised Nights

Vacation/Holiday Romance

The Empire State Series

Indigo Nights

The Ruthless Gentleman

The Wrong Gentleman

Love Unexpected

14 Days of Christmas

The Hero + Vegas = No Regrets

An American in London

Holiday/Christmas Romance

14 Days of Christmas

British Hero

The London Man (American Heroine)

Promised Nights (British heroine)

Indigo Nights (American heroine)

Hopeful (British heroine)

Duke of Manhattan (American heroine)

The British Knight (American heroine)

The Earl of London (British heroine)

The Wrong Gentleman (American heroine)

The Ruthless Gentleman (American heroine)

International Player (British heroine)

Mr. Mayfair (British heroine)

Mr. Knightsbridge (American heroine)

Mr. Smithfield (American heroine)

Private Player (British heroine)

Mr. Bloomsbury (American heroine)

14 Days of Christmas (British heroine)

Mr. Notting Hill (British heroine)

Dr. Off Limits

Dr. Perfect

Dr. Fake Fiancé (American heroine)

Dr. Single Dad

The Play + The Pact = I Do (American heroine)

An American in London (American heroine)

Sign up to the Louise Bay mailing list on my website
www.louisebay.com

THE LONDON MAN - SNEAK PEEK

CHAPTER ONE

CORMACK

I hang up the phone and sit back in my chair feeling pretty bloody good about myself. Everyone told me there was no way I could get approval to demolish the Stamford building. My contact at the planning office just told me, it's now a sure thing. For two years I've worked on these plans. And now it's finally going through. It's a victory, along with everything that comes with it.

Power.

Control.

Money.

My brothers and sisters are going to hate me even more than they usually do. Once the new Stamford building is developed, it's going to be the single biggest and most profitable development the Hart Group has ever seen. That means it will guarantee that it will be me not my siblings that heads up the Hart Group when my father retires. It's what I've worked my entire life for.

There's a knock at my door—it will be my assistant or my sister. I don't want to see either. I want to be on my own to bask in my success a little longer.

"Come in," I snap.

It's Jenna, my assistant. It could have been worse.

"Goldie wants to see you. Says it's urgent," she says, tilting her head slightly, letting me know that my head of PR is behind me.

I roll my eyes. I hate the entire idea of having someone in charge of PR—official ridiculous title: Chief Reputation Management Officer. What the hell does that mean?

Goldie mutters something behind Jenna.

I shake my head, exasperated. "I have five minutes."

Goldie comes in with the iPad he's never without. I swear he sleeps with that thing.

"We have some activity on social media around the Stamford building."

At least he gets right to the point. I hate wasting time on how-are-yous and did-you-have-a-good-weekend. Because the answers are always the same: I'd be better if I wasn't wasting time chit-chatting with you. And what I do with my weekends is none of your bloody business.

"@LondonSavvy has posted from outside the building saying how there are plans in place to demolish it and she's complaining," Goldie announces.

I stay quiet. My question is implied and it's always the same question—why do I care?

"I'm concerned about the rate at which it's gaining views and likes. And some of the comments are...they're talking about contacting the planning office and they're blaming Hart Group for everything from the destruction of a piece of thirties architecture to the potential fall of democracy."

My jaw tightens, but I don't speak. Because my question is implied: What are you going to do about it?

"We have people in the comments giving the counter view obviously," Goldie says. "And we have other people posting a pro-Hart Group stance. We're doing everything we can."

I still don't speak. Because my question is implied: Why are you in my office taking up my valuable time.

"You should be on notice," Goldie says. "Government departments are increasingly taking..." He makes air quotes with his hands. "public opinion into account. Basically, they don't want their decisions to go to the judge and jury of social media. We're seeing growing capitulation by local and national governments in the face of social media criticism."

I've just been told my plans are almost complete. So this social media criticism is too late. I pull in a breath. Except, I don't like to count my chickens until they're properly hatched and showing up on the profit and loss account.

"Can't we just call Zuckerberg and get this account taken down?" I ask.

"We need to let it burn itself out."

"But what happens if it picks up traction? I will not lose this approval."

"It's a risk," Goldie says.

I don't want risks like this when it comes to the Stamford building. I have no control. I hate that. There's too much at stake.

"Tell me again why I can't pick up the phone and have this blogger cancelled."

"Influencer," he corrects me. "We need to use our power wisely. If it gets out, it could play into the narrative that big business is bad and it becomes even more of a David and Goliath situation. You know what Brits are like. They're always rooting for the underdog. We don't want to create that underdog. We want her to be a slightly hysterical voice on social media."

I cringe at his use of the word hysterical when attributed to a woman having an opinion. Hysterical is never a word used when describing a man. "Don't describe her as hysterical, please. Insignificant is a better alternative in the context."

"Of course," Goldie says. "Insignificant."

"We'll go with your strategy," I say, "but there's a lot to lose in this situation. Everything looks positive in relation to the application. I wouldn't want that to change." I fix him with a look that tells him his job is on the line when there's another knock at the door.

It will be Jenna making sure Goldie doesn't overstay his welcome.

Except then I hear an excited squeal and the door busts open to reveal a head of tumbling golden curls and a smile that could melt even the coldest heart.

"Uncle Cormack!" Maddie shouts, running toward my desk.

Before I have a chance to get out of my chair, she climbs into my lap.

"Spin, spin, spin!"

I lift her up, give her kiss on the forehead before plonking her back down on my chair, and spinning her around.

My sister, George appears in the doorway. "You'll make her sick."

I don't reply, but pull out the drawer under my desk and pull out a Freddo. I look my sister in the eye, as I open the wrapper and present it to Maddie. "Hey beautiful, have some chocolate."

"You're a terrible uncle," my sister says. "And a worse brother."

"He's the best!" Maddie says, taking the chocolate frog from my hand.

I shrug and smile sarcastically at my sister.

My siblings and I are not the archetypal happy family. We've been taught since we were Maddie's age to be competitors. Instead of saying grace at mealtimes, my father would lecture on his philosophy on life.

How business is a zero-sum game.

How coming second is losing.

How there are no second chances.

And then he would go around the table and get us to tell him what our wins were for the day.

I've never asked, but I hope my sister doesn't take the same approach with Maddie. Sometimes I think it must be nice to have siblings that celebrate each other's successes and cheer each other on, instead of what we have between us.

The ice.

The distrust.

The distain.

If it wasn't for Hart Group, I'm not sure any of us would still be in each other's lives. Hart Group brings us together. The business has us compete against each other and anyone who dares to come up against us.

The upside is we all have skin as thick as a rhino and no matter how many times we get knocked down, we get back up and fight on.

"Are you coming to family dinner on Sunday?" George asks. "I need to know if to prepare the poisoned potatoes."

"You're hilarious." I know she's joking, but there's always an edge to our banter, and honestly, if George thought she could get away with murdering me, I wouldn't put it past her. My siblings know I'm most likely to head up Hart Group when my father retires, and none of them are happy about it. It means I have to watch my back. I'm the common enemy that unites them. Individually, I can handle them. But together? I have to be careful.

Maddie thrusts the empty chocolate wrapper at me and I lift her from my chair. "Are you going to Grandpa and Granma's on Sunday?" I ask. "I'm not going if you're not going." She's the only reason I'd go. That and my mom. I have enough of my dad in the office.

"Of course. I love Grandpa."

I let out a half laugh at the same time as George does.

"Who would have thought he'd be soft as shit as a Grandpa?"

"Mummy, shit is a bad word."

George rolls her eyes at her daughter's admonishment. "Sorry."

"You two need to get out of here so I can make this company some money and keep your mummy in her nepo-baby corner office."

"Fuck you, Cormack," George says.

"Mummy!" Maddie protests.

"See what you've done?" George says to me.

"Oh yeah, your swearing is definitely my fault." Just like when we were children and my father was in a bad mood it was because his kids didn't know how to behave.

I put Maddie on her feet and give her a kiss on her head. "See you later alligator."

"See you Sunday, Uncle Cormack. Not later. I have to go home for my dinner now."

I laugh. "Okay, sunshine. You go home with mummy."

Maddie always lightens my spirit slightly. And it's just what I needed after Goldie brought me the news he did.

I need to demolish the Stamford building and get started on the new one. Then everyone can stop jostling for the crown.

It will be mine.

Read More

ABOUT THE AUTHOR

Louise Bay is the USA Today and international bestselling author of contemporary romance novels that make you laugh. Louise was inspired by such bonkbuster authors of the eighties as Judith Krantz and Jackie Collins, but wants to be Emily Henry when she grows up. Writing is just a side hustle to her full-time career as a personal butler/driver/chef to her kid. IYKYK.

For more information, visit www.louisebay.com.

Instagram and Facebook: @authorlouisebay

TikTok: @authorlouisebayofficial

Made in United States
North Haven, CT
30 December 2025

86053501R00204